Clan of the Wolfdogs

BOOK ONE

TOM BERQUIST

MANHATTAN
BOOK GROUP

Published by Manhattan Book Group
447 Broadway | 2nd Floor #354 | New York, NY 10013 | USA
1.800.767.0531 | www.manhattanbookgroup.com

Printed in the United States of America
ISBN-13: 979-8-9861392-4-1

To Peggy, Pal, Moo, Wally and Ollie, who befriended
me and to all the dogs who brighten our lives.

Thanks to my wife, Ellen, for enabling me to write. To my daughter, Emily, who not only inspires students and scholars with her writing, but has instilled the craft into her children, Zoey and Xander. Much gratitude also goes to my editor, Lynn Croxton*. Every writer ought to be graced with her artful coaching.

*LynnCroxton@protonmail.com

Foreword

OVER 100,000 YEARS AGO, WOOLLY mammoths and saber-toothed cats roamed a large portion of our planet. One early species of humans—*Homo neaderthalenis*—dominated vast areas of present-day Europe. Some 30,000 years later, a new species of humans—*Homo sapiens*—migrated from Africa, competing with their earlier cousins. Advancing and retreating glaciers and widespread volcanic eruptions caused extraordinary climate swings. Survival was extremely difficult, requiring an intimate understanding of plants and animals.

Constantly on the move to find food and better shelter, both species hunted the same animals and were hunted by the same predators. Children had to grow up fast, and lives were incredibly short due to injuries, diseases, starvation, and hypothermia. By 40,000 years ago, the Neanderthals had disappeared, displaced by what we call modern humans. We became the apex predators, most scientists agree, because of our superior intelligence, cooperative culture, and innovative weapons. As posited in my 2015 book, *The Invaders*, I believe we may also have had an unexpected ally, *Canis lupus*—the wolf.

Clan of the Wolfdogs borrows from my research to tell an action-packed fictional tale that imagines how our earliest ancestors became today's humans and how wolves became dogs and our best friends. Looking back with a good story, we can enjoy speculating how early humans and wolves must have watched and learned from each other. From hanging around campfires for food scraps to warning humans of intruders, wolves and humans slowly came to realize we could benefit from each other. In his novel, Tom Berquist pens moving images that show how two different species with similar social and pack traits hunted and survived through teamwork. Seeing how wolves tracked their prey and held them at bay inspired us to tame and train them to become living tools. And, by caring for them, we gained their undying devotion in return.

To be sure, Tom's novel takes dramatic liberties by condensing what took many thousands of years to evolve into a few generations. His story offers to take you on a fascinating journey through time. By vividly picturing the trembling hand on the shaft of a spear and marveling at the first taste of a mustard seed, his engaging book opens our eyes to ponder how we may have evolved. And by showing readers early humans not as simple brutes but as feeling, striving people like ourselves, Tom hopes to stimulate young people to study and learn about our roots. I know you will find Tom's novel thrilling, but you will also learn from it.

No one knows for sure how and when humans first invented certain tools, first farmed and domesticated animals, but if you love dogs as I do, you can join in one clan family's struggle to survive with wolfdogs at their side. Savoring a sweep of colorful, revealing vignettes, you will find yourself lost in a distant era that impacts us still.

Dr. Pat Shipman
Adjunct Professor of Anthropology, Penn State University

Pat Shipman, *The Invaders: How Humans and Their Dogs Drove Neanderthals to Extinction* (Cambridge, MA: The Belknap Press of Harvard University Press, 2017).

Chapter One

*Location: Paglicci cave, near present-day Rignano
Garganico, Apulia, Italy 39,000 years Before Present*

SCRAMBLING DOWNHILL, YOUNG IRIK DREADED what he might find when he reached the plain. Moments ago, he'd stood above, watching a roaming village of caribou innocently graze—fawns hungrily nursing—each trusting the whole of the herd to keep them safe. He hated to witness the killing of a magnificent caribou buck, which had held his head defiantly high to protect his brood. But as the herd migrated north, the clan hadn't eaten meat for days. When Chief Brul, his father, shouted up for him to join the men, Irik recognized the buck's death meant the clan wouldn't have to move again. At least, not yet.

Wiry and quick-footed, he raced toward the clearing with thoughts of his friend, Arol, who didn't believe he should watch the carnage. She cried over any killing, necessary or not, but as the chief's son, he must learn. Dodging past thorny locust trees, he reached the edge of the plain and froze.

There, dead and alone, sprawled the caribou buck, reeking of blood and swarmed by buzzing flies. Spears punctured his throat, his majestic crown of antlers splintered on the ground. Several paces away, Irik's father and the hunters bent in a fervid huddle. Screams Irik knew all too well rose from the center. His mouth dried as his eyes bulged. Not only the caribou bled today.

"Father! Father!" Irik cried, running to his side, prying his way past the sweaty, hide-covered legs of the four men.

His older brother, Reto, sat rocking his upper body, wailing in pain.

Irik looked up to his father. "What happened?" His eyes welled, but he took pride in no tears falling until he lowered them. By then, Chief Brul had looked away.

"The buck gored him hard, but Reto is a fearless hunter. He gave the buck the final spear."

Hearing his father's praise, Reto stopped crying and tried to stand. Grabbing at his chest, he stumbled, and the men broke his fall.

"Load him onto one drag sled," the chief commanded, "and put the buck on the other."

Irik cringed at Reto's cries as the men lifted him. "Can I help pull his sled, Father?"

The chief patted the top of Irik's dark, bristly head. "Yes, as long as you don't get in the way. We need to be back before nightfall. Before the lions smell fresh blood."

Irik took hold of a lower end of the sled pole behind the men, and they began their long trek back to camp. Usually, the hunters had high spirits after a kill, but Reto's injury dragged on their hearts.

With afternoon sun reflecting off the gravelly path, the men in front removed their drenched and smelly tunics, allowing Irik a clearer view. Beyond the shrubs that dotted the bare steppe, Irik caught sight of another hunt. A pack of wolves chased a caribou yearling to the side of a mesa and circled the exhausted animal. Irik knew wolves culled out weaker prey and pursued it for hours. Working as a team, they took turns playing lead wolf to save energy and make sure they didn't lose the quarry. Then they'd go in for the kill. Although both he and his friend, Arol, felt it cruel, Irik knew slaying the yearling only meant food to the wolves. Also magnificent animals, wolves could fall prey to cave lions or scimitar cats. *Killing means survival for all animals, including humans.*

A quick-moving female sank her fangs into the young caribou's rear leg and pulled. As the yearling tried to free itself, another wolf grabbed a front leg. The caribou dropped, splayed on the ground, kicking and crying out. The rest of the team piled on to keep the

2

animal down for the pack leader. The huge male with silver-tipped fur and large chunks missing from one ear clamped his jaws on the struggling caribou's neck.

From afar, Irik didn't hear the growls of the predators or the death rattle of their prey, but soon the caribou lay still. Not wanting to watch the pack rip open the animal's soft underside and gorge on its guts, he trudged forward, eyes to the ground. When he eventually glanced back, a tiny smile curled his lips. The rest of the trailing pack—young pups and one wolf crippled with age—had joined the feast, the adults moving aside to leave an opening for them. *The wolves act like a clan. I should tell Arol and maybe Father. We could learn much if we watch wolves, perhaps become friends.*

The fatigue in Irik's legs drifted away when he saw the swirling trails of smoke rising from the home camp. As the hunting party reached the outskirts, women and children rushed to greet them. Within a few breaths, his mother, Mata, and Reto's woman, Tra, bent over Reto, weeping. His mother didn't notice Irik still holding a lower part of the sled.

"Drag Reto to our fire," Mata pleaded.

While she prepared a poultice for Reto's chest and Tra washed his body with lavender-scented water, the men rested and chatted with their families about the hunt. Irik went to see the handsome buck before they cut him up. As he knelt beside the caribou's head, the open eye gave him a chill, so he focused on its long, hairy snout. He ran his fingers along it until he came to the long rough tongue that drooped to the ground. Sliced and cooked, that meat was highly prized.

Irik gaped at the buck's massive rack of antlers. They spanned six adult hands high and almost as wide. Most of the points were chipped, and many were missing from battles with challengers. *Your will to win must have been strong.* Irik dragged his fingers up and down the crown. Knowing the antlers would be broken up for tools, he stroked the velvet on them. *Soon, another buck will take care of your brood.*

Irik lay next to the animal's head to gauge its size. His legs fell several hand-lengths short of the buck's, even though he was tall for his age. The round hooves far beyond where Irik's feet reached made him feel small and awed. Brushing away dried speckles of blood, he dug his hand into the thick, white fur under its chin—like his mass of hair, only softer and less tangled.

He kneeled and stroked both hands over the animal's back, starting with the high bulge of bone at the shoulder blade. Lower, he handled the long sinews at the haunch, noting how they connected muscle to bone for traveling fast and far. He trailed a hand along the bumps of the buck's spine to the end of the stubby tail, admiring the smooth, dark brown coat. Last time the herd came through, their coats had been mottled. *Where do they travel to and from each season?* Walking his hand along the length of the body, Irik tried to remember how majestically this animal had stood and run. Could he capture his form and his spirit?

"Enough. Move away, Irik," his father yelled.

Irik flinched and flushed. "He's fourteen hands long, Father, enough food for five days."

"Good," Brul said with his usual stern voice and a tight-lipped smile. "Once we cut him open, you can help with the butchering."

Irik's heart beat faster as he stood aside and watched the men roll the animal on its back, knowing what would come next. Creta, a boy of his brother's age who always pushed Irik around, jabbed a pointed flint blade into the buck's rear. He cut a line up the belly, grunting and grinning with each stroke.

The whole clan stood watching except old Uncle Okra and Arol. He was probably resting, and she might be sulking while concentrating on her collection of found objects. It comforted Irik to picture her endlessly organizing her elk teeth, broken bird bones, seeds, and pebbles.

As the intestines oozed out, Irik's stomach turned, and he looked away.

"Stop when you get to the windpipe, Cret," Chief Brul said. Wet, hacking sounds and a gassy stench pervaded the air.

Irik's eyes snapped open at his father's command. "Take this blade and cut here so we can remove the entrails." Irik looked at his piercing eyes and hooked nose—traits they shared—and tried to keep his hand from shaking.

As he placed the blade where his father pointed, the smell of bloody innards seized his throat.

"Go ahead," the men shouted.

Irik's stomach pumped bile. Gagging, he retched.

Cret guffawed through his missing teeth.

Irik lowered his head to his chest, eyes and throat burning.

The men groaned, a couple snickering.

Chief Brul pushed him aside. "Go to your mother, Irik."

Trudging back toward the cave, Irik found his Uncle Orki seated and leaning against a rock. Except for a bare spot at the top of his head, his long hair and beard blended into his shaggy tunic of mammoth hide. He flashed a yellow, uneven, yet warm and welcoming smile.

"Butchering all done?" he asked, waving the boy to sit.

Irik shook his head and dropped next to his father's much older brother.

Orki thoughtfully stroked his beard. "I never liked butchering either."

Irik perked up at the understanding tone. It amazed him how much Uncle Orki looked like his father but—unlike Chief Brul—often shared Irik's feelings.

"It's not just that," Irik said, "but how I don't fit in. I can't please my father."

Orki nodded slowly and looked him in the eyes. "As clan chief, your father needs hunters. He expects you to become a man soon."

Irik shuffled his feet. "But when—?"

Orki took a deep breath. "You start now, by learning to kill with a spear, and later you take a woman."

Startled, Irik asked, "But how do you—?" He looked to the ground, scratching his head.

"Learn to kill?" Orki asked. "That comes with courage and practice. Take a woman? You first feel her in your loins."

Too embarrassed to talk about some dreams he'd had and the morning wetness in his crotch, Irik said, "I don't want to kill animals."

"Look, Irik, you must kill to live, and not only for food." Orki scratched his beard and squinted. "Hunters must be warriors to protect their clan and home. Not only from predators but from other people."

"Other people?" Irik had never seen a human outside of the Valley Clan.

"Yes, there are, but not like us. The Lessors are strong, quiet, came here before us, and will fight to keep their land. The fierce White Clan does horrible things to their enemies."

"W-what do they do? Irik asked, trembling.

"They..." Orki choked up, then patted his nephew's knee. "I can't speak of it. But don't worry, they don't live near us."

Irik shuffled his feet. "Was it the White people who killed grandfather?"

Orki slowly shook his head. "No, our father, Rolf, was killed by the Fox-tail clan."

"Why?"

Orki looked away, tears forming in his weary eyes. "They... they made off with my woman, Kiki, Nara's mother. You never met her."

Irik trembled. "You mean that other clan stole her?"

Orki pulled hard on his beard and nodded.

Eyes widening, Irik leaned in. "Why?"

"Probably because they needed a woman to make more children."

"You let them?"

Orki gave a long sigh. "Your grandfather, Rolf, formed a search party of your father, me, and two other Valley Clansmen." He gazed into the distance. "But we were attacked in the forest by a much larger force of warriors. Only your father and I survived." Orki forced a swallow. "We ran. We had to get back to the rest of our women and children."

Stunned, Irik fixed his eyes on Orki's still-grieving face. "Why can't these people be good like us, Uncle?"

With the back of his hand, Orki swiped his tears. "I don't know, but they are few and far away. You're too young to worry about them." He groaned, eased his sore body up, and gestured toward the cave. "Enough talk, Irik. Go be with your mother and brother."

Confused and anxious, Irik sulked on his way home. What made some people bad? Would Cret become like the Fox-tail or White people? Why did they steal women and fight over land all animals share? What terrifying things did the White Clan do? He would ask his father.

Reaching the entrance to the clan's cave, it soothed Irik to step inside stone walls. He found his mother and Tra beside Reto, still lying on the drag sled covered with ibex pelts. Tra cooled his forehead with a clump of wet moss as he twitched and muddled.

"How is he?"

His mother glanced at Tra and back at Irik. "The ribs will heal. He's asleep now." She narrowed her eyes. "Why aren't you helping the men?"

Irik stared at the ground. "They didn't need me."

"Come here, Son." Holding up his chin, she asked, "What's wrong?"

He wanted to see Arol, but he was supposed to stay with his father, showing strength and helping the clan. He answered haltingly, "Do you believe Father will always keep you safe?"

She wrinkled her brow. "Of course. Why would you ask that?"

"Just wondering." He stifled a yawn.

"You need a nap, Irik. I'll call you when the feast begins."

Grabbing a tallow lamp, he retreated to his family's section deep in the cave. The familiar bumps, crevices, and ledges in the gray-brown rock always comforted him, and he needed their security more than ever. The walls also provided the perfect canvas to capture the spirits of his beloved animals. He placed his hand on the cold rock until it warmed and communicated to him. He imagined caribou grazing on the landscape and wolves working together in the hunt—only taking what they needed. He caressed the rock and felt the body of the buck and the frenzy of the pack. *This is where I will place them.*

Checking the consistency of his ochre paints, he began dabbing and shaping the colors into form. Frightening images of those bad people vanished. Slowly, the muscle and movement of the buck and the wolves emerged and danced in the shadow of the walls. Gazing at his creation, he sighed with satisfaction, stretched out, and descended into deep sleep.

Chapter Two

S HE WOKE, HIS HEART knocked against his chest. The lamp
had burned out, the grass of his bed scattered across the floor.
Had he been thrashing again? He sat up and rubbed his eyes, trying to
wipe out the nightmare of being chased by White warriors who had
killed his parents.

"Irik?" His mother's call echoed along the cave walls. "The feast
will begin shortly."

Irik shot up, relieved to hear her voice. Having eaten only wild
grapes and plant tubers for the last two days, he was famished. Meat,
even the fallen caribou's flesh, roasted and juicy, sounded delicious.
And, if he hurried, he might catch Arol before she got there.

"I'll stay here with Reto and Tra," his mother said. "Your father
wants you to sit next to him during the ceremony."

"Will do," he said, eager to take that privileged position for the first
time. Running out, he stopped at the cave entrance and returned to
give Mata a kiss on the cheek.

Sprinting to Arol's campfire, he found her parents dressing up in
their best furs. Arol sported a yellow flower above her ear and flashed
a bright smile.

"Hi, Pral, Leta. Can I walk Arol to the feast?"

"Sure," her mother said, "but don't be late."

Pral smirked in his quiet, pleasant way.

Irik took Arol's hand. "Come on. I'm hungry." He halted. "What
will you eat?"

"Nuts and berries." She held up her pouch. "I heard you had a hard time at the butchering."

He looked straight ahead, not answering.

"It's all right," she said. "I'm proud of you."

He let go of her hand. "You know, we all can't live on plants."

"You could. I do."

He scoffed. "There's nothing wrong with eating meat. It's tasty and makes you strong. Some say smarter. It's not fair to shame anyone for killing animals." He slowed and turned toward her. "What would you wear? How would you keep warm at night?"

She took his hand and met his eyes. "I know, Irik. And you know, by wearing their hides, I feel I'm honoring them. Keeping their spirit alive in me. Just as you do with your cave drawings."

"I do understand, but men…" he tapped his chest, "…have to kill animals to provide for the tribe and to fight to protect the women."

Arol drew back. "What's gotten into you? I never heard you talk like that before."

They walked in silence to the community fire. As Irik guided her toward the women's side, he said, "I'm sorry. See you later?"

A grin dispelled her unease, and her amber eyes twinkled.

The community fire sparked and sizzled. Caribou flesh hung from spits, dropping its juices onto the flame, and the smoky scent made Irik's mouth water. The smell, warmth, and dance of the flames brought each member of the clan together to reflect on their bounty. These men and women were not only his family and his clan but his universe. He would likely never encounter another human being. His life would intertwine with and be determined by his relationships with the thirteen of them and their offspring.

The men, who tended the fire, bared their chests and muscular shoulders tapering to thin waists. The flames' flickering made their brown bodies look like they were rising out of the red earth. Now ten winters old, Irik had gained the right to sit with the men. Taking his brother's place beside their father, the chief, made him reflect on his role among them.

In the middle of the men's side of the fire sat his father, wearing a bear claw necklace to convey the chief's strength and courage.

Next to him sat Orki, his wise older brother. Reto, his firstborn son being groomed as the next chief, would normally sit on his other side. But tonight, Irik served as a puny substitute for his stronger brother. Next to him sat Pral, Arol's father, a quiet, steady man who'd left another clan to join theirs. Lastly came Cret, a brave but hotheaded boy who'd lost both parents to coughing sickness. Sitting among these men, Irik felt both safe and insignificant. He tried to see himself older, how he'd have to quickly become a hunter, a man, a mate to a woman, a father, and a protector of the clan. Looking inward, as he was advised not to do, he sized up a self that did not seem to be enough.

His father stood, and with Orki's help, rotated both sides of meat on the spit, making the fire hiss and sputter.

On the other side of the fire, the women sat holding hands and swaying together as they hummed from deep in their throats. Normally, his mother, Mata, the great storyteller, would be sitting across from her man. Tonight, it was Pral's woman, Leta, Arol's equally pretty mother. She breastfed her yet-to-be-named infant boy while Arol caught Irik's eye and smiled. Then came his father's mother, Molo, a widow the clan depended upon to find and cook herbs and use plants to heal. Finally, there were Orki's three daughters. Tra, the oldest, was Reto's woman, and Koto, the next oldest, had been frail since birth. The youngest, Nara, was Irik's least favorite cousin—and the girl Irik's parents talked about becoming his woman.

All eyes rested on Chief Brul to begin the feast. He stood with a blade in his hand and bent over a spit. He would test the meat for wellness and honor one hunter with the heart. Cutting out a piece from a blackened haunch, he blew on it and put it in his mouth.

"It is ready," he said.

The clan let out a chorus of 'ayahs' but remained seated.

Brul pierced a stick into another small blob of meat and cut it off the spit. Holding it high in the air, he proclaimed, "We give thanks to the animal that died so we may live. Its heart goes to the bravest hunter, my son, Reto."

"Reto! Reto! Reto!" The people cheered.

Brul held up his hand. "Reto is resting but will enjoy his prize later. Let us eat."

Shouts broke out as the preparers spread cooked meats out on rocks. The women cut them up, handing the dripping pieces to their men and children. Laughter and cries of pleasure abounded. Irik's teeth and tongue enjoyed the savory meat, but his eyes kept drifting across the fire to Arol. She was gazing away, having finished her sparser meal. Irik felt guilty for enjoying the caribou's flesh, even if his father had thanked the noble buck for giving its life to feed them.

Soon, his father and most of the clan had finished eating, rubbing their rarely protruding stomachs and dozing off.

Irik caught Arol's attention, and they took in each other's eyes, smiling as though of one mind. He considered what Orki had said. He did have a sensation when he touched her unlike with anyone else. For now, the flames separated them.

"Irik? Irik!" his father called, poking his shoulder. "What are you dreaming about now?"

Irik snapped to attention. Knowing his father rejoiced in the bounty of the feast, he answered, "The success of the hunt."

"Yes, tonight we celebrate."

Irik dug his bare feet back and forth into the earth. "I was thinking about ways to make the killing easier and safer."

Brul narrowed his brow. "I know you feel bad for Reto, but you've only watched the hunts. You can't see things we experienced men know."

"Yes, Father, but when I saw some wolves killing a caribou, it made me wonder—"

"What has that got to do with us?"

"They culled out one animal far away from the herd, and working together, stayed clear of hooves and antlers."

"So?" his father barked.

Irik took a deep breath. "We could learn from them, Father. The males pair up with only one female. They are like us."

"No, they are what they are—animals. Wolves are vicious and kill for meat."

"But do they prey upon humans?"

"No, because we won't let them. We protect our own."

Brul got up and retrieved a long leg bone. Gnawing on it to extract the remaining meat, he measured Irik with intensely dark eyes.

Irik dug his fingers into his scalp, debating whether he should broach what bothered him. "Are the White people our enemies?"

Brul threw his bone into the fire. "What makes you ask that?"

"Uncle Orki said they do horrible things to people, but he wouldn't tell me what."

His father sighed. "I shouldn't tell you either, but it's time you learn about these things."

Irik's eyes widened.

Brul gazed into the distance. "Many winters ago, there was a boy named Eby from the River Clan, Arol's cousin. He was about your age when he went exploring and never came back."

Irik leaned forward, goosebumps on his arms.

"The clan searched for days and finally found his body."

Irik drew back from his father's grim expression.

"The boy's head had been removed, his heart cut from his chest."

Irik gasped. His sympathetic heart leaped from his chest to his throat, and it ached to swallow. The bloody image seared his mind, shattering his illusions of human kindness. "No animal scavenger could do that. Was it the Whites?"

"No one knows for sure, but our long-ago ancestors spoke of White savagery."

Shuddering, Irik struggled to ask, "W-why would they do that?"

Brul shrugged. "Who knows? Maybe to send a warning." He raised his hand. "Point is, Irik, you have to learn to kill or be killed to protect the clan."

Irik sensed a lecture starting. "Yes, Father."

"Son, I killed my first red deer at ten winters, bonded with your mother at twelve, and fathered Reto at sixteen. The clan needs children to grow fast and strong to survive."

"Yes, Father." Irik hoped the next advice wouldn't be to bond with Nara. "I will try."

"You must do more than try. Start by learning the spear. Enough talk. Go home and go to bed."

"I'm sorry, Father. Goodnight."

Chief Brul gave him an affectionate half-smile. "Ask your mother to join me. Tra can watch Reto. We'll be home later."

Irik grabbed a piece of charcoal from the edge of the fire pit and left. Away from the fire, in the dark, he ran. The earlier nightmare of being chased nipped at his heels. This time, the White warriors came for his head. Panting, he reached his mother.

"What's wrong, Irik?" Mata held him. "You look like you've seen a lion."

"I'm just..." he caught his breath, not wanting her to leave. "Nothing. Father wants you to join him at the fire."

"All right" She gave Irik a squeeze, nodded to Tra, and left.

Still shaking from foreboding, a new feeling for him, Irik retreated into the cave. Maybe the prancing of his animal figures on the wall would comfort and inspire him to draw. Staring at a jagged, vacant space above his elk sketch, the only image that occurred to him was the decapitated body of that boy. Nagging questions circled. *Who were the White people? Why would they do such a thing?* He found them scarier than any hungry, wild animal because they could outthink and outnumber victims. What had turned these people into beasts, giving them senseless anger, unfathomable cruelty, and a brute force beyond needing to survive?

The back of his head throbbed. He held up the charcoal. From a dark corner of his mind, he stabbed at the wall.

The stone seemed to fracture. A scream broke out.

It can't be. No, the scream's in my head, making me draw.

A man's body. Chest, arms, legs, penis.

Jab harder. It will go away.

Draw, Irik. What's inside you.

It needs a head.

Cret's ugly face emerged amid dread and hate for his brutish ways. You must fight back.

No. It's not Cret. Irik dug his palms into his temples. Maybe they'll go away. Jab harder.

Yes, Irik, let out your hate. Release the—

No more. I can't.

He dropped to his knees, covered his eyes, and shook. Looking at what he'd drawn frightened him even more than the screaming in his mind. He picked up a rock and slashed at the figure until he collapsed, disturbed and exhausted.

———————◆———————

Much later, Irik half slept as his parents returned for the night. They adjusted their bison-skin blankets and whispered between them.

"Brul, don't put the lamp out yet," Mata said.

"What?"

Irik's eyes opened a crack.

"Look," she said and pointed to the cave wall. "He's been drawing again."

"Mata, I'm tired. Put out the lamp and go to sleep."

His mother went over to the wall and held the lamp to get a closer look. Irik watched her examine the wall from every angle. She beamed. His heart burst with pride.

She turned around.

He snapped his eyes shut, hoping she didn't see the last drawing he tried to destroy.

She nestled up to her man and whispered, "Irik drew the head of a caribou, antlers and all. You should see how real it is."

"In the morning," his father mumbled.

"And he drew a pack of wolves chasing the caribou."

"Not surprised," Brul grunted.

"Strange though," she continued, "he also drew what looked like the body of a man with the head of a roaring lion." She took a deep breath. "It scares me."

Irik shuddered.

"Huh! It's just a picture." Brul scolded. "The clan needs men to hunt animals, not draw them."

"Yes, but he can picture things in his mind—make them come alive. That talent might help the clan someday."

Brul grunted. "He must learn to be a man. Use a spear to feed and fight for his people." He rolled over. "Goodnight, Mata."

Irik winced at his father's decree, but he held dear what his mother had said. She saw he'd captured the spirit of the buck and wolves. He felt a release—sure their spirit would live on in the cave. *Maybe the buck's surviving fawn will grow up to become great and proud as well.*

Chapter Three

I N THE DARK, WHILE THE tree toads still creaked, the men of the clan got ready for a long day's journey. They needed to find a new source of flint to make more blades for tools and weapons. Not wanting to face night predators, they left as soon as the cicadas shook their noisy wings at the rising sun. The youngest children remained with the women at work scraping and sewing hides. Cret, the oldest boy at fourteen winters—already an experienced hunter—was left in charge, guarding the camp and the older children from any danger.

Nearby, at the shore of the river's oxbow, Irik sat talking to Arol. Pretty, petite, and one winter younger than Irik's ten, she had been his best friend as long as he remembered. The sun's low rays made the red in her hair glow, and Irik's heart warmed with each glance at her. He drew in the sand with a stick like an extension of his hand. Looking up, he'd catch her honey eyes with dark brown flecks watching him intently, and she smiled up to her dimples.

On the hill above, Irik caught his older cousin, Nara, at it again with Cret. Nara broke off their snuggling and yelled down. "Irik, Arol, are you ready to play find me?"

"I guess," Irik called back, wishing the two of them would become a pair. "In a while."

Cret shouted in his usual gruff voice, "Don't forget, we have spear-throwing practice later."

Irik groaned and stared off. He got out of that as often as he could. How can Nara stand kissing someone so obnoxious, always wanting to push others around?

"They bother you, don't they?" Arol asked.

"Yeah, Cret doesn't really care if I learn the spear, and Nara always finds me." He slapped his stick hard on the ground, frustrated that Orki hadn't yet given Nara to Cret.

His cousin had glossy, dark hair and symmetrical features, but Irik didn't care for her nose, too much like his own. She had rankled him since toddlerhood, expecting to win every game and stealing his playthings.

She wheedled Uncle Orki for gifts from the hunt his other daughters needed more. Nonetheless, her sisters often braided her hair just to silence her demands. And so, she traipsed about in the family's best furs, holding her elaborately styled head high.

"That stick isn't a spear," Arol said, "Why are you frustrated?"

His eyes widened at her perceiving the stick as an extension of his hand and mood. "Cret's a bully, and Nara bosses me around when she's only two winters older."

"But you're smarter than both of them."

He smiled shyly. "Maybe Cret."

"For sure, and I bet Nara cheats when we hide."

"Maybe," Irik said and then whispered, "Shhh. She's coming."

Nara scuttled down the hill and pointed to the grove of thick pines. "Your turn to run and hide." Seeing a way to catch her cheating, he asked, "A twenty finger count this time?"

"All right," she agreed. "I'm closing my eyes now. One, two…"

Arol and Irik dashed to the trees. Barely into the woods, Irik motioned to Arol to keep running while he doubled back quietly over the carpet of pine needles. He crouched and secretly watched Nara count. Before she was halfway to twenty, she opened her sharp eyes and started creeping into the trees.

"Nineteen, twenty. Here I come!"

Irik jumped out in front of her. "I caught you. You had your eyes open."

She spun around and faced him. "I did not."

"I saw you. You're a liar besides."

Nara's face reddened. "No, no, that's—"

"AAROOK!" A howl shot up from the direction of the camp, cutting Nara off.

"What was that? Irik, you know the animals."

"I don't know this one." He scanned the area. "Where's Cret?" Dashing into the pine grove, he yelled, "Arol, come back. Hurry!"

Another strange, gurgling sound broke out. Then a raspy squawk. Irik and Nara's eyes darted in every direction.

Arol broke out of the trees. Irik put one arm around her and held his spear with the other. They stood together listening.

From afar, Cret shouted, "Go!"

A shriek.

Nara gasped. "Where is Cret?"

Irik pointed. "It came from the direction of the camp. Sounds like the cry of a wolf. We better get back." He took Arol's arm. "Our fires will protect us."

As they reached the women, Cret clamored down from the hillside. He was carrying a limp body the size of a fox, but black and white with only two legs. No spear.

"Cret! Cret!" The women called. "What happened? What is that?"

Cret held up what most recognized as some sort of large bird.

Arol cringed and covered her eyes.

"I took it from a she-wolf," Cret said, expanding his chest, emphasizing the deformed shoulder Irik's mother told him resulted from being beaten as a child.

"Ooh," the women gasped. "Tell us."

"I was at the river's edge when I spotted this strange thing slowly waddling along the shore. An easy target for a nice meal. As soon as I raised my spear, the she-wolf jumped out from the brush and pounced on the bird." Holding his muscular throwing arm in the air, he continued. "The wolf shook it dead by the neck. When she saw me, she let go of the bird and snarled."

"Oh, my," Irik's mother blurted. All eyes remained on Cret.

"Before the wolf attacked me, my spear hit her. She howled and ran away with it dangling from her side."

"Good work, Cret," another woman said, "you are a brave boy... man."

"Where did the wolf go?" Irik asked. Cret might be making it up.

"It doesn't matter, Irik. Far away." Cret kicked the bird in the air, and it fell at Irik's feet.

Arol gasped and walked away, the red in her hair glinting as it swayed with each step.

Cret scowled, making his pockmarked face all the more repulsive. "Start plucking that ugly thing, Irik. No spear practice today."

Although Irik resented the way Cret treated him, Irik's mother had explained that a poor orphan had to show his power. Once Arol was out of sight, Irik took the bird in his arms. Hefting it, he judged it weighed as much as a one-winter-old human. An auk, he thought, his father having told him about an animal like this that lived near the sea. At the end of one of the bird's stick-like legs, Irik spread a wide webbed foot between his fingers. How it moved faster in the water. Holding its almost severed head in his hand, he admired the white patches below each eye.

Why did you wander far from your home and family?

He ran his hand over its heavy, hooked beak lined with parallel grooves. The bird could easily crack open those hard shells his Uncle Orki once showed him. Moving along its plump body and memorizing its oblong form, he came to the tiny wings.

The maker of birds somehow didn't want this one to fly.

Ruffling the white down feathers on its belly, he knew they would make a great liner for a baby sling.

With Cret no longer in view, he carried the auk to his mother, whom he trusted would pluck and butcher it.

That night, after the smoke from the family fires had settled, he went to the rear of the cave and found a bulge in the wall. Holding one of his father's hand axes, he stared into it for several moments. With two fluid swipes of his sinewy arm and skillful hand, he carved the perfect profile of the auk. A sharp nick gave it an eye. Intending to paint it later, he went to bed and dreamed about how the she-wolf would give her life to protect her children.

Irik awoke when the first streaks of morning light penetrated the cave, and he rushed to find Arol. She sat at her family's fire, using two sticks to drop heated stones into a birch bark bowl, hissing and steaming.

"Smells good," Irik said, thinking sticks are sometimes like long hands.

"Mother made porridge for me with forest herbs," she replied, stirring the bowl. "Would you like some?"

"No time for that. Gotta go." He held out his hand. "Let's see if Nara wants to join us."

Arol bounded up and easily took his hand. "Where are we going?"

Already running, pulling Arol along, Irik answered, "To where Cret said he got the bird and speared the she-wolf."

When they approached Nara's family area, she was covered in blankets. Irik nudged her shoulder with his foot. "Wake up, cousin."

Pulling the bison-skin blanket below her dark eyes and prominent nose, she groaned, "What for?"

"Arol and I are going to see if Cret really did spear a she-wolf."

She sneered. "Are you stupid? She could be alive and attack you."

Irik held up his spear. "Are you scared? If Cret did spear her, she's probably dead by now." He sneered back. "I'm not afraid, and you're not my mother."

Before Nara could reply, he took Arol's hand. "Let's go."

Once over the hill and following the river shore, Irik spotted where the sand had recently been disturbed. He knelt and placed his fingers in the depression of a five-lobed paw print. "I thought Cret might have made up a story, but there was a wolf here, all right. The size and depth of the heel print makes me think she was young, maybe two winters." He pointed at a gap in the sage brush. "Over there."

Arol bit her lip, eyes wide and turbulent in myriad shades of gold and brown. "Are you sure we should…?"

He nodded. "Look, the wolf's lost a lot of blood. Come on." Holding his spear out front, he gestured for Arol to stay behind him, and they trudged off.

Coming to a rock outcropping with scraggly junipers poking out of the crevices, Irik pointed. "See the pool of dried blood?" He put a finger to the blackened patch. "Cret wasn't lying, so he is pretty brave. She probably tried pulling the spear out right here, last night." He looked up. "Maybe there's a den nearby."

They crept along the rocks.

Irik froze. Arol bumped into him. He whispered, "Did you hear that?"

"Yeah, it sounded like chirping quail birds."

"Or a litter of squealing wolf puppies. This way." He led toward a wide gap in the rocks where the trail of blood ended.

Arol gulped.

Cret's spear lay at the entrance. The she-wolf must have scraped it out on the rocks.

The squeals intensified.

Irik put his ear to the opening, nodded, and stared into the dark hole.

"You're not thinking of going in there, are you?"

"I could fit."

"But what if the she-wolf's in there. She'll protect her babies."

"True, but if she were alive, she would have heard and smelled us by now. Given a warning growl."

"Are you sure?"

He was sure about the female but not about her partner, which might come back at any time. He poked his head farther into the hole.

"Irik, please don't."

He looked into her expressive eyes. "Trust me," he said and pulled off his vest. Setting his spear aside, he grunted as his shoulders scraped and groaned as his rear end passed through the entrance.

"Oh!" he cried, seeing the pups.

Excitedly, he dug his feet into the earth and propelled himself the rest of the way in.

"Irik!" Arol screamed.

As he moved deeper into the hole, whimpers from the litter of wolf pups echoed in his ears. He reached out, and his fingertips met the warm fur of squirming babies. As his eyes adjusted to the dark, he could make out their dead mother. He bent closer, and their little legs crawled along and tickled his arm. Eyes still closed and blind, the few days' old pups began licking Irik's face and trying to suckle on his nose and ears. It tickled, and he kicked his legs.

Arol shouted, "Are you all right?"

"Yes. I can see the mother is dead." He laughed as the pups smelled his ears.

"That's not funny," she said.

"No, it's her cute puppies—they're all over me."

He started wriggling out of the den.

"You're all scratched up, Irik," she said, running her fingers along his shoulders.

He flipped over and smiled at her. She wrinkled her nose at the smell of urine.

"Wait," he said, reaching back into the hole.

Laughing, he handed her a wiggling, squealing, black ball of fur.

She took it to her chest. "Aww!"

Another pup.

"Ohhh!" She hugged both, letting out her irresistible giggles.

Another.

She kissed all three and cooed as they licked her delicate, tawny face. The babies bore thicker fuzz and rounder features than adult wolves. A mingle of brown, black, and gray fur yielded to lighter shading on their bellies and stubby legs. Their still-folded ears—no larger than Arol's thumbnails—had yet to gain hearing, but their little noses sensed a hundred times more than a person could. They mouthed Arol's fingers in search of nutrients, winning her heart forever.

"Two more coming," Irik said.

"I...can't..." she said as they squirmed in her arms, "...can't hold them anymore."

"Here," he said, handing her the fourth and fifth puppies. "Put them in your lap."

Sticking his head and arms back in the den and straining, he said, "I think that's all."

He grunted. "No, wait." He stretched far in. "Aha, here's the littlest one." He pulled it out of the crevice, held the last pup high in the air, and laughed. "It's a girl, I think, and she's got a dirty white streak on her chest."

The pup let go of her pee.

"Ha!" Arol laughed. "Look at *your* chest now."

"I'll call this one, Meeri," he said. Ignoring the wetness, Irik sat up and put his legs around Arol's lap to make a barrier. They watched the litter of six squealing wolf pups scramble over each other.

Arol pointed at the largest. "Look at this one. He's a boy, and he pushes the rest of them aside.

"Like Cret." Irik laughed. "And this girl never stops squeaking."

"Like Nara," Arol said, blushing because she seldom made fun of anyone. "They're probably hungry."

He let out a long breath and reached for his water skin. Loosening the rawhide at the top, he gently squeezed a dribble of water in front of one pup's nose. Soon, they'd suckled until both water skins were empty. Eyes still closed; the pups settled down into a heap. Arol and Irik stroked their heads and backs, and they all fell asleep.

Irik looked up from the puppies to find Arol frowning. A tear drop trickled to the end of her tiny nose.

Irik put a hand to her shoulder. "What's wrong?"

"They will need milk, you know." She choked back more tears. "How can they live?"

Irik ran his hand back and forth through his dark, bushy hair. "I don't know, but we can't leave them here. The father, if there is one, will abandon them. A weasel or a badger might…" He stopped talking as alarm lit Arol's amber eyes, and she shuddered.

He squeezed her hand and gazed into the sky. "I got it," he said with excitement.

She wiped her tears. "What do you see?"

"You know that sheer rock ledge below the oak tree where we used to hide from Nara? It's hard to reach, and we could border it up, make it safe from prowling animals."

Arol smiled in agreement and admiration. For the second time in his life, the mesmerizing depth of her eyes drew him in. For a moment, he was lost.

Shaking his head, he broke the spell. "Come on," he said, piling the pups into his vest. "We'll make them a new home."

At dawn three days later, Irik and Arol knelt at the rock ledge and pulled away the leafy branches that covered the entrance to the new wolf den. Irik heaved the large boulder aside, and two pups scrambled to greet them. As the little pups licked their fingers and whined, Arol took them into her arms. Peering into the back of the den, Irik reached for another pup.

Holding a limp, cold body to his chest, Irik said. "I'm sorry."

Arol let out a sob.

Irik closed his eyes and nodded slowly.

"So, there you are," came a shout from above. Nara jumped down to the ledge.

"Go away," Irik said, seeing Arol try to hide her tears.

"Listen, Irik, your father asked me where you've been these last few days." She pointed a finger. "What are you two doing with those smelly wolf puppies?"

"We saved them after Cret killed their mother."

She poked the dead pup. "Doesn't look like you've done a good job," she scoffed. "You know they'll die without their mother's milk."

"Leave us alone, Nara."

"Huh!" She squinted her almost black eyes at him. "If your father knew you were playing with wolves and not practicing your spear-throwing—"

"Shut up. If you tell my father, Arol and I will never play with you again."

She turned, walked away, and mumbled, "Stupid kids."

Arol put her hand to Irik's arm. "You know she will tell. Then what?"

He drew a deep breath. "I'll figure something out."

The skinniest of the remaining three pups stumbled and fell flat on its belly.

"It's Meeri," Arol exclaimed, picking her up and kissing her on the nose. "Oh, Irik, Nara's right. They will die if they don't have the right food. They're too small to take in the pieces of meat we bring them."

"I'll find a way," Irik said, patting her arm.

A frown concealed her dimples. "I can't keep coming here, Irik. For three days in a row, we've found one dead, and only three remain." Her chin trembled. "Look at your favorite, the runt. She can hardly climb on you anymore."

Irik slapped his thigh. "Come on, Meeri."

With a wobbling gait, Meeri of the white chest streak found it to Irik's hand and licked it.

Arol was crying hard, her body shaking. "I can't bear it anymore."

He hugged her. "I understand. You don't have to come here again."

When she quieted, he asked. "Will you stay with them until I bury this one? Then we'll go home. Okay?"

She nodded. "I'm so sorry, Irik."

Trudging a distance away, Irik scooped loose dirt to make a place for the latest casualty, covering the little body with rocks to discourage predators.

The next morning when Irik woke, he didn't rush over to the pup den. He had been dreaming of the wolf mother and had an idea.

Walking to the side of the cave where grandmother Molo slept, he didn't find her. Amazingly alive at forty winters, she was sitting outside, mashing up dried flowers in a stone bowl. She was the clan's knower of herbs and plants, where to find and how to cook and heal with them. He sat down next to her and took in the familiar smell of her wild garlic necklace and hair braided around sprigs of rosemary.

"Molo, what are you making?"

"A wood lily paste. It adds good flavor to old meat. What are you doing up so early?"

"Can you tell me if anything grows nearby that tastes sweet and… and makes you feel strong?"

She ground the flowers for a few moments before saying, "Down by the river where we wash out hides, I saw some new milkweed coming up, next to old plants. The young ones would be tasty if the shoots are not more than two hands high."

He stood up. "What do they look like?"

"The new plants look like spears sticking straight out of the ground. Two petals on either side."

"Thanks, Molo," he said and snitched a couple of acorns floating in a nearby bowl.

"Uh-uh," Molo grunted, "they're not ready. The water is still dark. Eat those, and you won't be able to go for days."

Dropping the nuts, he kissed her forehead and stood.

"Hold on," Molo said, "bring back some of the horn-shaped pods from the older plants next to them. We need to make sure you have the right plant."

Returning with a handful of shoots in one hand and pods in the other, Irik asked, "Are these the ones, Molo?"

"Yes, let me show you." She cracked open a pod and plucked out a fingerful of silky stuff embedded with tiny seeds. "See, these seeds carry tiny plants that come from the ones that went before them." She opened a pouch at her side and added the pod. "Someday…"

"Molo? That's interesting, but can you tell me or Arol later? I have to go."

She smiled and waved him off.

When he returned to the den and pulled the branches and boulder aside, no pups came. Not a sound.

He reached into the clumps of fur, his heart beating in his throat. He held the first limp pup to his face. He was still warm. Sleeping?

No breath. Irik laid it down.

The second one. Also dead.

When he picked up the smallest one, Meeri squeaked and tried to open her eyes.

"You're still alive!"

Holding her under his arm, Irik reached into his pouch, pulled out a piece of dried meat, and began chewing. When it became soft, he took a spear of milkweed and chewed until he had a sloppy mouthful.

Holding Meeri up to his lips, he leaked a few drops of the warm soup on the pup's nose.

No reaction.

He stroked a finger along her nose and tried to imagine seeing her pink tongue. *Come on, Meeri, open your mouth.*

A few more drops.

Meeri whimpered, mouth still closed.

Irik tried humming a soft song like his mother sang to her, all the while picturing in his mind Meeri opening her mouth. He'd seen birds and a spotted hyena feed their babies this way.

Yes, the pink tip of her tongue poked out.

A few more drops.

Meeri took it in. Would she swallow it?

Irik waited.

Meeri's tongue stuck out again, farther.

More drops.

Yes, again.

A squirt. Irik fought back a smile, so as not to lose Meeri's meal.

More.

Meeri pressed her snout against Irik's lips, and the food flowed.

When Irik's mouth was empty of the milky mass, Meeri began squealing and pawing at Irik's face.

"Hold on, girl," Irik said, took another piece of meat and milkweed, and chewed.

Several mouthfuls later, Meeri fell asleep.

Irik held her to his chest, hoping the little runt might now live. She was the one who'd peed on him, but she was also his favorite with the white blaze on her tiny chest. He closed his tear-filled eyes.

Chapter Four

IRIK SHOOK HIS HEAD AT the boulders strewn on the ground that once kept the pups penned and safe. He slumped at the entrance of the den he and Arol had built for the litter three moons ago and looked at Meeri in amused disbelief. She'd broken loose and stood to lick his face.

"What am I going to do with you now, girl?" He scratched her under the chin and gazed into Meeri's powerful golden eyes, remembering their former delicate blue. "You're growing up, my friend."

Irik had fed the pup by mouth for almost two moons—sleeping with her at night when he found weasel tracks above the cliff. Meeri's shoulders now reached above Irik's knees when she was on all fours. Still, if she got out at night and jumped down the cliff, she could be easily caught by any number of predators. The pride Irik felt from saving the runt and seeing her grow was tempered by fear of what might happen next. When he took her for walks, she followed him everywhere like a duck trailing its mother. It was both a wonder and a problem.

Irik patted her head and said, "Sit."

"Woof!" She sat.

He liked how she obeyed him, as though he were the leader of her wolf pack. But when considering her future, he worried if the bond was right.

Meeri's ears shot up straight.

Knowing how keen the wolf's senses were, Irik looked up. It was Arol. She waved at him from above, grabbed hold of the exposed oak tree roots, and climbed down the embankment. Meeri waited at the bottom, whimpering and wagging her tail. When she reached the ledge, Arol opened her arms, and Meeri jumped up, putting her front paws on Arol's shoulders. She kissed the wolf's nose and ruffled her neck.

"Phew! You need to wash up in the river." Glancing over at Irik, she said, "What's wrong, Irik. You don't look happy." She sat close to him.

"It's Meeri," he said, giving her a half-smile. "She needs more than a bath."

"What happened?"

"She broke out last night." He gestured down the cliff. "She'll be heading there next."

"What are we going to do?"

He shook his head.

She put her hand on his, and Meeri nudged them both with her cold nose.

Irik patted the wolf's head. "She needs to be free, but we can't just let her go." Looking at Arol's concerned eyes, he added, "Will you help me?"

"Sure, what do we do?"

He got to his feet and pulled Arol with him. "We show her the wild. How to find prey and not become it."

"Can we do that?"

"Why not?" We've already taught her lots. Come, Meeri."

They both laughed and said, "Good girl," as she shook herself and pranced in place, eager as ever to do their bidding.

———✕◆———

The next day, in a faraway thicket of beech trees bordering a meadow, he and Arol began Meeri's wolf training. Using mice and voles that Irik had trapped overnight, the first step was easy. He would let Meeri follow her instinct to chase. Before Arol joined him, he released the little creatures one by one and watched the half-grown wolf dash after them. Meeri didn't catch them all at first, as the mice often scurried under a rock or a tree stump, but she was fast and persistent. She appeared to relish the capture and the snack, always spitting out the tail.

After Arol arrived, they trained her to track. That morning, Irik had taken a fresh rabbit pelt his mother was going to clean along with a rope of twisted hemp. Tying the hide to the line, he gave Meeri a good scent of rabbit. Taking turns, one held Meeri in place while the other ran through the trees, dragging the pelt on the ground, then hiding. Once Meeri realized she'd get a piece of dried meat for following her nose to the rabbit, she found it every time.

For strength training, they let Meeri grab onto a thick piece of bison hide with her jaws, and they tugged away until their arms ached. Later in the day, they built stamina she'd need to chase herd animals over distances. Taking turns, one held Meeri while the other ran far across the meadow and into another stand of trees. When Meeri found Arol, Irik called her back. Meeri's tongue hung down to her chest, so they gave her water and rested.

"Irik," a voice echoed down from the hillock near the edge of the meadow.

His father.

Irik shuddered. What would Chief Brul do when he found him not working with his spear? Raising his second son to become a hunter like Reto was the most important thing to Brul and the clan.

"Come here, Son," he commanded, holding up the dirty rabbit pelt.

Closer, Irik could see anger in his eyes and resolve in his stiff jaw.

"What are you doing here with this rabbit skin? Your mother told me you took it."

Before Irik could answer, Arol appeared in the meadow, Meeri jumping playfully alongside her.

Brul raised his spear, bolted toward them, and shouted, "Run, Arol, I will kill it."

"No, Father!" Irik shouted. In a few paces, Brul would be within a spear's throw. "Arol, stop! Meeri, sit!"

Arol dropped beside Meeri, patting her head.

"Are you all right?" Brul asked as he slowly approached them—spear in hand. The chief stopped cold and looked back and forth at Irik and Arol.

Meeri growled.

Brul pulled his spear back, ready to throw.

"Down!" Irik yelled, and Meeri obeyed.

"It's all right, Chief Brul," Arol said. "This is Meeri. She won't hurt anyone."

Irik smiled at Arol, but he wasn't so sure. The two of them had bonded with Meeri, but his father was a stranger and perhaps perceived as a threat.

Brul stood speechless. Irik knew his father was at war with his instincts to kill the beast. At last, Chief Brul said, "That wolf is dangerous."

"Not anymore, Father." Irik braced himself. "We have trained her. Watch."

"Come, Meeri." As the wolf approached, Irik reached into his pouch and gave her a piece of dried meat. "Good girl. See her wagging tail? That's her sign that we are friends, like… like members of her pack."

Brul scowled. "It's a wild animal, Son. It belongs with its own kind."

Irik nodded. "You're right. But we found her as a blind, newborn puppy. Arol and I fed and took care of her…"

Arol joined in, "It's true, Chief Brul. Meeri thinks of us as her mother and father. She has no fear of humans."

Needing to show him, Irik reached into his pouch. "Here," he said, handing him a piece of meat. "Just say, 'Come Meeri,' and hold it out."

Brul took the meat and looked hard at the animal.

"Father, maybe you could lay down your spear?"

Brul's icy glare gave the answer.

Irik grabbed another piece of meat. "Watch." Kneeling alongside Meeri, he said, "Stay," and placed his hand in the young wolf's jaws.

Meeri drooled but did not nibble the meat.

Irik grinned proudly.

"See, Father." He let her take the meat, still anxious she might bite someone she didn't know.

Brul held the dried meat toward the wolf.

"It's all right, Meeri, go." Irik worried his father would show fear, cause Meeri to react badly, and he would kill her in an instant.

The wolf advanced one step, and Brul's hand began to shake.

Irik had never seen his father afraid before, but he knew how humans dreaded wolves. His nerves began to strain, but if he panicked, Meeri might become protective and attack.

Meeri, tail lowered, crept slowly toward Brul.

"Good girl," Irik encouraged.

With one step between them, Brul jerked his hand.

Meeri snarled and crouched, hackles up and fangs bared.

Brul raised his spear.

"Father, don't!" Irik yelled, jumping between them.

Brul grunted in exasperation and lowered his spear to his waist.

Irik put his arm around Meeri and stroked her bristled head and neck. "It's okay, girl." He gave her a little shove.

The wolf's eyes darted between Brul's outstretched hand and doubtful face.

Irik's heart beat against his chest like a thundering stampede.

Brul kept one hand steady while clenching his spear with the other.

Meeri tilted her head and gently snatched the treat.

Brul let out a long-held breath.

"Yes!" Arol shouted, clapping her hands.

Irik remained silent and waited for his father's reaction.

"Son, I don't understand it. What you and that wolf are doing is unnatural." He looked to the ground.

Irik's heart jumped into his throat.

Brul continued, "But, it is a... a wonder."

Irik closed his eyes, feeling every taut nerve and muscle in his body begin to loosen. "Thank you, Father." He sighed. "Can I keep her?"

"Irik, you won't be able to prevent her from growing up. An animal that needs to kill to eat would be dangerous to our clan."

Irik tensed again, knowing his father was right about animals following their instincts. What he was doing with Meeri contradicted the way of the wolf. But if he let her free now, she could not feed or protect herself. Concern for her fate tore at him.

Arol put her hand on Irik's.

"Father," he said, "I could build a pen away from camp. Tie her up when I'm not training her to hunt on her own."

Brul shook his head and dug his fingers into his beard.

"Train a wolf?" a distant voice shattered the silence.

They all looked to the top of the hillock.

His mother.

"What is going on, Brul?"

"Our son has brought us another problem." He walked uphill to join Mata. Irik's parents talked together—his father often raising his voice and gesturing toward Irik.

Irik and Arol stroked Meeri and looked at each other nervously.

Finally, his parents ambled back down the hillock, Mata smiling and Brul stone-faced.

"Your mother's belief..." his father said and looked at Mata. "...Our belief in your ability to understand animals has saved you again."

Seeing his mother smile, Irik wanted to run to hug her, but he knew his father wasn't finished.

Brul shook his finger at Irik and spoke in the chief's voice. "On one condition, young man. You have until next full moon to pass the first test as a hunter. Either you reach the tree-level of spear-throwing, or the wolf goes."

Irik swallowed the lump in his throat. Hitting a softwood aspen tree at ten paces and having the spear stick and stay in the trunk was difficult, especially for someone with a weak arm who hadn't been practicing. His brother, Reto, hadn't accomplished it until he was twelve winters.

"Thank you, Father."

***

At daybreak, Irik stood ten paces from a two-hand wide aspen tree. Meeri, tied to a nearby tree, watched. Knowing how poorly he would do at spear throwing, Irik didn't invite Arol to his practice session and already missed her. Glancing at Meeri, who tilted her head with curiosity, Irik planted his feet and drew back his spear.

Whoosh! It flew wide and to the ground only halfway to the tree.

Picking up the spear, he threw again, hard. It flipped end over end and hit the ground, breaking off the stone blade's tip. Leaving Meeri tied and whimpering, he went back to camp and brought back another blade. Sitting at Meeri's side, he fastened the blade into the notch at the end of the shaft using loops of rawhide.

He got up and stepped off only five paces from the tree. Maybe he needed to hold the shaft closer to the tip as well. He threw.

Whack! The middle of the spear shaft hit the tree, and the stone blade flew off.

Irik knew he couldn't keep breaking his Father's spear blades, so he would throw the bare shaft at the tree. After several throws, he hit the tree trunk straight on but splintered the notched end. He would have to carve the wood tip again if he wanted to affix another blade, so he kept throwing.

And throwing.

Different arm positions. Different stances.

Throwing again.

By mid-morning, he was able to hit the tree occasionally. With greater confidence, he backed up to ten paces and threw. It landed five paces short and many hands wide. Irik didn't think he was weak, but he needed more power in his throw.

He backed up beyond the ten-pace mark and ran hard. The spear landed farther but way to the side of the tree.

He slumped to the ground, looked over at Meeri, and put his head in his hands. He didn't have the strength, the form, or the practice behind him. *You're a fool, and you're going to lose your wolf.* He looked at Meeri, who had begun to tug at the rope, and said, "I will not fail you."

———◆———

That night, Irik thrashed in his sleep, as he always did when something bothered him. He got up before dawn and took one of his father's hand axes to a remote wall in the cave. There, gritting his teeth, Irik slashed at the wall, snarling under his breath with each cut in the rock. These were not like the marks left by others to enumerate their kills or children. Stroke after angry stroke, he made random, straight lines representing the out-of-control spears he had thrown. *There has to be another way.* Enraged, Irik didn't sense his brother Reto approaching.

"Had a bad night, brother?" Reto asked. "You were jabbing me in your sleep."

Irik dropped the hand ax. His face burned even hotter. "I did? Sorry."

Lifting a tallow lamp to the wall and running his fingers along the streaks, Reto said, "Not your usual fine drawing. What is this?"

Irik shrugged his shoulders. "Nothing."

Reto smiled. "How's the spear practice going?"

"Bad."

Reto put his arm around his brother. "This is important to Father and the whole clan. I thought Cret was supposed to train you."

"He doesn't want me to learn, and if I don't in twenty-eight more days..." He averted his eyes.

"I will help you, Irik."

He thought of how inferior he always felt to his much stronger brother. His voice cracked, "You will?"

"Yes, tomorrow I have a break from our daily hunting. I will show you how to get started." He narrowed his eyes. "But after that, it's up to you."

"Thanks, Reto," he said and put out his arms.

Reto took him into a hug. "Come on. I want to meet your wolf friend."

***

Irik's spirits ran high on the way to the aspen grove, where he introduced Reto to Meeri. Reto, having heard about Irik's success with their father, was relaxed. He easily took to and was accepted by the wolf.

"Quite a feat, Irik. I suppose you'll soon have her talking."

"Speak!" Irik said.

Meeri woofed.

Reto's eyes widened.

"She'll let you pet her," Irik said, scratching Meeri behind the ears.

Cautiously, Reto gave the animal a gentle pat.

Meeri pressed her head into his hand for more.

Reto shook his head. "I never thought humans could communicate with animals, especially dangerous ones. You have a special way, my brother."

Reto's words filled Irik with pride. He had done something his big brother could not. "You know, Meeri is special, and I think she can help the clan someday." Attaching Meeri's rope, they headed to the aspen grove.

Irik tied up Meeri and pointed at the wide tree he had been trying to hit.

"Good target," Reto said, "let's start at five paces. Now show me your stance."

Irik faced the tree head-on, knees locked, holding the spear straight up in the air and shaking.

"No, no," Reto barked. "You have to start with the right stance." He twisted Irik's body and positioned his throwing arm at an angle behind him. "And your other arm…" He directed it forward. "…here, pointing straight out at the target. Good, now spread your feet about two feet apart and bend your knees slightly. More. That's good, now relax. You have to memorize this stance and do it the same every time you throw."

Irik narrowed his eyes at Reto. "How can I relax when I've got to remember?"

"Shut up. You've got to. Now relax."

Irik sighed.

"Good, now onto the spear hold." Reto adjusted Irik's upper and lower arm to form a right angle above his head. "Hold it. You have to get into this position every time. Now stay like this and let your body remember how it feels."

After several minutes, arms aching and spear wobbling, Irik cried out, "How long do I have to—"

"Until you tell me you have it."

"I've got it."

Reto kicked Irik's legs. "No, you don't."

"Ow! That hurt."

"Your knees were locked again, brother. I told you to bend them and relax. Now get back into your stance, or you'll never learn."

Once Irik got comfortable with the stance and the properly balanced spear hold, they worked most of the morning on the critical throw position, still not letting go of the spear. Reto showed him how to angle his arm back and pivot his body and back foot to whip the spear for maximum speed and distance. By late afternoon, tiring of the posing and repeated slow-motion drills, Irik asked, "Are we ever going to throw the spear?"

"Are you sure your body remembers your perfect stance and throwing arm position?"

"I think so."

"Show me," Reto asked and stood back. "Good. Now, just before you pivot…" Reto took hold of his throwing arm and slowly moved it forward and upward. "Where your arm straightens out over your head to…" He moved Irik's arm farther out. "…here. Then you release the spear, but all in one smooth movement."

"I got it." He began pulling his arm back.

"Not so fast, Irik. You need to concentrate your sight on the center of your target and raise the tip of your spear slightly above the target because the weight of the tip will pull the shaft downward." Reto narrowed his eyes and stared at Irik. "You got that?"

Irik nodded, but he didn't. All the dos and don'ts muddled in his mind. Part of the problem was the thrust needed to hurl the spear far enough.

"You'd better get it, Irik. Because once you know when to throw, you are on your own. Now throw."

Whoosh! The spear landed short and wide.

"You let go too soon. Try again."

Whoosh!

"Too late this time. Again."

Whoosh!

"More pivot."

Whoosh!

"Concentrate."

Whoosh!

"Relax."

"Reto, how can I concentrate and relax at the same time?"

"You have to, Irik. Come on, throw. It's almost dark."

Irik bounced on his knees and shook his arms.

Whoosh!

"Again."

Whoosh! Whack! The spear hit the tree trunk. Irik watched wide-eyed as the spear end began to droop and dropped to the ground. He kicked the dirt and growled.

"Congratulations," Reto said, "you've done it. Let's go home."

Irik stared at him. "But…"

"You've proved to yourself you can do it, and you can do it again."

"But… but I'm only at five paces."

"Right," Reto said, waving his arm. "Now you have to back up one pace at a time until the spear sticks and stays in the trunk at least half of the time."

"My arm's not strong enough, Reto. There must be another way."

"No other way but practice." He put his arm around Irik. "Let's go."

Chapter Five

THE FULL MOON IRIK HAD dreaded since the last one was still visible in the morning sky. He didn't sleep well that night, dreaming his arm was a stick, but he woke up knowing all he had was his mind and his arm to rely on. With the ever-present racket of the ravens, the men of the Valley Clan gathered at the aspen grove. All were required to watch and maybe celebrate the budding of a new hunter. Irik stood at a ten-pace mark his father had stepped off, realizing Brul's long strides made the distance to the tree even farther. Focusing on the fat aspen that was both his challenge and Meeri's salvation, Irik felt as stiff as the tree.

Uncle Orki and Pral—both yawning—strolled in, followed by Reto.

Putting his arm around Irik, Reto spoke quietly in his ear. "Remember everything I taught you, and above all, you must relax. You'll have many more tries at this. It took me six and almost a year."

Irik nodded but blocked a shudder, knowing he only had this one chance to save Meeri.

His father raised his hand to quiet the muttering men. "Men of the Valley Clan, we are here today to support Irik in his quest to join our team of great hunters. Let the test begin."

He gestured toward Irik. "You have five throws."

"Hear! Hear!" the men shouted and pounded their spears on the ground.

Brul waved his spear, and stillness resumed.

Irik asked his body to remember the perfect stance, the exact position of his arms, and the proper hold and release of the spear. He glanced over to Reto, who gave him a nod.

Returning his focus to the target, he stretched back, pivoted, and threw.

Whoosh!

The toss was short, but straight to the tree.

"Ooh!" the men cried out. His father looked surprised at the good throw.

Irik sighed with relief, but it didn't release all his tension. He must relax.

What or who could he picture in his mind that would calm his nerves? He got into his stance and pictured Arol, who always made him feel right.

Whoosh!

This one flew past the tree and wide to the left.

"Argh!" the men cried.

"Three more tries," his father shouted.

Irik tensed up again. Maybe he needed a blank mind. Eyes pinned to the target, he threw.

Whoosh! Crack! The spear shaft glanced off the trunk.

"Ayee!" the men cried.

Feeling angry at himself, Irik got back into his stance, bounced on his knees, and shook both arms.

"Come on, Irik!" Reto shouted. "Relax and think about why you're here."

That's it. Meeri's happy, panting face appeared in his mind. He could almost feel her licking his face.

Whoosh! Thwack! It stuck right at the bottom of the tree trunk.

"Ohh!" cried the men.

"Hold on," his father said and gestured for the clansmen to follow him to the tree. They huddled and talked among themselves.

Irik's heart pounded.

His father pulled out the spear and walked it back to Irik. "Sorry, Son. You almost had it, but the men and I agree if the target were a deer, you would have missed its chest." Handing over the spear, he said, "Your last shot, Irik. Make it good."

This was it. He had the stance, the power, and the distance. He only needed the aim. As he spread his feet apart and lifted his spear, he recalled his mother's words. "He can see things before they happen." She always believed in him.

This throw had to work to save Meeri and his pride. He fixed his eyes on the tree and pictured his spear sticking hard right in the middle. He could see it flying through the air in the perfect arc. He could feel his hand releasing it at the exact right moment, his body pivoting in one powerful movement.

Whoosh! Whack!

Irik closed his eyes. Would the spear hold in the trunk?

"Hea-Ya!" the men shouted and raised their spears in the air.

His father, Reto, and all the men came running to him and patting him on the back.

"Ten winters old and soon to be a hunter," his father proclaimed as he held Irik's arm in the air. "Now, you must study our hunting ways, close up."

"Thank you, Father. Thank you, men." Irik hugged Reto and thanked him for his help. "I must go."

The men cheered.

Running to Meeri's pen, he embraced her and dried a tear on her soft shoulder fur. "You're safe, Meeri. I did it." Tying the rope around her neck, he rushed into the camp.

Some of the women gasped while others laughed, but they all knew what Irik had done.

When he found Arol, she put her arms around both him and Meeri. Tears trickled down her cheeks as she hugged him.

"Why are you crying, Arol?"

She shook her head. "You're going to be a hunter now."

Chapter Six

TWO WINTERS LATER, IRIK SLEPT deeply, worn out as usual from learning to become a hunter. Jolted awake by a low rumble, he lifted his head and brushed the hair from his eyes. He concentrated on the sound, outside the cave and becoming louder, then a "yip" from Meeri. Tossing his bearskin blanket aside and sprinting to the cave entrance, he found Meeri straining at her deer hide rope. Irik's heart hammered as he placed an ear to the ground.

Nodding, he jumped to his feet and dashed back into the cave. He poked the mounds of fur covering his sleeping parents. "Father, they've come! The big shoulders are heading into the valley."

Eyes still closed, his father mumbled, "What are you dreaming of now, Irik?"

"I know the sound. The bison have come, just like last spring."

Brul groaned and rolled over.

His mother smiled up at Irik, then jabbed her husband in the back. "Brul, wake up! Irik knows about animals. The clan needs food. Time to ready the hunt."

His lingering sleep gone, Brul leaped out of bed and took Irik by the shoulders.

"Is it true?"

"Yes, Father."

Still naked, his father rushed out of the cave, Irik at his side. Meeri lunged and barked in the direction of the valley. Gray dust clouds appeared in the distance, blurring the thin light of dawn. The ground trembled beneath Irik's feet. Thousands of heavy, pounding hooves announced the advancing wedge of beasts long before he could see them.

Watching his father's reaction, Irik knew the hunter's heart raced with fervor for fresh prey. Brul's wide smile revealed how he reveled in providing for his clan. The long winter had taken another hunter, depleted their provisions of dried meat and nuts, and brought a new baby to feed. The strength and spirit of the Valley Clan were near a breaking point.

Brul patted his son's shoulders, almost equal in height to his. "Thank you, Irik. You're twelve winters old and almost a man. Time for you to join the hunt."

Irik's chest swelled with his father's recognition. "Can I bring Meeri with us? She's been a great guard for our camp." Seeing no change in his father's expression, he spoke again, "Meeri catches rabbits on her own. She could help with the bison hunt by culling out one animal and keeping it at bay."

"No, Son. We don't hunt that way. Your wolf could just as easily scare the whole herd to run." He gestured toward the cave. "Come on. We need to wake the men and get ready."

Irik ran to Meeri and hugged her neck. "Sorry, girl. No hunting for you yet." He sighed. "But for me, it won't be just watching and drawing animals anymore."

Irik had undergone nearly two years of shadow training, only listening to the men's plans and watching them hunt. With Meeri at his side, always anxious to get into the action, he'd made careful mental notes on strategy and how well they executed the hunt. Still, he dreaded the day he'd have to participate.

Irik patted Meeri on the head and rushed back into the cave. He slipped by his preoccupied family, grabbed a lamp, and headed into the dark recesses where he'd drawn the animals. To the hunters, this alcove was a trophy room. They met here to gaze at Irik's paintings, remind themselves of previous conquests, build courage, and plan for another safe, successful hunt. But to Irik, the room meant much more. The walls formed a sacred canvas where he poured his heart into his work and connected to their spirits.

As he rounded a corner, the lamplight gave life to his paintings. He gazed lovingly at a savannah where animals flourished in abundance. Standing at the center of the room, Irik slowly turned around and watched as the light glimmered, making the animals frolic. A flock of goats grazed on a hillside. An auroch proudly displayed its massive, curving horns. Red horses romped through sweet grass. A fat, pregnant mare stood, ready to give birth. To Irik, drawing these figures not only recorded their beauty but captured their spirit. He sensed a force beyond bone and breath all living beings possess, including humans.

When the flickering light met the charging herd of bison, Irik reached over and felt how the contours of the stone added muscle and movement to their images. He hoped his drawings of last year's great bison hunt would inspire the men. They needed every advantage, as once again, herds had become scarce.

He smiled, pivoting to see the egg-filled raven's nest he'd drawn during sparse winter days, and the snake he depicted after Meeri chased it out of the rocks. Almost full circle, he came to the wall of the Valley Clan, and his heart warmed. There, framed in red and yellow, blazed the handprints of every member of the clan, everyone he had ever known. Living spirits, Irik called them. He remembered when he first showed Arol how to mix the fine sandstone powder with water, swirl it around in her mouth, and blow it over her hand onto the wall.

Hand-painting became a clan ritual. Chief Brul insisted each member paint their own, saying, "This is me. I lived here with the Valley Clan. Remember us."

"Are you there, Irik?" His father's voice echoed down the chamber, followed by the wobbling light of his lamp. Brul's eager, smiling face peered around the corner. "The men are on the way, Son. Let's get the fire going."

Once Orki arrived, all six of the clan hunters were seated around the fire. Dressed in lighter deerskin cloaks without leggings for agility, the men gazed at the wall while they waited for Chief Brul to speak. The dancing light made the cave paintings of horses, aurochs, and big shoulder bison come alive and leap off the walls.

Brul turned to Irik. "Give me the elk bone." The chief silently ran his fingers back and forth over the carved shoulder blade.

On it, Irik had captured a simple scene of hunters throwing spears at an elk herd. Many moons ago, the clan asked Irik to carve the bone for the chief to carry on hunts. The men soon became convinced it brought them good luck and much game. Irik was proud to provide something that lifted the hunters' spirits.

Chief Brul's bear claw necklace rattled as he raised the elk bone with both hands, reminding the men of their leader's bravery and vision. He spoke solemnly. "Our four-legged brothers and sisters have come again to give of their own so that we may live among them."

Spreading his fingers out toward the men, he continued, "Each of us must now gather our strength and courage for a successful hunt. As the past has shown us, the big shoulders will remain in our valley for only one day before their trek to the north. I have taken into account each of your thoughts to come up with a plan. We will hide near the birch grove and wait until the bison graze on the tender steppe grass shoots and rest in the midday sun. Do we agree on two teams to ambush them?"

"Yes," the men shouted in one voice, pounding their spears on the cave floor.

Irik closed his eyes and inhaled the musty cavern air to seal this moment in his memory. He felt a deeper connection to his father somehow, a sense of pride. For the first time, he saw him as not only an appointed ruler but a natural leader.

Chief Brul continued, "Because Irik is now twelve winters old and adept with the spear, he will join us in the hunt."

The men turned to Irik, who forced a smile. He feared he could never be the leader his father was or what his brother would become.

Brul gestured to his right. "My good brother, Orki, along with Pral and I, will lead the first wave of attack, followed by the second team of Reto, Cret, and Irik. We must execute this plan with speed and no mistakes. If we frighten the herd, not only might the animals trample us, but we may also lose our first chance in moons to eat well. And, to allow Pral and Leta's new baby boy to grow." He glanced over to Pral.

Pral blushed and nodded thanks.

"Now," Brul explained, using the tip of the elk bone to indicate directions, "Orki, Pral, and I will slowly move down into the valley here. Near the birch grove, we should find some cows resting with their calves. Once our team attacks an animal, the tree barrier means the cow has only one way to run—back toward the valley. We may not be able to bring a full-grown bison down with our first spears, so I will signal to the second team, hiding up the valley in the low hills." He pointed to the second team. "You will either join us to finish the kill, or if the injured animal can run, I will call you to jump out and meet it head-on."

Irik trusted this two-team approach—one he had witnessed with the wolf packs and promoted—but he still felt nervous. When he glanced over and saw his old, frail Uncle Orki slumped over the fire, he told him, "Maybe you'll find an old or injured big shoulders—that'll make the kill easier."

"Good idea, Irik," his father said, "we'll keep our eyes open." He turned to the group. "Both teams must watch for packs of hyenas or lions out for the same prey. Cret, you will guide the women farther up the hills before the hunt to be ready to bring drag sleds down and help butcher the kill." Brul, who had kept talking louder and faster in his excitement, concluded by shouting, "If all goes well, we feast tonight."

The men cheered.

Brul laid the elk bone down, picked up a stick of charcoal, and rubbed it on his face to conceal himself from the animals. The men did the same. When they finished, Brul turned to Irik, put a blackened finger to the pink tip of his nose, and laughed. "There," he said as he grabbed some leafy branches. "Let's cover our heads and get ready."

Embarrassed, Irik finished disguising his face and head before walking out with Orki.

"Don't worry," Orki said, "your father was only trying to be playful."

"I guess, but I fear I will never live up to him."

"I understand, Irik. As the oldest son, the clan expected me to become the chief, but Brul showed special abilities."

"To get the men to follow him?" Irik asked.

"Exactly. Each one of us has to serve our fate, give our special skill to the clan." Orki put his arm around Irik. "You will find yours when the time comes."

After the teams had woven their hair with leafy twigs, they grasped their spears and hiked down to their positions.

Reto, Irik, and Cret took their places up the slope of the valley. The women, with their butchering stones and sleds, moved up the hill above the two teams. From the higher location, Irik apprehensively watched the first team creep down to the valley where the cows grazed near the birch grove. The sagebrush turned thicker and higher near the animals, so Irik could no longer see the hunters moving. His breathing grew heavy, and his spear slipped in his sweaty hands.

Screams shot up from the valley floor—high-pitched human cries mixed with the bellows of a beast. Reto jumped up and dashed in the direction of the birch grove.

Irik dropped his spear, his body shaking.

Cret turned to him and said, "Stay put." Noticing Irik's spear on the ground, he added, "You coward." He pointed his spear up the hill. "Go to the women."

Irik grabbed his spear and thrust it into the air, still shaking. "I will not. I am ready."

More shrieks rose from the valley.

Cret leaped to Irik's side and slapped his face. "Go, I said. I am the oldest here."

"But Reto ran to the grove, so maybe we should—"

With a swing of his spear, Cret swept Irik's legs out from beneath him. "Go! Or I'll tell your father."

Irik scurried up the hill, tears running down his cheeks. When he reached the women, he saw deep worry on their faces.

"Why are you here, Irik?" his mother asked. "We heard the cries."

Out of breath, Irik struggled to answer. "Not sure. Cret sent me up here. To protect you."

His cousin, Nara, rushed to him, studied his face, and whispered, "I'll stand by you, Irik."

He didn't answer, searching for Arol, hoping she wouldn't learn Cret sent him away.

"Aiee!"

Irik stiffened. A new sound echoed up the valley. One he knew too well. The roar a predator makes. The scream of death.

A lion.

Irik heard his father cry out and saw Cret run down to the birch grove.

His father's screams resounding in his head, Irik ignored Cret's order and sprinted down to join the men.

Only twenty paces behind Cret, Irik spotted a large lioness. *A second one?* It was stalking something from the edge of the birch grove.

More shrieks.

Tree branches slapped Irik's face as he ran. He broke through the bush and froze. Father lay on the ground, blood flowing at his neck, deep lion claw marks across his shoulder. Next to him lay a dead cow, two spears in her throat. Beyond, Reto and Cret dashed toward the trees.

"Father! Father!" Irik screamed and ran to him, placing one hand on the gushing wound and propping his head up with the other.

Choking for breath, Brul pointed past the birches. "Orki, Reto…"

Irik turned.

A lioness had Orki's head in her mouth, dragging his limp body along the tree line.

Reto let out a terrified yell and threw his spear, which landed wide.

Irik knew Reto needed help, but he couldn't let go of his father's head in his lap. The lion—three times the size and strength of a human—dropped Orki's body and lunged at Reto. Cret held back his spear throw.

The lion grabbed Reto's leg. With one twist of its massive head, it pulled him to the ground. Jumping on top, it faced Reto's scream with open jaws.

Whoosh! Cret threw his spear, and it stuck deep in the lion's belly before the animal could sink its teeth into Reto's neck. The lion roared at the spear dangling from its side, let go of Reto, and grabbed Orki's lifeless body, carrying it away through the trees. A few paces away, Pral lay motionless, spear still in his hand.

Brul, barely conscious, his head in Irik's lap, grunted out a few words.

Reto tried to pull himself up. "Irik, what is Father saying?"

Irik placed his ear next to his father's lips. "Sled. I think he's trying to call for the sled." He shouted up the valley, "Sleds! Bring the sleds!"

The women were already on their way. At the grove, Mata gasped and rushed to help Brul. Leta and Arol ran to Pral. Tra hurried to Reto's side and helped him wrap rawhide around his bleeding leg.

Orki's two other daughters kept yelling, "Where's my father?"

Irik could not answer. He'd fixed his mind on what must be done.

Brul tried to speak with blood flowing down the side of his mouth. Mata, kneeling at her man's side, put her ear close. She listened, then turned to Irik. "Your father wants you to care for your brother and the clan."

Irik was stunned. He was to care for his brother and the clan? He stood with his jaw open, unable to think or act.

His mother slid her hand under Irik's to hold the blood flow from Brul's wound. She looked at her younger son and ordered, "Do it."

Irik hesitated. He couldn't leave his father to be ripped apart by scavenging hyenas.

Brul raised a shaking hand to Irik's cheek. "Go, Son. Take care of the clan." He let out a long breath. "My time is gone."

Looking at the blood-soaked cloak, Irik knew these might be his father's last words.

"Yes, Father," Irik whispered and rose. He turned to the women and shouted, "Patch their wounds." Irik grabbed a stone butchering blade out of the sled. With the noise and smell of blood, he knew scavengers would soon be upon them.

"Pral is all right," Tra announced, helping her man to his feet, "He was only knocked out by the bison's kick."

Irik turned to Cret. "Get a blade and start with one haunch. I'll get the other." Irik dreaded cutting up the kill but didn't hesitate. Looking up at the circling vultures, he yelled, "We must hurry."

By the time the women were done patching the men's wounds with leaves and rawhide, Cret had finished cutting the cow haunch.

Irik turned to Reto. "Can you and Pral manage to drag the meat back? Cret and I will pull Father."

They loaded his father onto the sled, and Cret pointed to Brul's waist. "Look, your father forgot the elk bone."

Irik shuddered and froze. The lost protective powers of the bone meant nothing. The attacks were his fault. He had unleashed the power of the man-beast from the walls of his mind. He made the lion-headed image come alive and devour his people.

Brul let out a faint cry.

Irik glared at Cret. "Shut up and grab the pole." He lowered his head next to Chief Brul's. "We are taking you home now, Father. Also, the meat."

"Father?"

He waited. The only sounds were the weeping of the women and the distant howls of hyenas. He kissed Brul's cheek, then grabbed the two poles at the front of the sled. He glanced back at his dying, maybe already dead, father and his severely wounded brother. He felt the pain on his mother's expressionless face, the sorrow in Arol's bowed head, and the trauma in Orki's daughters' tears.

He leaned forward, dug his feet into the ground, and lunged one step ahead. He stumbled, but he got up. It didn't help to think Meeri might have been able to warn of the lions. His carved elk bone and cave of animals didn't protect them.

Despite his injury, Reto took charge of the burial. As their stoic chief would have demanded and tradition required, the clan took no time for mourning. Death and life were closely intertwined and readily accepted with little ceremony. The bodies were sledded far from the cave, above a dried creek bed, and laid side by side. Together, the clan gently set boulders and rocks over the bodies, each saying silent goodbyes. Protecting their dead clan brethren from scavengers was important but recovering and hunting again was critical.

As expected of the men, Irik didn't cry. He could only partially experience the deep sorrow of his mother and Orki's three daughters. He kept picturing how his lion-headed figure cast a violent spell on him and his clan. But the women, too, must get on with the work of surviving. Once the rocks were piled high, Reto and Irik walked Mata back home.

Irik did not return to the cave that night to draw. After the lions, animals never meant the same thing to him. He had connected with their spirits, but now he brought out their anger with humans. Finding his way to the wall of the clan, he placed his hands over his father's and uncle's handprints, crying in solitude.

Later that evening, he found his mother by the fire. She looked drawn but not in tears. He thought they could comfort each other, but he didn't know how to approach her.

"Come here," his mother said, beckoning him with open arms and understanding eyes.

He buried himself in her warm bosom and took in the scent of lavender she had picked and rabbit she had cooked earlier in the day. He knew his father would want him to be strong, but he had to say something. "I'm sorry, Mama."

She held him tighter and slowly rubbed his back. "You have nothing to be sorry for, Son. Death is part of life, and we must stay strong and move on."

Not only her steady ways and love comforted Irik. She had a way of magically casting out his troubles and carrying him into another place and time.

"What story would you like to hear?" She lifted his chin. "How about the time when I knew your father was the one for me?"

"I know." He nodded, wondering how she could talk about her man without crying all over again. "It was when he gave you his share of honeycomb when you lost yours in the river."

She chuckled. "Yes, I knew then he'd also be a good chief. Would you like the story about why our ancestors left the jungle and journeyed north?"

He looked up at her. "I like hearing about what they faced to find a new home, but..."

She tousled his hair. "But you know the ending."

He grinned.

"Oh, I suppose you want to hear why the wolf howls at night?"

He perked up. "Could you tell me again?" He snuggled closer.

"At the end of a day filled with both hunt and play, the father wolf waits for the moon. When it rises in the sky, he greets it with a long, mournful call. When people hear it, they quake, fearing the mighty wolf." She looked down, waiting for Irik's response.

"But I don't fear it, Mama."

"I know, Son, but most do."

"Why is the wolf howling?"

"He may be warning other wolf packs or animals that he and his pack are strong and hold this territory. That's what your father used to think." She inhaled deeply.

Irik waited, fearing she would start crying. He wanted to ask what they would do without him but was afraid. After a moment, he said, "Father knew a lot of things and taught me much, but could the wolf be howling for some other reason?"

"Like what?"

"Maybe he lost his family and is calling to join a new pack. Or for a new mate?"

"Maybe."

"Mama, could he be crying as we do, in sorrow? Sometimes I feel so sad when I hear it."

"Well, we could never know. Wolves are different, but I suppose one could have grief."

"I'd have to *be* that wolf before I knew what he meant with his cry."

"That's right, Son. You can't be a wolf, but knowing you, you'll learn what every wolf is howling about. Now, are you ready for bed?"

Seeing tears forming in her eyes, he said, "Yes, Mama," and kissed her cheek. "You tell the best stories."

Getting into bed, Irik realized things would be desperate now. His father and uncle were dead, and his brother injured badly. The clan had gone from five able hunters to two and himself. Plus, he had unleashed a beastly curse on it by listening to those screams from beyond the cave wall. With ten mouths to feed and game scarce, the clan might not make it through the winter. They must move again, and he would have to leave his misery and paintings behind.

Chapter Seven

I RIK, CRET, AND PRAL STOOD speechless at the ruckus before them. Despite it being mid-winter, the sunlit plain erupted with hundreds of fat, gray rabbits, thumping their hind legs and scurrying through the grass to reach their burrows. Meeri caught several in moments and charged down the endless meadow for more.

"The heavens have favored us," Pral declared, waving his spear. "What are we waiting for?" He sprinted ahead.

Cret ran after Pral while Irik stood, taking in the scene. To find a vast plain covered in green grasses and crowded with small game in the middle of winter was an unexpected gift. Although Irik had experienced other wild swings in temperature, he worried about the strange cracks in the ground spewing hot, foul vapors. But what did it matter when food was scarce? Watching Meeri chomp and drop rabbit after rabbit, Irik considered the power of hunger and the instinct to kill prey to satisfy it.

He was thankful, earlier in the day, that Meeri had followed her nose, forded the rushing river, and brought them to this bountiful place. Although he couldn't bring himself to throw his spear, he followed Meeri's trail of dead rabbits and began filling the sled.

By nightfall, it was half full, and the men sat around the fire eating roasted meat for the first time in more than two moons. Meeri preferred the meat raw and had long ago fallen asleep, legs twitching in dreams about the chase.

"Your wolf is smart," Pral said, patting the bloated belly protruding from his rib cage.

"She was hungry too." Irik poked the fire embers with a stick. "I can picture how happy Reto and the women will be when they eat rabbit around the home fire."

"Yes," Pral beamed. "If we gut the game first thing in the morning, we could be back home in three days."

"Or, we could stay another day and have a full sled to take home," Cret suggested.

"We need to get this meat back to camp," Irik said. "Our people are hungry."

Pral nodded vigorously, lips pressed and eyes burning toward Cret.

"Look," Cret argued, "the sled is half empty. More is better. The clan can wait."

"Uh-uh," Pral grunted. "Think of our hungry women. We can come back for more once the clan is fed."

"I agree." Irik crossed his arms. "The clan comes first, and the plain is hidden, so it should stay teeming with rabbit."

"Hidden?" Cret asked.

Irik pointed in the direction from which they came. "The raging river we crossed winds almost all around this plain, and the mountains on the other side are sheer rock."

Cret narrowed his eyes and shook his head, unconvinced.

"With that river as a barrier and little forest cover," Irik explained, "the rabbits are safe from their fox and coyote predators. We can return for another catch."

Cret opened his mouth to protest, but an eerie howl echoing from the mountains cut him off.

Meeri jumped up and whined.

"A wolf pack leader." Irik's voice was hesitant, his eyes shifting about. "Probably claiming dominance of his territory or seeking another mate. We need to keep the fire burning all night and leave in the morning."

"No, I want more rabbit," Cret demanded.

Pral sneered. "That's greedy. We have enough for weeks. The clan is starving."

Cret shrugged his shoulders. "What's another day?"

"Huh!" Pral glared at him. "Easy to say when your fat face is full, and you have no family to worry about. You just want to have fun spearing rabbits."

Cret got to his feet. "Watch what you say."

Pral stood and faced him, never a coward despite a retiring disposition.

"Hold on," Irik yelled, wedging his hands between them.

Meeri barked.

Cret poked Pral in the shoulder. "You're not the big chief, old man."

Pral shoved him to the ground. "Neither are you, boy."

"Okay, okay," Irik said, jumping between them and giving Cret a hand up. "We can't resolve who will be chief until we meet with Reto when we get back."

Cret and Pral sat on opposite sides of the fire, seething.

"Get some sleep," Irik said, throwing on another log. "I'll take the first watch." Tending the fire while scanning the dark for the reflecting eyes of scavengers, he thought about the clan. Not having a chief divided it, and the lack of migrating herds near home took its toll. Most of the clansfolk didn't want to move again with all the risks of predators and changing winter weather. But some, like Cret, wanted to relocate right away. Irik yearned for his father's wisdom and confidence.

As his eyelids drooped, he roused Pral for the next watch and went to lie down. Hearing only an occasional pop from the fire and a faint, distant howl, he fell asleep. He dreamed the howl was a call for help, to belong with others.

"Wake up, Irik," Cret yelled as he kicked his legs. "Your wolf left."

Irik wiped the sleep from his eyes and sat up. "What?" He looked where he had tied Meeri to a large boulder. During the night, she had chewed through her rope and was nowhere to be seen. He cupped his hands over his mouth and yelled her name in every direction.

"She couldn't have gone too far." Irik scanned the horizon. "I need to look for her."

"We figured you would," Pral said. "If you don't find her, meet us back here at high sun. We'll spear some more rabbits, gut them, and have the sled full by then."

Irik nodded, turned, and ran. "Mee-ee-ri! Come here, girl."

Making a zig-zag path across the plain between the river and mountains, Irik feared the worst. Desperate enough to chew through a rope, Meeri must be responding to her wolf instinct—perhaps to mate or join a wild pack. *Would the females accept her? Would a male mate with her or simply kill her?* Irik's thoughts swirled as he ran through the grass. *Animals are drawn to their own kind, even if it means death. Are people the same?*

He looked to the ground as a rabbit ran over his foot, nearly tripping him.

Poor, beautiful things. He heard Cret shouting, "Yea! Got him," with each throw of his spear. Is it his pride in accuracy or the thrill he gets from killing?

Looking at the scampering animals, Irik wondered if they had ever seen a predator, let alone a two-legged one. This huge colony of rabbits enjoyed such good fortune. They built their homes right in the ground under their feet, had an endless garden of food nearby, and multiplied. *They lived in peace until we came and will until the river dries or other predators find them.*

"Meeri!" Irik called with less hope of ever seeing her again.

When the sun reached the top of the sky, he reluctantly dragged himself back to last night's camp. As he approached, he heard Pral and Cret bickering while they gutted the last of the rabbits.

Seeing Irik, Pral broke off the argument. "No luck, I see."

Irik shook his head, dejected.

"Have something to eat," Cret said, "then you and I will head home."

Irik's brow wrinkled as he scanned their faces. He didn't want to show much emotion in front of them, but his heart felt hollow, his eyes stinging with unshed tears.

"Pral's turning his back on our clan," Cret said. "Thinks he has all the answers."

"No, I don't, Cret, just not your answers."

"Look at this place," Cret turned to Irik. "We should move here."

Pral sighed impatiently. "Without finding shelter beforehand?"

"Well, w-we…" Cret stuttered.

"Another topic to discuss with Reto," Irik said.

As they prepared the rabbit-laden sled for travel, Pral gestured for Irik to follow him toward the river.

"I'm leaving the clan for a while, Irik," he said, the rushing water covering his low voice.

"Where are you going? Is it because of Cret?"

Pral pointed into the distance. "See those two mountain peaks there? The smaller one sort of leaning against the bigger one?"

"I see them."

"Before I joined your clan, I lived with the River Clan on the other side of those mountains. We called them the Partners' Peaks, representing a man and a woman. I need to go back to see my old clansfolk."

"And leave Arol, Leta, and the baby?"

"Let me explain." Pral gestured toward the ground, and they sat. "I may have a way of strengthening the Valley Clan *and* my old clan."

"Go ahead."

"You see, I bonded with Leta when her father, Gelt, was the River Clan chief, and I expected to someday take his place. But Leta's younger brother, Mar, would most likely be chosen chief once he found a woman. So, Mar stayed, and Leta and I decided to leave with Arol and start our own clan."

Irik raised a finger. "That's when you joined us years ago, I remember."

"And it's been good for our family, but with your brother likely to take command, maybe there's another way."

Irik scratched his head. "I don't know why Reto doesn't just declare what our father expected before he died."

"He will, as soon as his leg heals. I'm hoping to convince the River Clan to merge with the Valley Clan."

"Makes sense," Irik said. Banding together could mean more successful hunts and less danger of attacks from animals or those strange people Uncle Orki and Father had mentioned.

"Good. I need you to carry my message to Leta and Arol. Tell them where I'm going, why, and that I'll return soon."

"Will they understand?"

"Yes. Leta knows me well. We have a strong bond of love." He put his arm around Irik. "And I know you can comfort Arol."

Would Pral ever promise Arol to me? Not while I'm unproven and haven't earned her.

"I will," Irik said, "but I'm sorry you'll be gone." They stood, hugged, and walked back.

Without saying goodbye to Cret, Pral headed out toward Partners' Peaks, rabbit meat dangling from his belt.

Cret and Irik, holding opposite ends of the heaping sled, pulled toward home.

"I can't wait until everyone sees the results of my hunting skill," Cret announced.

"Yours and Pral's, you mean. And don't forget Meeri's," Irik snapped back.

"Yeah, and you didn't kill a single one."

"Shut up, Cret. Don't talk to me the rest of the way home."

A few weeks later, the mild winter blossomed into early spring at the Valley Clan camp. Everyone had full bellies but drained spirits.

Holding Arol's head to his chest to soften her sobbing, Irik said, "Pral will be back soon."

She looked up at him, wiping her eyes. "Mother says the same thing, but coming from you, I believe it more."

He smiled. "Remember, it was three days out to the rabbit meadow, and Pral told me it would take him several more to reach the River Clan camp. So, he'll be back soon."

"I'm scared for him, Irik. I heard Nara talking about how dangerous it is for a man to cover long distances alone."

Irik shook his head. "Nara is more anxious than most. Your mother is the one to follow. Watch how she bears up in her man's absence."

"Mother trusts he'll do what's best for his family."

"I know he will," Irik said, staring off and admiring the powerful bond of Pral and Leta.

"Thinking about Meeri again?" Arol asked.

He nodded.

"I bet it feels like… a hole in your heart."

"Exactly," he said. "You're the only one who relates to animals."

"Pral!" Leta screamed and ran past them, baby bouncing on her hip.

"See," Irik said as Arol jumped to her feet and darted after her mother.

As Pral set down his sled full of rabbits, Leta and Arol almost knocked him over, throwing their arms around him. The family hugged as if they'd never let go until the baby let out a cry. Pral lifted his boy in the air and laughed. By this time, the entire clan had gathered around to share in the joy.

Reto spoke. "We are happy to see you, Pral, and thankful for you bringing us food."

"Of course," Pral said, "I passed the plain of rabbits on my way back."

Everyone but Cret clapped and cheered.

"Did you meet with your old clan?" Irik asked.

"Yes, and it went well." Pral beamed as Leta kissed him on the cheek.

Reto coughed loudly. "Why don't you take some time with your family, Pral, and meet with the men later to talk about our clans?"

Irik watched the close-knit family head to their part of the cave. He could see, feel, and rejoice in Arol's happiness as Pral hugged her, but a wave of regret swept over him. He missed Uncle Orki and Meeri, but it pained him most to have seldom received affection from the strict Chief Brul. Now it was too late. He'd also have less of Arol's attention with Pral home, but he'd never begrudge her time with a loving father.

Sitting around the community fire, Reto, Irik, and Cret listened intently to Pral talk about his meeting with the River Clan. He explained how, moons ago, Leta's older brother, their chief, fell from a rock and drowned in the river.

"The clan has three other young men—my son, Mar, being younger than Vir and Uro. Old Chief Gelt, Leta's father, is infirm, passing the incredible age of forty winters. He wants to keep leadership in his family. Unless Mar finds a woman to have a child with, it would fall to Arol someday having a son. Gelt is open to bringing our clans together and says he'd consider me becoming their new chief."

The Valley Clansmen cheered, but the modest Pral held up his hand.

"But there is a condition. Gelt wants to see his daughter again and his new grandson. He needs to be sure he has a boy from his family that will someday become chief."

"That makes sense," Reto offered.

"You would be leaving again, Pral?" Irik asked, thinking about those other boys. If Arol was to go along, maybe they would steal her. "How would we know if the River Clan agreed?"

Pral smiled mysteriously and replied, "That depends upon another promising opportunity and whether or not the Valley Clan is interested."

"Let's hear it," Reto said, "but not before we share a drink of sun tea."

Reto held up a large gourd and sprinkled dried flowers into the vessel. Irik loved the tea made from a flower with a bright yellow center and white petals, as though the sun were peeking through puffy clouds. As Reto added hot water, the brewing aroma wafted among the men and relaxed them even before taking a drink. They toasted each other as they passed the gourd. Irik took the last drink and looked to Pral.

"On my trek passing through Partners' Peaks, I noticed a wide swath of dried, fairly recent auroch tracks—a sizeable herd—moving west. I headed that way for half a day, bunking for the night under a chestnut tree. The next morning, I woke to the smell of roasting meat. Following my nose like a stalking lion, I climbed over a rise and looked down on a lush valley and smoke rising from a fire."

"Humans?" Irik asked breathlessly.

"Wait." Pral waved a hand. "I crouched behind a stand of prickly bushes. Soon, a woman—only some ten hands high—emerged from a cave below the rocks. Holding a baby to her bare breast, she tended the meat hanging over the fire."

"Was she a Lessor?" Reto asked.

"I've never seen one. I crept along the brush to get a closer look."

The clansmen leaned in, eyes wide.

"A man came out of the cave in a rough-cut cloak with no leggings or shoes. He was broad, muscular, and sort of plodded, making me think he's not fast on his feet. When he approached the woman, I got a better look. And yes, he appeared similar to what Leta's father described as a Lessor—bulging forehead over deep eyes, broad nose, and no chin."

Irik gasped, his hair standing on end.

Cret laughed. "And ugly."

"I guess you could say that," Pral considered. "They're not tall and slim like us, but they act much the same."

"How were they like us?" Irik's throat was dry, his voice hoarse.

"When the man came out, he hugged the woman and patted the baby on the head, and they talked to each other."

The men muttered among themselves.

"Pral," Irik asked, "what else did Leta's father know about them?"

"He said they seemed secretive, stayed by themselves mostly. He told me they…" he put a finger to his temple. "…may be a little slow."

"Were there more?" Cret asked.

"As I watched, more came out and sat around the fire and ate. There were four men, one quite old. Also, three women and two children."

Reto asked, "What is the opportunity?"

Pral nodded as if recalling something he'd almost forgotten. "I didn't recognize it then, but as I circled their camp to get back on my path, I came across another rocky outcrop." He reached into his pouch and handed Reto a piece of dark blue stone. "Perfect shale for new cutting and hunting tools, isn't it?"

Reto passed it along, and everyone grunted in agreement.

"That's not all," Pral said. "Further on, in the southern hills above their camp, I came upon a stream, eight-hands wide. It flowed down from the foothills to within only twenty paces of their camp."

"With aurochs migrating through the area," Reto said, "it sounds like a perfect home site."

"Exactly what the River Clansfolk thought when I told them about it." Pral's hands curled into loose fists at his sides, and he shook them excitedly. "They've been thinking about moving, so it could be ideal for both of our clans."

"Living near the Lessors?" Irik asked.

"No, stupid," Cret said. "We'd take it from them and make it our home. What weapons did they carry, Pral?"

"As much as I could see, several spears, but thick and roughly made, only for thrusting."

Reto raised both hands. "Hold on, Cret, we're jumping ahead. The site could be promising, but both clans need to meet first and do more planning before we consider it. We don't even know if the cave could fit us all."

"True," Pral acknowledged. "The River Clan, including my family, has five men, three women, and two children." He counted on his fingers. "With the Valley Clan's three men and five women, that makes sixteen."

"So many people," Reto chuckled softly, "and in a year or two, we'd have even more. If the cave's big enough, it sounds like a great chance for our two clans to merge and grow."

"What do you mean?" Irik asked, feeling he'd missed something.

"The River Clan has two men needing women," Reto said with a grin, "and our clan has two single women." He looked at Irik until realization dawned on his younger brother's face.

"That's right," Pral said, "another plus for uniting our clans."

Irik felt like he'd been kicked in the gut. *What if one of those other boys wants Arol?*

"When will you leave, Pral, and how long will you be gone?" Cret's craggy face barely concealed his eagerness to be free of the older man.

"The weather is good," Pral answered, "so, tomorrow."

"How will we know when and where to meet?" Reto asked.

"I suggested to Leta's father that if the Valley Clan agrees, we meet at the end of summer, at the rabbit meadow, only two days from the Lessor site. Would that work?"

Reto turned to Cret and Irik. "Do we agree?"

"Yes," said Cret.

Irik ran his hand through his hair. "I guess."

"It's settled then," Pral concluded. "When the birds begin to head for their winter homes, and the days are as long as the nights, look for the bright autumn star. When it makes its lonely path across the dark evening sky, we will reunite."

"Don't be sad, Irik." Arol turned to wave back to her calling parents against the sunrise. "I will wait for you, and in a few moons, we'll be together again. Like always." Her flushed lips trembled as tears seeped from her amber eyes, radiant in the dawn light. The surrounding dark lashes and sepia flecks within drew him as deep as he dared to look.

Seeing her feelings burst forth, Irik had to dry his cheeks as he shakily said, "Promise?"

"I promise." She leaned in, he thought for a hug, but kissed him goodbye. It was the first time she had brushed his lips with hers, and it filled him with a warm tingling as they wrapped their arms around each other and held tight. He wavered on his feet against her, letting the new, dizzying sensations course through his body and ignite his heart. As Arol broke off their embrace to trudge away, he had to force himself to let go of her soft, brown hand.

Irik stood at the edge of the cave with a lump in his throat, watching Arol and her family shrink into specks on the rosy horizon and disappear.

How dull and empty a world without her. Already he yearned for another kiss. They had always meant so much to each other. Arol awakened emotions stronger than anything he'd glimpsed before with other people, his art, or the wolves. She took her rightful place at the center of his mind, the core of his being. How would he bear the separation?

A tap on his shoulder startled him. Cret surveyed him with skewed lips of either pity or disdain.

"You, Reto, and I are meeting tomorrow at high sun to pick a new clan chief."

Irik stiffened.

"We have to have a leader to work with Pral." He flipped a hand at Irik. "See you then."

Dismayed by Cret's swagger, Irik rushed to Reto.

He found his brother trimming a rabbit pelt while his woman, Tra, sewed another.

Breathing fast, Irik exclaimed, "Cret told me about the meeting tomorrow."

"Yes," Reto acknowledged, running his blade along the pelt.

"Can we talk alone, Brother?"

"Sure." Reto kissed Tra and got up to follow Irik.

When they reached a secluded spot, Irik asked, "You're going to be chief, right?"

Reto took a deep breath. "No, I've decided I can't and don't want to."

"What!" Irik cried, looking around to see if anyone heard him. "Your leg is getting better, isn't it?"

"No, Irik, it's not. I still limp badly after many moons, and I could never lead a hunt or cover long distances. Being slow could make it dangerous."

"But, Reto, you're the oldest. Father had chosen you before he died."

"I know, but things change, and Tra and I have decided…" he put his hands on his brother's shoulders "…we are having a baby, and I need to be with her."

Irik wondered how Reto could be so dedicated to his woman. "I…I'm happy for you, but the clan?"

"I can contribute without being a burden. Flake blades, butcher, and help in many ways."

Irik's jaw tightened. "You'd let Cret become chief?" He raised his voice. "You know he's not bright, and he's hotheaded and… and cruel."

"Yes, but he is brave, strong, and wants to be chief."

"Reto, please."

"No, Irik, it will be up to you. You may only be eleven winters old, but you are much smarter than Cret, and I believe you could grow into a good chief. I know it's a tough challenge, but if you're willing, you have my vote."

Irik stared into his brother's face. He didn't seem to be teasing.

"You should think it over," Reto said, patting him on the arm and walking away.

Irik slumped against a tree, utterly overwhelmed. What kind of chief could I be? How could I lead a hunt? But if Cret became chief, what might that mean?

He shuddered. Needing to calm his racing mind, he ambled back into the cave. He ignored his mother's greeting and sought the only place of comfort he knew.

Without a lantern, he found his way into the room of the animals. He walked slowly around the cave walls, feeling the contours of the creatures he'd painted, remembering how he connected to their spirits. His fingers traced the curved horns of the auroch, the bristly manes of the red horses, and the powerful shoulders of the bison.

The animals meant something different now. Their flesh, not these images, kept the clan alive. If he were chief, he'd have to lead the killing.

A fluttering lamp light approached.

"Irik. Are you there?" his mother called.

He didn't want to answer, but when she peeked around the corner into the alcove, and he saw her warm smile and kind eyes, he smiled back.

"Hello, Mother," he said and gestured for her to sit.

She placed the tallow lamp between them with a sigh. "Reto told me of your disappointment."

"Yeah, I don't understand why Tra's more important than the whole clan."

She patted his leg. "I know it feels that way, but the bond between a man and a woman is what makes up the clan."

Irik wrinkled his brow.

She put her hand to her heart and closed her eyes. "Your father used to tell me he wouldn't be a good chief without me."

Irik respected her feelings and waited.

She gestured toward him. "Someday, you will come to that place and find a relationship that makes you a stronger, better man." She nodded slowly. "You will find that person. You just have to be open."

Irik pictured Arol, hearing her say she promised, then waving goodbye. "But…" he said and groaned.

"You know what your father wanted."

Irik heard his mother, but he didn't want to respond.

"Nara," his mother said, "has already had her moon flows."

Irik recoiled. No, not her again. Arol is the one…

"She is a strong woman and would make you—"

Irik shot up. "I don't like Nara!" He bolted out of the cave.

———✦———

Irik sat on a tree stump in the pine grove two days later, hidden from the clan and brooding. Knowing he could not lead a hunt, he'd told Reto he would not be chief. The thought of Cret in charge still troubled him. Cret was a great hunter, but it took more to be a leader. Yet, hunting was what fed the clan, and without it, they would perish. Cret had to be chief, even though he didn't seem to understand how important goodwill among people was. Irik simply had to live with it. But he felt he was giving up on his beliefs, giving up on himself.

"Irik." It was Cret. He had found him. "No more hiding. You and I are going hunting to the rabbit field tomorrow,"

Irik nodded slowly.

"Be ready to leave at dawn."

He nodded again and watched the new clan chief disappear into the cave.

Needing to rest up for the long journey, Irik waited for the sun to drop under the horizon, and he went to bed.

He awoke in the middle of the night to what he thought was the howl of a lone wolf. Thinking it sounded more like a male's cry for a mate, he trudged over to the community fire. He added some kindling to the smoking embers, and soon the flames lit the hillside. Watching their dance, Irik became entranced and thoughtful.

A rustle in the nearby bushes perked him up.

A whine.

From a wolf? He grabbed the back end of a burning branch and crept toward the sound.

A familiar 'yip' greeted him.

He sprinted toward the curled blob of fur.

There, lying on her side, was Meeri, tongue hanging out and panting, tail trying to wag.

"Meeri, you've come back." He knelt, hugged her neck, and rubbed her side. Her whimper sounded the same, but her body felt and looked different. She was pregnant, fat with teats growing from her belly.

"Are you okay, girl?" Her tail lifted but soon fell.

"Now I know where you've been." Stroking her head, he watched Meeri's eyes close and her chest rise more slowly. *Why would you come back? Well, I'm just glad you're here.*

Joy surged through Irik's veins. "Let me get you some water." He jogged back to the cave entrance, where a goatskin water bag hung.

Grabbing it, he turned. Meeri pulled herself up, and with her rear end dragging along the ground, struggled with her front legs to reach Irik.

"Hold on, girl," he said and saw why. There, some thirty paces behind Meeri, the fire reflected in a pair of yellow eyes piercing the blackness.

In the dark, cloud-covered skies, he could not make out a figure, but he knew the eyes were of a wolf. The male must have chased her here. *Does he want to bring her back to his pack? Kill her? I need to get between them.*

Remembering a stack of spears the clan kept for emergencies at the side of the cave entrance, Irik crept slowly toward it. The wolf's eyes didn't move, so he knew it must think it remained unnoticed. With the water skin under his arm and spear in hand, he skulked toward Meeri. He sprinkled drops on her lips, and she lifted her head to lap them up, then collapsed.

The male wolf's eyes began to move slowly up and down, indicating he was stalking. *Does he only want to protect his mate? Am I in his way?*

Irik stood and raised his spear.

The yellow eyes shot upward and quickly became bigger as the wolf began his charge. Irik couldn't see the lupine body in the dark, but he knew the wolf, with excellent night vision, could surely see him. And take him down.

He shuddered, realizing he couldn't tell where to throw his spear.

The wolf's paws slapped the ground. Meeri snarled.

Irik knew the animal would use its body to knock him over and go for his neck.

Closer, Irik saw the glint of fangs rising. "Meeri. Stay!"

The wolf lunged.

Irik stepped back. He fell into a crouch, planting the base of his spear angled into the ground.

Meeri growled and tried to get up.

Irik held tight to the spear, screaming as he sensed the wolf leaping at him.

The spear tip bore into the wolf's chest. A liquid crunch and shrieking howl hung in the air as the wolf writhed on the spear and went limp, falling to the side.

Shouts rang from the cave as people hurried to the scene.

Irik reached behind him, felt Meeri's licking tongue, and dropped between her and the dead wolf. He lay there, chest heaving, struggling with what he'd done. Looking at the pitch-black fur of the dead wolf, he wondered why he'd left his pack. *Did he want to bring Meeri back? Whatever his plans, I ended them. Forever.*

He had killed.

He had to.

Following many hours of devoted attention, drinking and eating, Meeri slowly recovered from her escape. With her at his side, Irik retold the clansfolk how it all happened, then retreated into the pine grove.

Once again, Cret found him. "You've proven yourself, Irik. No rabbit hunt tomorrow. We'll feast on your wolf." With a slight flash of mangled teeth, the chief-to-be added, "Thank you."

Irik nodded, dazed by everything, especially this unexpected courtesy.

As Cret left, Nara approached. Irik stood stoically, not wanting to talk anymore.

"I always knew it, Irik. You are brave and smart, and you should have been chief."

"Thanks, Nara," he said and started walking away.

She grabbed his arm. "It would be my honor to make that wolf's fangs into a necklace for you." Her pleading gaze and soft tone almost made him forget he despised her.

He combed his hair back with his fingers. "I guess."

She smiled and reached for a hug but dropped her hand between Irik's legs and rubbed.

The sensation alarmed but excited him.

Chapter Eight

IRIK BLINKED HIS EYES OPEN at the damp warmth of Nara's breath on his face. Still deep in the night, he wanted to wake her to take him in again, to experience the pleasure he'd only heard about before through the giggles and moans of his parents.

He considered the face he had known all his life—his older cousin of fourteen winters who used to play tricks on him. Her once darting eyes now stayed fixed on him. Her beguiling face and full hips captivated him as she gave of herself. Irik no longer saw her with a child's eyes. Like his father before him with his mother, Irik had become a man at only twelve winters old because of Nara.

Seven months had passed since the first time she touched him so unexpectedly. Last night, she'd told him his mind made him better than any hunter. And, she promised to bond with him, not Cret. She gave him a sense of power and pride he'd never imagined before.

He raised his chin, inhaling deeply. The autumn star had signaled the Valley Clan to leave and meet with the River Clan to consider becoming one and finding a new home. Today, he must face his challenger and begin to play a more critical role.

He tucked his hand under Nara's long black hair and lifted it to his nose. Closing his eyes, he recalled how that fragrance—oils from a spiky plant—intoxicated him when they first touched. Gently laying his fingers on her cheek, he admired her nose—which had a similar hook to his but more delicate. He placed a finger on her lips and loved how they parted for him.

Nara woke, smiled, and took his hand. They embraced.

When his heart finally slowed and their sweat cooled, she wrapped her arms around him, and they slept.

At dawn, a blast of cold air penetrated the cave, waking Irik. Winter had chased autumn away. Watching his sleeping woman, he regretted it was time to go. He slipped out of the bearskin blankets, put on a heavy buffalo hide tunic, and padded to the other side of the cave where Cret slept. He didn't find him there, but Cret's woman, Koto, pointed to the entryway.

Outside, at the sight of Irik, Meeri tugged at her rope. Her five, almost-fully-grown offspring jumped up in their pen, eager for a training session and the meat that followed.

"Sorry, girls and boys," Irik said as he walked past. "You will have to wait."

Cret sat beneath the branches of a beech tree, wrapping wet rawhide strips around his spear blades, fastening them to shafts. He laid the weapons in a row on the frost-covered ground to dry and tighten in the sun.

He didn't look up when Irik spoke. "Cret, you and I have a problem."

"I'm busy, Irik. Making sure our weapons are in the best shape."

Irik wrinkled his brow. "For what? We haven't met with Pral and the River Clan yet."

"Huh," Cret grunted with a snide laugh. "As chief, I will convince Pral to attack the Lessors and take their home for us."

"Maybe you will, and maybe you won't, but that's not why I'm here."

"Why then?" Cret's gravelly tone betrayed growing irritation.

"Nara and I have decided to bond."

Cret shot up, spear blade in hand. "You don't decide that!" He pointed it toward Irik's face. "I am the chief."

Cret was stocky, muscular, hotheaded, but slow. Irik had to be careful, so he slyly backed away a step, closer to the row of spears on the ground. "I know, but we want each other."

Cret chuckled, exposing his missing front teeth. "Both of you are children."

"I am twelve winters now, and Nara has flowed with the moon."

Cret spat at Irik's feet and growled, "Nara is mine to take."

"No, our clan has a one-woman rule. Like the wolves, you have to be loyal to your mate for life. You already have a woman."

"Huh! Childish wolf talk. I am the pack father and will mate with any female." Cret stepped closer, his pockmarked face burning red.

"Cret, you know my Uncle Orki never promised any of his daughters to you, let alone two. Koto agreed to bond with you, but…" Irik glared at Cret. "…you will not have Nara."

"You think you can tell me what I can have?"

Irik glanced again at the row of spears by his feet and shifted his sinewy legs alongside them. "Not me, but the clan—my father made that bonding oath with all the Valley men before you joined us."

Cret shook his head, contempt burning in his eyes.

"You know that oath says each man will only bond with one woman." Cret scowled. "I didn't take that oath."

"Right, the clan took you in as a young orphan. But the Valley Clan oath is what ensures the men will work and hunt together as a team. Having more than one woman would cause in-fighting."

Cret jabbed his blade closer to Irik's chest. "Your father is dead. He failed us, and now I decide who bonds."

"Cret, you must respect him and the rules of the clan. You may be chief, but no one respects you."

Cret roared and lunged.

Irik deftly stepped behind the row of spears.

Cret's bare feet slipped and rolled on the spear shafts, and he fell hard on his back.

Irik picked up a spear, jumped on top of him, and laid the shaft across his throat. With Irik's wolf-fang necklace dangling in front of his crimson face, Chief Cret choked and struggled for breath.

The wolves barked, and the women of the clan came running. Koto screamed for Irik to stop, but Nara caught his eye and gave him a little smile.

"Get off him, Irik," Reto yelled, limping toward them.

Holding his leg in pain, Reto scolded, "How can our clan survive if the last of our men fight each other?"

"I am chief," Cret bellowed, "and your brother cannot bond with a woman without my permission."

Orki hadn't promised Nara to him, but Irik knew that was what his father wanted. "Reto, Nara and I have already bonded with our bodies."

The women gasped, but Nara didn't blush.

Reto glanced at Irik but fixed his eyes on Cret. "That is true. The clan agreed to make you chief. But I know you respected my father and are bound by the rules of the Valley Clan."

Koto and the women glared at Cret, who did not respond.

Reto continued. "Before our father died, he said he wanted Irik to bond with Nara."

"But..." Cret blustered.

"No, it is done. We must respect our father's wishes. The clan's rule is clear, and we have bigger issues facing us. You two will soon meet with Pral and the River Clan to plan our futures." Reto waved his hand over the group. "All of us depend on you."

The women, including those who'd collectively raised Cret, stared at him reproachfully until he hung his head.

Nara flashed an adoring smile at Irik, and they walked away hand in hand.

After hiking hard for three days, Irik, Cret, Meeri, and all five of her fully-grown brood arrived at the once-swollen river that bordered the rabbit meadow. The rainless summer and early winter had dried it into a ditch of rocks. The snow-covered field beyond was barren of grass and rabbits. Nature, humans, and other animals had turned it into a dusty home for termites and lizards. Meeri, confused or disappointed, looked to Irik, seemingly for an explanation. He shook his head. *Did some of the rabbits find a new home?*

In the distant direction of Partners' Peaks, Irik spotted a trail of smoke. They'd soon meet Pral and his River Clan. Cret had initially argued against bringing the wolves, expecting the other clan to fear them. But, for many moons, Irik had trained them hard and convinced Cret they'd be of value. Coming to within waving distance of the River Clan, Cret reluctantly agreed to go ahead, explaining to them that the wolves were tame. Irik and the pack remained still.

When Cret waved him on, Irik sprang into action. Commanding Meeri and her brood to stay, he backed up halfway between the men and the wolves and called out, "Pack, come!"

"Ooh," the men exclaimed when they saw the wolves playfully jump on Irik and wag their tails.

Irik waved his hand around his head and said, "Circle."

Meeri and her children raced in a ring around him.

"Aah," the men cheered.

Irik held his hand out toward the wolves. "Pack. Stay." He backed up to the men. Pral gave Irik a big hug and introduced him to the River Clansmen. Their aged chief, Gelt, was not able to stand and had a hard time speaking without any teeth. Mar, Arol's younger brother, shared her red-tinged hair and kind eyes. Uro, a hulking twelve-hand-tall man with a beard to his waist, exuded a serious demeanor. Vir, the third hunter in Pral's clan, looked to be Irik's age, of slight build and wearing a perpetual smile. When each man greeted Irik, they touched his wolf-fang necklace and told him how much they admired his power over the dangerous animals.

Irik knelt and said, "Let me introduce each of my wolves. Deego, come." The large, pitch-black male bounded over to lick Irik's face. Irik marveled at how much he looked but didn't behave like his feral father, the wolf Irik had killed. "This is Deego, the big man of Meeri's family, always bossing his brothers and sisters around." He chuckled. "But not his mother." Irik took Deego and every other wolf around to greet each man. "Paw," he'd say, and the man and wolf would shake hands.

Next, he called Fola, the second male in the pack, fastest learner and best tracker. After Fola shook everyone's hands, Irik introduced Bika, the first of three females. He described her as shyest in the litter, but once she got to know someone, most loyal. Slar came next, biggest of the females, also fastest and most fearsome. The last female was Deela, the wolf with the best traits from her mother and father. Like her mother, she had a white streak on her chest and superior intelligence. Like her father, she displayed tremendous tenacity and strength.

Once the littermates had gotten to know the River Clansmen and gathered around Irik, he looked at Meeri. "And here's the wolf who started it all." He braced himself firmly on the ground, patted his chest, and opened his arms. "Come on, girl."

Meeri raced to Irik and leaped into his embrace. Catching her, he wobbled a bit, then laughed and kissed her on the nose. The men hollered and guffawed.

After shaking Meeri's paw, the River Clansmen wanted to learn how Irik accomplished such an incredible feat. He described he and Pral's daughter, Arol, finding Meeri as a newborn, feeding and caring for her. He explained the potential bond he recognized between human and wolf when he threw a stick, and Meeri fetched it back to him.

"You see, we can become their pack leaders. Only other wolves might be able to divert them from minding us. Fortunately, Meeri passed her obedience to humans on to her children, and because they saw how their mother acted with me, they were easier to train. Someday, I believe we can teach wolves to hunt with us."

"Enough, Irik," Cret interrupted. "We need to talk about our clans and a new home."

Pral held his hand up toward Cret. "We'll get to those matters, but first, let's take a tour of our cave home, meet our families, and get to know each other better. Afterward, we'll have a delicious stew our women are preparing."

As they entered the cave, Irik's nose wrinkled at the unfamiliar smells, and the heavy air clutched at his throat. At the fire, cutting up pieces of white flesh, sat Gelt's considerably younger woman, Cici. Poola, her young son, was at her side. The women laughed while covering their mouths and closing their eyes out of embarrassment.

With pride, Pral showed Irik and Cret what was being cooked in the simmering pot. Several flat, black heads, three fingers wide, bobbled on the surface. Their beady eyes and worm-like spikes made Irik force back a gag at the thought of eating whatever it was.

"It's catfish," Pral announced, "a staple of the River Clan and one of my favorites."

"How do you hunt them?" Cret asked.

Pral reached behind Cici and held up a woven reed net. "We run this through channels in the river and catch them."

Pral led them farther back into the cave to the sleeping chambers. Because this cave was shallow, rain dripped down from the earth above, making for soggy beds. A stench of wet, sweaty furs repelled Irik.

"Oh," Pral said, looking at Irik's graying face, "you're probably smelling the bat droppings from back in the cavern. Can you hear them squeaking? We share our home with them during the day. They fly out each night to feed and wake us up at first light."

At that moment, Irik wished he had wings and appreciated his clan's dry home. Following a light dinner that he merely pecked at, the men shared hunting stories and the sad retelling of the Valley Clan's disastrous encounter with the lions.

Arol's younger brother, Mar, asked, "Is it true your clan has available women?"

Cret answered, "No, only one. She's older, a widow."

Pral asked, "You mean Mata? She's twenty winters older than Mar. How can there be only one? Before I left, there were Koto and Nara, Orki's daughters."

"No longer," Cret said. "Koto and I have bonded, and Irik is with Nara."

Pral's eyes and mouth widened from surprise to dismay. He glared at Irik. "Is this true?"

Irik looked to the ground. "It's what my father wanted."

Pral opened both hands toward Irik. "I always thought you and Arol were close."

"You never promised her to me, Pral. I assumed she would bond with one of the River Clan boys." He clamped his lips and shook his head, turmoil clouding his eyes.

"She didn't."

Irik's heart shattered, and he could not speak.

During the silence that followed, Irik couldn't have cared less about the man-woman balance between the clans or whether ill will between Pral and Cret would jeopardize an alliance. He had broken the promise, not Arol, and he must live with it.

Pral let out a breath through gritted teeth. "As you know, I have been chosen the River Clan chief, and both our clans have more urgent needs."

Reluctantly, Cret deferred to the older chief. "That's what I say."

Pral gave Cret a slight smile.

"We need to find a better territory. With the start of a long, cold winter, the herds have already been taking routes beyond us. We need a more reliable meat source. Nuts and fruits are not enough."

The men nodded and murmured.

"Absolutely," Cret said. "And you told us the Lessor camp had shelter, stone for tools, water, and auroch migration trails nearby. You said their weapons looked inferior to ours. We can defeat them and take their territory."

"Yes!" Pral's men said, waving their spears.

"It is our right!" Mar shouted. "The Lessors can find another place to live."

Pral waited for quiet. "It's possible we could sneak up on them at night from the rocky hill above their camp. Hide in the rocks and throw our spears."

"That could work," Cret agreed.

Irik asked, "Wouldn't they defend their home and family?"

Cret shot Irik an angry look. "They are lower people."

All except Pral nodded and narrowed their eyes at Irik.

Cret sneered. "Don't you think we could defeat them, Irik?"

"We could, but should we?"

Cret huffed in disgust, the men grumbled, and Pral chewed his lower lip.

Irik's stomach churned as he gathered his thoughts. "My father told me he once saw a lone Lessor take down a full-grown elk." He turned to Pral. "Were they big?"

"Yes, the Lessors look big and strong." Pral frowned thoughtfully.

"I'm not afraid of those ugly brutes," Cret declared.

"Of course," Irik said. "You are an expert spear-thrower, but if the first attack doesn't take them down, their greater strength would easily best us in hand-to-hand fighting."

Cret agreed, "They do know their territory, and there could be more than four men."

The group rubbed their heads and mumbled.

"And," Irik lowered his voice. "Will you kill the woman and children?"

The group fell silent until Cret yelled, "We can make slaves of them."

Cret's cruelty and greed appalled Irik. Such methods would never unite people.

Pral scowled at Cret. "Do you have a better plan, Irik?"

Irik rubbed his neck, then scanned their anxious faces.

"All of you knew my father to be a great chief. He knew injuries to our men could result in losing a hunter. It happened to my brother, so we must be careful."

Pral nodded. "True. But what would you do?"

Irik inhaled slowly. "I think we should scare them away."

Cret laughed. "How childish."

"Let's hear him out," said Pral.

Irik rose slowly and scratched his jaw in deep thought. One of his cave paintings—the man with a lion head—flashed into his mind. "We can make them afraid, so they leave their home. It'll take a few days to gather our women and children here."

Pral gestured for him to continue.

Another image appeared to Irik. He recalled playing during a rainstorm, using a stick to cut a groove in the sand, and making the water form a second rivulet. "Moons ago, you told us about their small stream. If the uphill water is not frozen and has earth on either side, we could dig a trench right up to the edge of the stream bed. By adding some large boulders—"

"What?" Cret glared at Irik, then Pral.

"It's only the first step," Irik explained. "The second day, we'd instruct both clans to gather their ceremonial clothes—furred tunics, headdresses with horns, and noisemakers—all in the brightest colors. Molo could crush some berries or flower petals to make dye, and we have red and yellow ochre. Combining brilliant, contrasting shades of plumage, leather, and flax fibers, we'd have plenty to wear or wave to draw attention and make an impression. We could make the two-day trek to hide nearby and spend the night."

"What is this?" Cret asked. "Are we going to entertain them?"

Pral said, "Cret, we need to listen. Then decide together."

Cret shook his head and muttered to himself.

Nodding his thanks to Pral, Irik continued. "Early morning of the next day, Mar could go to the head of the stream and divert it by rolling the boulders onto the old route of the water. It would flow down the other side of the ravine."

"Ahh!" the men uttered, looking to Irik to continue.

"By the time the stream runs dry in front of the Lessor's camp, our clans will have hidden behind the rocks at different heights on the hill above. We will paint our faces with red and yellow ochre, cover ourselves with furred hides, wear ibex and reindeer headdresses, and wait for daybreak." He raised a finger. "If the Lessors are isolated and superstitious people, we can scare them with drums and jumping up and down like a pack of half-human, half-animal beasts. When we all scream and roar, they will fear us and flee."

"Ha!" Cret interrupted. "How can you see ahead like that? We have no past to teach us."

Irik sighed. "I can imagine it."

"What is that? Imagine. Know what's coming next?" Cret let out a belly laugh. "No one can do that. What if they aren't afraid and run up the hill after us?"

Irik thought hard as he fiddled with his necklace. The wolves, always nearby, looked up at him. He shouted, "Meeri, pack! Come!"

They rushed toward him, a furry mass of wagging tails but with fearsome fangs and claws. Startled, the men straightened their backs.

Irik smiled. "See, even you who know my wolves get nervous around them. All people, including the Lessors, are afraid of wolves."

"But how would—?" Pral began.

"For moons now, I've been training them to circle squirrels and rabbits to prevent their escape." Irik glanced fondly at his panting crew. "I bet I could command them to bark and snarl around the Lessors as though ready to attack. When the Lessors ran, I'd call them off."

The men grunted and nodded, impressed by Irik's prowess with the wolves.

"Then, when they discover their source of water has dried up, they will believe the man-beasts with unearthly powers caused it," Irik finished.

Pral said, "That would surely do the trick."

Cret asked, "How will we know they've left?"

Irik was ready. "I say Mar, who knows the terrain well, stays hidden at a distance up the hill during the day to watch if they leave or not. If they do, we have a good new home. If Mar sees them return, he can get away, and we'll all come back and fight for it."

"What is there to lose?" said Vir, the friendliest of the River Clan men.

Irik frowned. "Much if we have to fight. My father taught me thinking and skill are more powerful than strength and weapons."

"Not always," argued Cret. "As all of you know, lions killed Irik's father and uncle, and his brother was injured on a poorly planned big shoulders hunt. I think Irik has concocted this nonsense because he's afraid to fight."

Irik jumped up and charged at Cret, ramming him in the stomach with his lowered head.

Cret let out a painful gasp and fell backward. Getting up took him a moment, but he barreled at Irik, punching him hard in the face.

Meeri rushed at Cret, pushing him over and standing on his chest, while the rest of the pack circled him, snarling.

Pral shouted, "No more."

"Off, Meeri," Irik said, blood from a split lip dripping on his chest.

Cret stood and spit at Irik. The young chief's fury stirred Irik's fear of the man-beast within himself.

"I like Irik's plan," Pral asserted. "If everyone agrees, we'll keep our clans and chiefs separate until we have a new home for all."

The men nodded. Outnumbered and sore, Cret shook his head but uttered no word.

Chapter Nine

HALF A MOON LATER, ALL members of the Valley Clan, except Reto and pregnant Tra, met up with the River Clan at the drought-stricken rabbit meadow. Only two days away from the Lessor cave, both groups displayed high spirits. Chiefs Pral and Cret agreed Irik would take the lead in directing his scheme to steal the Lessor home. After the women greeted their counterparts for the first time, they talked long into the evening about relocating.

Following a two-day hike to an oak-treed rise, the clans set up camp some distance behind the rocky hill overlooking the Lessor site. Unloading the drag sleds of hides, headdresses, provisions, and weapons, Irik relished everyone's enthusiasm for his plan. Still, knowing he'd eventually have to face Arol, he was gripped with shame and loathing. They often glanced in each other's direction but avoided eye contact. Irik hoped after the clan settled in, he would have a chance to explain to her what had happened. By nightfall, he was physically exhausted from the day's hike, mentally drained by guilt, and unable to make the effort.

After sending Mar to spend the night at the creek and dam it up in the morning, Irik joined Nara. As usual, she boosted his pride, telling him he'd be a better chief than Cret, but their lovemaking disappointed. Worry hounded him over Arol and whether his plan could succeed.

Restless, Irik woke before dawn to prepare the ochre face paint. Meeri and her pack joined him, sitting at his side as he ground up chunks of ore in a stone bowl to make the powder. Meeri licked drool from her chin, watching Irik squeeze blood from a hare killed along the journey. With plenty of red paint made, he used urine to mix a batch of yellow. Dipping his finger into the bowl, he placed a colorful dot on Deego's nose. "We'll be ready to go soon, wolves," he said, smiling at their wagging tails.

When dawn broke, Irik helped the clan prepare for the early morning assault on the Lessor camp. The women put on tunics fur-side-out to hide their feminine figures. Faces painted and wearing hats of feathers or rabbit pelts dangling from their heads, the clansfolk stood ready. After Irik fitted the ibex horn headdress above Vir's smiling face, he guided Meeri and her brood to a spot at the bottom of the rocky hill. Concealed behind it, they obeyed his command to stay.

Climbing back up, Irik directed each "man-beast" to spread out on the hill and hide behind ledges and boulders. "Move quietly and stay hidden until you see my hand signal to jump out and howl." With her comely face obscured by a headdress she'd made of dangling feathers and clinking beads, Arol only nodded.

Soon, the first Lessor left the cave and walked to the now-dry stream. It was a woman who carried an infant in one arm and held the hand of a young girl.

Irik gave the signal, and the clan burst from the rocks—shrieking, banging wooden drums, and swaying back and forth.

"Eeeyo!" the Lessor woman screamed, running back to the cave, almost dropping her baby. Irik signaled the clan to hide again behind the rocks. When the other Lessors emerged and Irik saw their bulk and unusual features, he hesitated and swallowed nervously. Then he raised his hand, and the clan jumped out again, showering the Lessors with animal roars.

The male Lessors jumped in place, whooping and hollering at the intruders, while their women screamed and children cried. Panic gripped them, not knowing where the next invader would emerge, how many there were, or what to do about them.

A big, gray-haired Lessor backed up toward the stream, turning to stare at the dry stones of the bed. He yelled to another man, and both thrashed about in disbelief, shaking their feather-decorated spears toward the recently exposed rocks.

Worried the flummoxed men might try to attack, Irik sprang up and shouted, "Meeri! Pack!" and waved his arm around his head. "Circle now!"

The wolves shot out from behind the hillside and formed a growling, snarling semi-circle around the Lessors. The four stocky men shielded the three women and two children as best they could without throwing their spears at the wolves. They jabbed the points at the pack to keep them at bay, always checking if the hill "creatures" would attack.

Irik realized the wolf pack had created a standstill rather than chase the Lessors away. *How could I make such a dumb mistake? Is everything doomed to fail?* He motioned for the clan to hide behind the boulders again.

When two of the Lessors began to retreat toward the base of the hill on the right side, he shuddered. They climbed slowly up the rocks toward Pral and Arol. Roaring like a lion, Irik scrambled to protect his people. "Meeri, Slar, come!" he shouted.

The wolves bounded toward Irik. *Will they know, without training, to get between us and the Lessors? Yes!* Meeri and Slar wheeled around to face the enemy. Dodging spear thrusts, the wolves lunged, instinctively trying to move the Lessors back toward the hill's base.

Irik held his breath as Meeri and Slar forced a retreat. *Good girls! What would we do without you?* Once downhill, the rest of the pack joined their mother in the chase. With the clan "creatures" continuing their cacophony and adding a barrage of loose stones and pebbles, all the Lessors shifted away from their cave.

The four warriors and their frightened families had given up. Running awkwardly, they turned around every few steps to see if the man-beasts or wolves followed. The pack held back at a word from Irik, and the Lessors headed for a distant, grassy field.

Patting each of the wolves and giving them meat rewards from his pouch, Irik watched the Lessors trudge out of sight. Triumphantly, he signaled for the clan to retreat behind the hill and hike back to the field camp.

Calls for celebration abounded upon their return. Irik felt it was overhasty, but the clan couldn't stop buzzing about their victory and new home. Pral suggested they build a bonfire to dance around. Irik agreed to head up wood gathering, for which the clanswomen quickly volunteered, eager to support and spend time with their new hero.

Moving deeper into the oak grove, Irik noticed Arol trailing behind the crew. If possible, she's grown even lovelier. *I wish I'd painted her face to have something to keep and compare. Not on a cave wall but maybe a flat rock I could hide. No, I don't deserve any part of her after what I've done.* Once he staked out an area to deposit the wood, he sent the crew gathering.

"Arol, can I tell you something?" he asked, heart throbbing in his throat.

"What?" she snapped. "My father already told me." Her kind, honey eyes had frozen.

Irik reached to touch her arm. "May I explain?"

She pulled away. "About breaking a promise?" She sneered. "Because you had to."

"I…" he choked, looking down, realizing nothing would ever be the same between them.

"Were you that desperate to find belonging in the clan?"

He winced and put his hand to his heart. "I'm sorry, Arol."

"For what? Needing Nara to make you into a man?" She narrowed her eyes at him. "I once thought you were your own man."

Irik couldn't speak. He'd chosen a lover over his dearest friend. His throat ached, and his eyes misted. *Can we never be close? Does she hate me?*

She walked off but turned to say, "What made you special is gone. Goodbye, Irik."

He slumped to the ground and put his head in his hands. *She's right. I did what most men do, even if I believed it was for the clan. She's beautiful in every way, but I lost her.*

"Are you all right?" Vir asked, not smiling for once. He dropped an armload of wood and rushed to Irik's side.

Anxiously, Irik got up and wiped his eyes. "Sure. Thanks, Vir."

They returned with the wood and got the campfire blazing. Cret and Pral commended Irik for a plan well-executed, and one by one, the clan members thanked and congratulated him. Irik savored his success but worried the Lessors were unpredictable. The clan enjoyed dried reindeer meat brought by the River Clan and Juneberries picked along the route.

Mar asked, "Can I keep watch on the rocky hill overnight in case the Lessors return?

"Why don't I join you?" Pral offered.

Cret cackled. "Why? Because your boy's grown up, Pral. He didn't need you at the creek, and he doesn't need you tonight. Sometimes young men want privacy. Remember?"

Mar blushed but didn't ask his father to come along.

Irik chortled. "Take one of the wolves, Mar, just to be safe."

"I would, but they make me sneeze," Mar said.

Pral crossed his arms and sighed.

Irik did his best to put Arol out of his mind, telling himself he had only done what he needed to do. He danced with Nara much of the evening, basking in her compliments. Tired from the exciting day, everyone went to bed early.

By morning, Mar had returned to the field camp with a reassuring report—no sign of the Lessors. Cret and some of the men wanted to move into the new cave immediately. Irik and Pral recommended waiting in the field camp another night.

Vir offered to spend the night on the rocky hill, but Mar insisted he liked being alone and felt the rest of the men should stay with the women. Pral bit his tongue, later telling Irik his son had always had an independent streak and striven to prove himself.

By mid-morning of the second day, Mar had not returned. Irik brooded more than he let on, remaining calm and discussing options with Pral and Cret. Field provisions were low, so they agreed the women, children, and Cret should head back to their respective clan homes and prepare for the move. Uro would escort them until they later split up.

Helping load the sleds, Irik didn't spot the tall, curved horns of the ibex headdress which had crowned one of them. He turned to Vir, who had worn it. "Where are the ibex horns?"

Vir lowered his head. "They were hurting, so I took them off."

"You left our prize headdress on the rocks?"

"I...I," Vir stuttered and blushed.

"Go on," Irik said. "I'll find it, but please be more responsible from now on."

Waving goodbye to their clan's women and children, Irik, Pral, and Vir grabbed spears and water-horns to head to the Lessor site. They had grown accustomed to going days without food, so they traveled light and fast to size up their new home. When finished, they would head back and join in the return trip to the valley and their old cave with their families.

As the men approached the rocky hill, Irik spoke in a low voice. "Keep quiet, and don't call out to Mar—the Lessors might be near." He climbed to the lookout, hoping to find Mar asleep, exhausted from all the night duty. Moving past the rock ledge where he'd positioned Vir, Irik looked for the ibex horn headdress. A chill ran through him when it wasn't there.

Meeri began whining, and she and Deego bounded up the hill toward the lookout. With each climbing step, Irik's heart beat faster as he searched for signs of Mar. As he stepped around a boulder, his worst fear proved true. Mar's body lay on the ground, many deep stab wounds in his back. A pool of blood dried in the sand, smelling like an animal carcass and drawing flies. Irik shooed the wolves away. The Lessors must have come back.

He knelt and stroked Mar's auburn hair, so much like his sister Arol's. Hugging the lifeless body, Irik spoke under his breath, telling Mar he was sorry and thanking him for his bravery. *How am I going to tell Pral? Leta and Arol will be crushed.* Irik's wracking guilt shifted to terror as he thought about the women and children. *Might the Lessors pursue them?*

Wiping back his tears, he signaled the men below to be quiet. As he reached the bottom, he whispered to them that the Lessors might be near and to keep their eyes peeled.

Irik took Pral aside and told him he'd found his son. Pral froze, his face slack and lips trembling. He closed his eyes tight, then snapped them open.

"I will tell Leta and Arol. Leave his body here. No time to mourn." Frantically, he pointed out some heavy barefoot tracks, heading in the direction of their field camp but veering off. "Look. Four sets of men's tracks, fresh from last night's shower."

"Pral," Irik said, placing an arm around him. "We both know what that could mean."

Pral, Irik, and Vir looked at each other, struck by the same jolt of fear.

"We must move fast," Irik said, waving them on. "They may be following the trail of our women and children, and they know the territory better."

He started jogging ahead but stopped and turned. "We have some advantages. The Lessors are heavy and slow over long distances, and they're ambush hunters, not spear-throwers. On the other hand, they have a head start." He glanced down at Meeri and the pack. "Like our wolf brothers, our people possess endurance to outlast prey. Speed and stamina are our only chance." He threw off his hides down to his loincloth and sprinted over the sandy ground.

The wolves bolted ahead and stopped short, noses to the ground. Catching up to them, the men found the start of the trail that Cret, the women, and the children were taking. Pral pointed and said, "The Lessor tracks follow but run to the side of our clan's at a distance. They're clever enough to try to escape detection."

Before Pral had finished, Irik shot into a full-speed run, shouting, "Let's go."

The men ran their fastest until high sun. Passing over a ridge, they saw the Lessors traveling parallel to the clan. Because of the terrain and distance, no one could tell how close they were to catching up to Cret and the families.

Irik halted. Bending their sweaty bodies over to fill their lungs after the long run, the men looked desperately to him. Their heaving chests and sunburnt skin spoke of limits to their endurance. Irik's responsibilities and self-doubt weighed upon him. He had failed to foresee how the Lessors would react, but now he knew them capable of killing. He must look ahead and vowed not to make the mistake of underestimating them again.

He rubbed his sun-swollen eyelids, trying to get a fix on their situation. *Has Cret already seen the Lessors trailing them and tried to speed up the clan?* Squinting back toward the Lessors and noting their bow-legged gait, he estimated how long it would take them to overcome the families. For a moment, he thought he saw one of the Lessors carrying the long, curved horns of the ibex headdress. It infuriated him, but he shook it off and said, "We can't… let them reach the women first." He faced his palms to the men as he drew in replenishing air. "We must catch up… deliver a surprise attack from the side."

The men looked drained and unsure. *Do they no longer trust me? What would Father have done?* Irik jabbed his chest. "Find it in your hearts, men. Together, we can save our clan."

He pointed to a mesa stretching alongside the Lessors' path. "We could run behind that. When we came to the end, we'd be between them and the women."

The men gathered their strength. Storing what breath they could, they grunted their determination for the fight ahead.

Irik ran at top speed with the wolves and other men at his heels.

Reaching the end of the mesa, Irik and Pral peered around low shrubs. They kept a prudent distance from the Lessors but between them and the clansfolk. The women and children had dropped their sleds to run away.

Cret and Uro hurried into position between the retreating women and advancing Lessors. They stood side by side, spears at the ready.

It was too far to hit the Lessors with a spear from the mesa. It might come down to a close contact fight with a stronger foe. Hearing the faint cries of the women and children, Irik's sense of self became one with the clan. The hammering in his heart shifted from fear to fury.

"Meeri! Pack!" he shouted, pointing to the Lessors, "Go!" He looked to the men and gave a battle cry, "EeeYii!" The men bolted.

The Lessors saw them, and two turned to face the charge. The other two continued advancing toward Cret, Uro, and the clan.

The wolves surrounded both pairs, barking savagely but maintaining their distance. Wide nostrils flaring, the Lessors thrust their spears, keeping the wolves away.

Five body lengths between them, Irik shouted, "Throw now."

Whoosh! Whoosh! Pral and Vir each hurled a spear.

The spears hit but bounced off the Lessors' thick clothing.

"Meeri, Slar, come," Irik shouted and ran toward Cret, some twenty body lengths distant. He could hear Pral and Vir fighting, plus the wolves snarling.

Whoosh! Whoosh! Cret and Uro launched the first of their spears at the other two Lessors.

"Ugh!" Cret yelled when his spear flew over the gray-haired Lessor's head.

With a dull thud, Uro's spear bounced off the thick, bear-hide vest of the younger, beardless Lessor.

As the clansmen grabbed for their second spears, the two Lessors fell upon them. Uro took a crude spear to the chest. He grabbed at the sharp head but fell, trying to pull it out.

Irik was gaining on them—ten body lengths away.

Cret charged at the older Lessor, waving his spear.

Whack! He deflected the Lessor's spear, knocking it out of his wrinkled hand. Aiming at a gap in his vest, Cret stabbed the gray-haired Lessor in the chest. The aged one fell to the ground, struggling.

The beardless Lessor came at Cret, who countered with a flint knife. The Lessor twisted his body in time to avoid a fatal stab, but the stone blade sunk into his thigh.

The young Lessor jumped on top of Cret, choking him with massive hands.

Irik dove onto the young Lessor's back, yanking his beardless head up by his long hair. Acting not from anger but cruel necessity, he slit the Lessor's throat with his hand ax.

Displaying incredible strength, the young Lessor managed to lunge upward, throwing Irik to the ground. He clutched at his torn neck, blood gushing down his hairy chest. Confusion contorted his face as his body quivered. Irik saw no beast behind the Lessor's eyes. Only sorrow to match his.

Irik looked away.

He had chosen.

Lying on the ground and wiping splattered blood from his face, Irik heard Slar barking wildly and looked up. Charging toward him, the gray-haired Lessor screamed with rage.

Slar lunged full force at him, but the Lessor thrust his spear into her chest. Slar fell limp.

Bloody spear still in hand, the old Lessor headed for Irik. Pral and Vir gave chase.

Whoosh! Whoosh!

With a cry, the old Lessor stopped, bent over, and fell with two spears in his back.

Meeri came to lick Irik's face, removing some of the young Lessor's blood.

"Good girl," he said with a surge of happiness that quickly vanished. Slar, who had saved his life, was dead. Even worse than a beloved animal, the clan had lost Uro and Mar.

Clutching his wound with one hand, Cret helped Irik with the other and said, "You have proven your courage and more."

Surprised by Cret's praise, Irik said, "Thanks," but feared he had only proven himself something he never wanted to be—a killer.

Pral hugged Irik. "You saved our families."

Irik patted his shoulder. "We all did," he said, thinking of Mar and Uro giving theirs.

Vir hugged Irik. Looking at his young, smiling face, Irik said, "You did great in battle," and wondered what challenges loomed in his future.

"All right," Pral said, "Let's go tell the women we've captured a new home."

Cret lifted his spear in the air. "Iyee!" he cried, "On to a new life."

Everyone but Irik cheered. He pictured Pral, Leta, and Arol placing a cairn over Mar's body. He could no longer imagine life without loss and untold dangers.

Chapter Ten

A S HE DID MOST MORNINGS before dawn, Irik quietly lit a lamp and watched the ceiling turn into a magical sky. He marveled at the shiny crystals embedded in the cave walls, catching the light and sparkling like stars. *How long did generations of Lessors make this glorious place their home? Were we right to take it, and how long will we keep it?*

Softly rising so as not to disturb Nara, he dressed and threaded his way past the chambers of sleeping clansfolk to explore the deepest recesses of the cave. Along the route, he recalled discoveries he'd made of how smart and inventive the previous occupants must have been. He'd found fire-burnished boxwood digging sticks, strings of white-tipped vulture feathers, and long auroch rib bones used to soften and waterproof leather. A cache of animal teeth with holes drilled and strands of flax had delighted Arol, amazed at their workmanship and eager to employ them.

All these were found in the first few chambers near the entrance. *Why are the rear chambers empty? They could have held many, many hands' worth of their people. Did they move? Die off somehow? Did people like us kill them?*

Following the last unexplored tunnel in the cave, Irik twisted his body and squeezed through a crevice into the unknown. A vast, spiked cavern emerged before him, sending chills up the back of his neck.

Long, jagged spikes hung from the ceiling, dripping water. Similar points reached up from the floor, creating an illusion of a deep earth monster, drooling and ready to bite. As he stepped warily into the chasm, plinks and plops of water met his ears. He touched a spike: cold, wet, and smooth, made of stone, not ice.

Negotiating his way around the columns, he approached a wide expanse of raised, dry earth encircled by round stones. Long femur bones stuck upright in the ground, each a body length apart. Nature sometimes produced regular patterns, but this arrangement bore the mark of human intervention. He knelt and ran his fingers along the length of a bone, clearly from an aurochs, as the rest appeared to be.

Irik wiggled it, and the soil crumbled beneath, revealing another smooth, oval bone surface. As he dug around it, his lamp flickered. Grabbing a pouch of spare tallow, he hurried to fill the lamp or lose the flame. He held his breath and eased a fatty blob alongside the fluttering wick. "Come on, melt," he muttered. It would be difficult to return so far to the clan in darkness, and he'd neglected to tell anyone where he was going.

Poof! The flame caught, and he sighed with relief.

Below, in the brighter light, rested the top half of a human skull, empty eye sockets staring at him.

He jumped with a gasp. No more exploring today. Scurrying back to the crevice where he'd entered, he rammed his knee against the tip of a stone column. He picked up the broken piece and held it, considering how this cavern spoke to him. It contained much more than the dots and scratches they'd found on the walls when they first entered the Lessor cave. He'd come back again soon to dig deeper and find out more about the people they'd frightened away.

As he approached light seeping in from the cave entrance, he stopped at Chief Cret's chamber. "You won't believe what I found," Irik said, handing him the stone column's tip.

"What good is it?" Cret felt the rounded edges of the cavern spike and bounced it from one calloused palm to the other. "Wouldn't even cut into a rabbit hide."

"No, no, it's not a blade. I discovered this and other amazing things in a cavern beyond the farthest tunnel."

Cret smiled but shook his head. "Finally found some smooth walls, I hope. Maybe you'll paint again?"

"No, the ones back there are worse than our pebbled walls—they were wet."

Cret tilted his head. "What, then?"

"I saw where the Lessors might have put their dead. Buried in the ground."

"So? We pile rocks on ours to keep scavengers away."

Irik sighed. "Those people are smarter than you think. Maybe we can learn from them."

"Like what? Flaking dull spear tips?" Cret mimed stabbing Irik from a wide, ungainly stance. He spouted gibberish and frowned to imitate a Lessor's heavy brow ridge. "Come on. They're savages who killed our people."

"And we killed them. Stole their home, remember?"

"I know you feel guilty, but…" he waved his hand over his spacious quarters. "…look what we have now." Cret's woman, Koto, lounged contentedly with their newborn on a thick pile of hides and fur. Nara sometimes spoke jealously of her sister, and Irik could see why.

He grinned sheepishly, acknowledging the clan's improved lifestyle. Cret's closed mind and insensitivity discouraged him as always, but the chief was right about Irik's doubts. To gain the cave, they'd had to kill and be killed. Watching Cret and Koto's giggling baby, Irik wondered how the Lessor women and children were managing since losing their men and home.

Cret chided him, "Wake up! Quit dwelling on the past," and waved dismissively. "Go, get those wolves trained—we need ones that can attack."

Irik tightened his jaw. He resented Cret ordering him around. Although they'd gotten along since the battle with the Lessors, Irik believed the wolves should be trained for hunting, not attacking. Cret was taking a path opposite of what Irik envisioned, but he had no desire to lead, so he accepted the young chief's dominance. "You're right. The wolves need more work." Irik turned and walked away, knowing he'd go back to the Lessor burial ground when he had time.

"Where have you been?" Nara asked, stirring a meaty stew.

"I was exploring the far reaches of the cave, past that narrow tunnel I found."

"What for? It's almost high sun. Why waste your time?"

He ran his hand through his hair. "Curious, I guess. I found what looked like the Lessors' burial ground."

"Who cares? They're dead and gone." She laid down the stir stick. "Focus on the riches we have, due to *your* leadership, not Cret's. We've got a great cave with water out front, aurochs grazing around, and shale for blades. Those are the things that matter."

He nodded along, thinking about how fast life can change. "I'll eat later. Going to work with the wolves."

"Fine," she said, managing a crooked smile. On Irik's way to the wolf pens, he considered asking Vir if he wanted to explore the cavern. The cheerful youth had an inquisitive mind, and Arol might decide to join them.

The wolf compound erupted with thunderous racket as Irik stepped out of the cave. He'd focus on training Fola's and Deela's litters: eleven one-winter-old juveniles. He kept the raucous bunch in separate pens based on training regimens. Shaking his head, he surveyed the furry faces clamoring for his attention. *They wouldn't be here if it weren't for that wild male wolf sneaking onto the grounds one night and impregnating Fola and Deela.* With two litters of young wolves, training had become Irik's main job in the clan.

Fola's litter already knew how to guard. After watching their mother's vigilant behavior, their instinct to follow had done the rest. Irik had made progress teaching them to hunt. After intense practice, each of Fola's offspring could pick up the fresh scent of prey. They excelled at tracking: chasing after live game while barking, so Irik could follow them. Some needed work on surrounding and holding prey in place until huntsmen arrived to make the kill.

One moon ago, after teaching the wolves to hold prey at bay via constant praise and treats, Irik had invited Cret on a trial hunt. At the end of a long chase of a snorting boar, they found the wolf pack had killed and eaten half the animal before they reached it. Worse, the boar put up a fight, so Geri had a badly bitten leg. To Cret, this proved the wolves to be unreliable hunters. He insisted they'd be more useful as attack animals. Irik dreaded the task, but bound by his leader's wishes, he set out to train Deela's litter to subdue any enemy on command.

First, he needed to exercise Meeri and her adult offspring: Deego, Fola, and Bika. Untying all four, Irik picked up his throw stick and set a pinecone into the cleft at the top. He whipped the supple willow branch over his head, sending the cone some fifteen body lengths down the field. The wolves dashed after it, Deego getting there first. Irik hurled another in the opposite direction, and the pack pivoted after it. Cones shot every which way, chased by all the wolves except the one who'd caught the last. Irik had trained them to bring what they retrieved back before running after another, giving the wolves the most exercise in the least time while saving his arm from tiring.

The longer he used his throw stick, the more accurate Irik became at hurling pinecones. It occurred to him the extra thrust the stick provided might help propel a spear, but he'd have to work on that later. He tied the exhausted adult wolves back up, left the penned younger ones yelping, and went back into the cave to find Reto.

"Hi, Ireek," little Clor said with a radiant smile.

"How's my favorite niece? Been good, I hope?" Irik picked her up and glanced at Tra.

"Good," Clor said, and her mother nodded.

Handing the toddler back to Tra, he asked, "Where's Reto?"

"Up the hill. Looking for blade stone."

"Thanks. See you both later." He winked and grinned at Clor.

She wiggled her little fingers after him. "Bye, Ireek."

He found Reto trying to pry loose a chunk of shale with a wooden stave. "Need a hand?"

With four hands and much grunting, the gray rock finally popped out.

"Thanks, Irik. What can I do for you?"

"A big favor. Can you be a bad guy?"

Reto wrinkled his brow.

Irik held up a hand and chuckled. "Not for real. Cret wants me to train some of the young wolves to attack, and I can't put it off any longer."

"What's that got to do with me being bad?"

"I need someone to dress up in heavy bison hides, wear a face mask, and pretend to attack my wolves until they—."

"What? Bite me?"

"Yes, but the hides will protect your arms and legs until I say, 'Off.'"

"Really?" Reto arched a brow.

"You won't be in any danger. I've already got them to sit, stay, and chase. They listen and follow well. Please? It'll help the clan."

Frowning, Reto looked away, then turned back. "All right, Irik, for the clan... and you."

Irik clapped Reto on the shoulder. "Thank you, brother. Oh, and you'll have to put stink berry juice all over your body."

Reto moaned. "Irik..."

"Can we start this afternoon?"

"Tomorrow morning," Reto growled. "I need to prepare Tra."

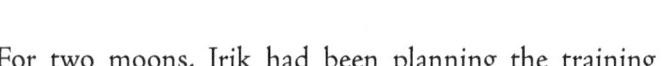

For two moons, Irik had been planning the training routine and preparing a protective costume for the attacker. He chose Cala as the first trainee. As the alpha male of the litter, Cala showed high confidence and independence while being responsive to commands. Irik had a strong bond with the young wolf, so Cala would be protective of him.

Waiting with Cala in a field near the pine grove, far from the clansfolk and other wolves, he listened for Reto's signal. He'd told him to whistle but stay in the pines, so Cala wouldn't see or smell him. That's where the attacker's disguise was stashed.

A whistle pierced the chilly morning air. Reto had arrived.

"Stay," Irik told Cala and strolled toward the grove, looking back to make sure he didn't follow.

Hugging Reto briefly, Irik whispered. "Thanks for helping. Can you strip down?"

Reto rolled his eyes, took off his vest, and nodded.

"Leggings too."

Down to his rabbit hide loincloth, Reto shook his head and groaned. "Boots."

"Come on, Irik."

"I know, but remember, it's important. Cala can't know who you are after this training, or he might attack you back at the cave." He handed him a bulging elk skin sack, confident the putrid pink berries from the moth-wing tree would work.

"Aaargh!" Reto said when he untied the rawhide at the top, covering his mouth and jerking his head back. "Smells like vomit."

Irik stifled a snicker. "More like rotten eggs to me, but stink berry juice will cover any scent, and it lasts a long time. Go ahead, squeeze the berries, and spread the juice."

Irik stood back, breathing through his mouth, and watched Reto grimace and grumble as he smeared the foul liquid on his skin. "Now, under your arms. Good. Dribble it down your back. More."

"Want to help?"

"Sorry, you're the attacker. I can't."

After Reto smelled like a walking latrine, Irik carefully wrapped layers of thick bison hide over his arms, legs, and feet, tying them securely with rawhide. Irik lifted a full bison hide, the kind the Lessors wore, over Reto's head to cover the rest of his body.

"Will it work?" Reto asked.

Irik poked him in the shoulder. "Don't worry, these hides are tough, just like you."

Chortling, Reto let Irik fit the striped badger mask—holes cut out for eyes, nose, and mouth—over his head. Irik explained how Reto should act around Cala and himself.

Reto nodded and grunted through the mask. Irik handed him a long willow branch with feathers bunched and tied at the end to resemble a spearhead and patted Reto's back. "Behave like an attacker. Listen to my commands. Act mean."

Irik casually led Cala along the perimeter of the grove where Reto remained hidden. He concentrated on staying calm despite what they were about to do.

"Now," Irik said in a low voice.

Reto jumped out from the trees, howling and pointing his spear at Irik.

Pulling Cala on his rope, Irik jerked back, feigning fear he hoped Cala would pick up on.

Surprised, Cala cowered and pulled back. Irik needed Reto to be more threatening to spur the wolf's defensive instincts.

"Strike," he said to his brother, who jabbed his stick at Cala's legs.

The wolf snarled and bared his teeth.

Irik hesitated. "Strike his nose."

Reto did, and Cala yelped and lunged against the rope toward the attacker.

"More," Irik said, cringing.

Cala snapped his foaming jaws at Reto.

Irik yelled, "Cala, attack!" and let go of the rope.

The enraged wolf sunk his teeth into Reto's arm and shook it violently.

As instructed, Reto dropped but hit Cala back to reinforce hostility. Snarls and screams rose from the ground. Feeling the furor of the attack in his gut, Irik shouted, "Cala! Off!"

Cala froze and glanced at Irik, Reto's arm still locked in his jaws.

Irik tugged the rope. "Off, Cala, off."

The wolf let go, and Reto limped away.

"Good boy," Irik said, kneeling at his wolf's side, patting his head as Cala snarled at the retreating villain. He stroked Cala, gave him treats, and talked softly to him until he calmed down. Leaving Reto at the hiding place, Irik went back to the pens to retrieve another wolf.

By late afternoon, Irik had returned the last of the littermates to the pen. He was exhausted and grateful to be done. Four out of five of Deela's litter had passed the first day's test. Cala, Ory, Cho, and Koro were on their way to becoming attack wolves, pleasing Irik immensely. Although he would need to reinforce the training over several days to make it stick, he—and, no doubt, the bruised Reto—needed a break.

He returned to the grove to help Reto undress and thank him for his excellent performance. Reto, happy to resume training later, delighted even more in a bath in the river.

Back at the cave, Irik found Cret, Pral, and Vir on their knees, finishing up butchering an auroch calf. "Hello, men. Another good hunt, I see." He subtly looked away. It troubled him to see younger animals killed, but only Arol might have understood why. *How cruel to take them from their mothers and waste their potential. If we could somehow keep baby animals safe, they'd have some kind of life before being devoured.*

The busy trio looked up, nodded at Irik, and continued cutting. Leta and Koto stood nearby, taking the chops and meaty ribs from the men, setting some aside for each family. Arol, of course, didn't help with the butchering, but she'd cook up a nice meal for her partner.

As Irik watched Vir deftly run his blade along sinew and bone to extract the meat, he thought how fast the boy had grown into a proficient hunter and brave warrior. *No doubt, he's a good man for Arol. Probably better than me. How can I blame him for wanting to bond with the brightest, most beautiful woman of all?*

Nonetheless, sorrow lanced Irik's heart when he recalled the day Pral gave his daughter to Vir. He was overcome with regret and jealousy, knowing Arol would lay with another man. The ache eased as he buried it deep, but it never disappeared.

Vir grunted, nicking his thumb with the blade and looking up to see if anyone noticed. Irik smiled reassuringly. He liked both Vir and Arol, rejoicing they had each other and wishing them happiness. He accepted, even celebrated, their relationship. His sadness stemmed from losing Arol as his friend and confidante. The pain sprang from a space she used to fill; the best part of him seemed to be missing.

Cret stood, blood dripping down his arms. "Pral, you and Vir finish. Need to talk with Irik."

Koto handed Cret a water horn. After rinsing his hands and wiping them with leaves, he turned to Irik. "How did your attack wolf training go?"

"Better than expected, Chief. I believe we can teach four of our wolves to fight."

"Good, we may need them soon."

Irik's eyes widened.

"On our way to the south field, we found many sets of human tracks, all heading toward Thumb Butte."

"Lessors?" Irik asked. The hairs on his arms and neck stood.

"We don't think so. All had foot coverings." Cret glanced down. "Pral?"

Pral's eyes glittered apprehensively. "Humans like us, not heavy Lessor tracks. Men, women, children. More than our clans combined. Even drag sleds." He sighed heavily.

"See, you must train the wolves," Cret said. We may need to defend our home."

Irik took in a long breath. "Maybe they're peaceful."

"Maybe, maybe not." Cret sounded more concerned than cocky. "Step up the training."

Irik nodded hard, pushing hair from his eyes.

Cret turned to the other men. "Pral, have Vir take all the bones and scraps over to the wolf pens. I've had enough for the day."

"I'll help Vir," Irik said, eager for a chance to ask about exploring the cavern. Secretly, he hoped once Arol found out about the Lessor graves, she'd want to go as well. He knew it wasn't right, but it was a chance to be near her.

———— ⋆◆⋆ ————

Body halfway through the crevice, Irik held the tallow lamp ahead of him with one hand and Arol's with the other. "Easy now," he said. "Twist sideways and shuffle your feet toward me." He tugged gently.

She whimpered, moving with him. The scent and texture of her brown skin reminded him of their childhood adventures, but her body had become curvaceous and mesmerizing. "Good, almost there," he said at the flicker of Vir's lamp from the cavern entrance.

When they'd all squeezed through, Arol hugged Vir, and they stood spellbound, gazing at the spiked columns on the floor and ceiling. Irik lit another lamp for Arol.

She swept the light across the vast chamber. "Irik, you're always discovering something."

Irik pointed to the tips of two columns. "See how the water drips from the roof column and meets the one below it? Like one feeding the other. Feel them."

Vir and Arol touched the wet stone.

Arol put her damp finger to her slender nose, making a cute wrinkle as she sniffed. "Hmm, I wonder..."

"Come on." Irik waved them toward the graves. "We're not the first people here. See all the upright bones? I believe there's a body beneath each one, and this remote place was chosen for more than keeping scavengers away." He knelt. "Look at this one."

Arol gasped, bringing the tips of her fingers to her heart-shaped lips.

Using his hand ax, Irik scraped dirt away from the bones. Vir and Arol joined in.

As they uncovered arms and ribs, Vir said, "The hands are holding a bunch of flowers."

Arol's delicate fingers explored the dried flower heads. "Looks like cornflowers. Someone had to place them here."

"And look between the bones," Vir said, pinching and holding up a bit of soil. "It's red ochre. Someone made it and sprinkled it over the body."

"Like some kind of ceremony," Arol offered. "Who were these people?"

Digging deeper, Irik unearthed a small rectangular stone. "They buried this one with tools as if he would work or hunt after he was dead." He examined the stone closer in the light. "Look, Vir, how blunt the edges are. Like the Lessors make." He waved a hand over the graveyard. "These all must be Lessors."

After they all stared at each other for a moment, Arol said, "And we only cover our dead with rocks."

Vir slowly nodded, unusually somber. "Let's open another grave."

At the next, they found a jumble of tiny bones. Digging deeper, they discovered larger ones—a rib cage. Then, a skull with strands of long hair beside it. Still affixed were several rows of tiny beads.

"It's a woman," Arol whispered, putting her hand to her soft brown throat. She choked back a sob. "And that's her baby." She swiped at the tears forming in her eyes. "They must have both died during childbirth."

Vir reached over to comfort her.

Pushing away his desire to hold Arol the way Vir could, Irik scraped more soil. He wondered if Arol was pregnant. At fifteen, she probably flowed with the moon. But would Vir's young seed be strong enough?

"Look at these," Vir said as he poked his finger into a pile of white objects.

"Beads," Arol said exuberantly. "Shells, bones, and teeth. They all have holes pierced in them." She picked up some long strands.

"Flax fibers, all twisted together. As if someone wanted her to make necklaces in…"

"In what?" Vir asked.

Arol shrugged. "In another life after… after she died."

Vir narrowed his brow. "What do you mean, another life?"

"I don't know. But they had feelings, cared about one another." She sighed. "Their bonds lasted after death."

"Like us," Irik broke in. "Even though they look different, Lessors may be similar to us. Just as human as we are."

"Maybe," Vir said, as he grabbed a handful of beads. "Here, Arol. You've been playing with making beads and necklaces."

She studied them for a moment. "I'll take one of each," she said and picked some out. "Leave the rest for the woman to do."

Irik and Vir stared at her. Irik had forgotten how much grace Arol had within her.

"Let's go," she said with a shiver.

Irik agreed. "We should leave this place to the Lessors."

Chapter Eleven

Two moons later, Irik and Nara had just finished stew made from wild turnips and deer meat Irik and his hunting wolves had secured that day.

Chief Cret stopped at their fire. "Hi, Irik, Nara. I want to thank you for the deer meat and all the game you've been bringing in."

Irik pointed to the ground. "Thanks, please sit and have some honey Pral brought us."

Cret looked stunned and raised a hand in a warding off motion. "No, no, I just want to see if you'd like to join me in a friendly contest."

"What kind?"

"A little game of hunting between you and me."

"Why would we do that? Food is plenty, and we're all bringing it in?"

"I'm thinking of going after that pack of boars we've seen in the area."

"Oh, them," Irik said with a shrug. "They'll forage and move on soon."

"But why let them go? Their meat is rich and tasty. Let's see who the better hunter is: you and the wolves or me."

Irik laughed. "You've always been the best hunter, Cret."

"Come on, Irik. Prove to me how great your wolves are."

Nara gave Irik a nudge.

"Well, maybe." Irik had learned to live with his old nemesis, but he could still be pushy.

"Give it some thought then. I'll stop by in the morning. Have a good night."

With Cret out of earshot, Irik turned to Nara. "What do you think has gotten into him?"

"Can't you see? He's jealous. You're outdoing him by bringing in more meat, and the clan respects you. Did you see the look on his face when you offered him the honey? Pral never brought him any. Take the challenge."

Agitated, Irik stood. "No good can come from that."

"Quit avoiding it. You know you'd be a better chief, and you've got the wolves."

"They're not proven yet."

"Irik, you've shown your command over them. You've had it ever since you killed Meeri's black mate. His teeth around your neck proclaim your power."

"Nonsense, Nara. Power comes from the clan, and Cret is our chosen leader."

"Just wait," she said.

"Enough." Irik walked away.

The next morning, while Nara gathered wild herbs, Cret showed up as promised. Irik put down the willow branch he'd carved with a stone blade.

Standing above Irik and tapping his spear into the ground, Cret said, "Ready?"

Irik looked up. Audacity shone on Cret's pocked face.

"You still want to have that contest, I take it?" Weariness tinged Irik's words.

"Yes," the chief hissed. "Something more important to do?"

Irik held up the notched end of the branch. "I've been working on a way to throw a spear with more power."

"What a stupid waste of time."

Irik gritted his teeth at Cret's actual stupidity. "More forceful spears could benefit the clan."

"Look, I've told everyone we're having this contest, so let's go."

Cret's bitter glare betrayed a deep need to prove his authority.

He's still a damaged boy beneath the bluster. Irik stood. "I'll get my wolves."

Cret pointed in two directions under the gray but non-threatening sky. "We've seen the boars in the south and east. You pick."

Irik shushed his excited wolves. "Are you sure you want to go alone? We always hunt in a party—much safer."

Cret expanded his already broad chest. "I've got my spears. You have your wolves."

"I'll go south," Irik said.

"Fine. Let's meet halfway at Thumb Butte around high sun. If no one has made a kill by then, we'll double back and hunt on the way home."

Irik nodded, pointed south, and looked to his wolves. "Pack! Go, hunt." His three best trackers—Labo, Ras, and Seely—took off through the brush. Cala, who he'd brought along for safety, lunged against his rope. "Easy, boy, you're walking with me."

"Good hunting," Cret said with a sneer and trotted off to the east.

Irik watched the chief's lurching gait ruefully. The shoulder wounded when Cret was little had never healed right and often pained him, especially in the cold. The last thing Irik wanted was to kill animals if no one needed meat, but he was stuck in a pointless game. If he came back empty-handed, Cret would smear his name and block any projects he proposed to help the clan. If Cret lost, he'd sulk, go on tirades, and make everyone miserable.

Irik's trek through flatlands, patches of pine and beech woods, and low hills was quiet, except for cawing ravens and chattering chipmunks. The wolves treed some squirrels and cornered a badger, but Irik didn't bother with small game, knowing Cret wouldn't either. He put the childish chief out of his mind and thought about his spear-thrower idea and Arol.

By late morning, he was within sight of Thumb Butte. Ruthless shrieks from a pack of hyenas shattered the quiet. Not far away. If they found Cret, he'd be easy prey, as they could surround him and attack from all sides. Cret wouldn't be able to throw his spears fast enough.

A scream. Not from the hyenas.

"Go, pack!" Irik shouted, running with Cala toward the sound. With wolves dashing ahead of him, Irik scrambled through a dense thicket of sagebrush, his heart beating faster with each step. Hearing his wolves barking wildly, he knew they'd circled the hyenas and were holding them at bay. Hyenas were as fast and fierce as any wolf. *How many can there be?*

Too many. Breaking through the brush, he saw Cret on the ground, being torn apart by two hyenas. The third was finishing off Ras, or was it Labo?

Irik pointed to the two fighting over Cret, yelled, "Attack!" and let go of the rope. Cala tore off, and before Irik could take two steps, the wolf had his teeth into one of the hyenas ripping at Cret. Cala and the hyena matched in size and power, their spotted and gray fur locked in a fight to the death. Irik hurled his spear at the other hyena, catching it in the haunches. With a yelp, it fled, two wolves chasing after it.

Irik threw a second spear at the hyena attacking Ras. It sunk deep in its side. With a howl, the hyena fell away from the lifeless body of Ras. Irik gulped and turned in rage.

Cala, the victor, stood on top of his hyena, jaws clamped on its throat. The hyena kicked its gangly legs and stilled.

Cret, body torn and bloody, lay dead.

Irik knelt beside his chief and unwanted rival. Blood was everywhere, Cret's throat a mass of torn flesh. His inner beast—acquired through no fault of his own—was dead. Tears welled in Irik's eyes as he turned and retched. Cala, Labo, and Seely came to his side. He patted them and stood shakily, wiping his face and scanning for more hyenas.

He saw none, but it was only a matter of time before the noise and smell of blood attracted more predators.

He bent down and pulled Cret's arms around his neck, over his wolf-fang necklace. Lifting Cret's body onto his back, he began the long journey home.

Chapter Twelve

F ULLY CLOTHED IN FURS, IRIK, Reto, Pral, and Vir huddled near
the fire. Holding their hands toward the flame, they exhaled trails
of moisture in the chilled air. Irik tugged his mittens on, leaned back,
and sighed.

"What's troubling you, Chief?" Pral asked.

Irik pressed his lips together. "Doubts about being leader."

"Ha, I've known those well," Pral said, "and I knew when I passed
them on to you, we'd have a better leader…" he pointed to his chest. "…
than this old goat."

Holding fingers to his head to mimic horns, Vir bleated softly.
Everyone chuckled.

"Seriously," Pral said, "you won this great home for our new clan,
and you trained wolves to work for us. Besides, you have that ability
to—?" He searched for words.

"Guess what lies ahead," Reto interjected.

"That's it," Vir said. "You're not stuck in the past. After Cret died,
our clan found it easy to unite behind you."

Irik's heart swelled at hearing Vir and Pral's words. Maybe he
could lead the clan on a path less strewn with blood.

Pral nodded. "And someday we'll decide a real name for the
new clan."

"Why not, 'Clan of Chief Irik and his Incredible Wolves'?" Reto
jested. Irik snickered into his mitten, so the others laughed along.

A blast of wind howled through the branches of cut pine trees propped against the cave entrance. Irik shivered, remembering the wolves outside burying their thick, winter-fur-covered bodies under insulating snow.

Pral went on, "Your orders to store plenty of dried meat kept us from starving this winter."

Vir giggled. "Now, it's all frozen like a rock."

Irik smiled at Vir, then turned serious. He looked each of them in the eyes. "I'm worried, men. Uncle Orki once told me his ancient ancestors suffered through a long period of winters where summer never came."

The men murmured and shifted.

"Such times may be here. With few aurochs and no other hoofers migrating through, we may not find enough game to feed the clan."

"What can we do, Chief?" Vir asked.

"Consider those mammoths over by Thumb Butte."

"You mean hunt them? We're too few." Reto's pitch climbed. "They're as tall as two men, twenty hands wide, and terrifyingly powerful. How could we—?"

Pral broke in. "Thumb Butte is where we found all those tracks. We've never seen other humans wearing shoes, pulling drag sleds, and in such numbers. They might attack us."

Irik wagged a finger. "Don't forget, Pral, you belonged to the River Clan, and we merged peacefully. Maybe they wouldn't be hostile. What if they joined us? I believe there's strength in numbers. If we killed just one mammoth together, both clans would eat well for a moon."

Pral's eyes narrowed, even as his stomach growled. "The River and Valley Clans had similar numbers. If this group is as large as it looks, they might not want our help and could trounce us easily. Chief, we've always gotten by on our own."

"True, but things change, and our new clan is too small." Irik ran a hand through his beard. "Listen, the mammoths are plentiful, but we cannot hunt them alone. If we separated a beast from the herd, surrounded it by wolves, and had many more men throwing spears, we could take one down."

The men straightened their backs and regarded each other quizzically.

"Many men, many spears?" Pral countered. "Even if we joined the other clan, we might not have enough. Remember that scavenged mammoth carcass we found last winter? Its thick hide covered with fur would be hard to pierce." He swung his arm upward. "And those huge, slicing tusks."

Irik weighed the risks to his men and wolves. "Just a thought. Let's make it a night."

He stood and walked toward the cave entrance while the others returned to their families. He always checked on the wolves before going to sleep. He could tell by the clumps of snow where each wolf—nose under tail—nestled with their siblings. Watching the snowflakes lay a glittering fleece over their beds, he admired how animals could adapt.

Back in the chief's quarters, he found Nara sitting hunched over and slowly rocking her body. She clutched an object between her legs and whimpered.

Irik sat and put an arm around her. She fell into his lap and sobbed.

"What's wrong, Nara?"

She wiped her eyes and looked at him. "I failed you, Irik."

"What do you mean?"

"I—I haven't given you a child. A chief needs someone to follow him."

It was true, and it did sting him, not in the first years, but after Arol and Vir had a baby girl. He avoided showing any disappointment, placed a hand under Nara's chin, and whispered, "It will happen. Stop crying now."

She put her arms around his neck. Something fell to the ground with a clunk.

"What was that?"

"Oh," she said, picking it up and handing it to him. "Arol gave me something."

At first, Irik couldn't make out the strange, lumpy thing that fit neatly into his palm. It was lighter than stone, and when he held it closer to the fire, it revealed the figure of a woman—a pregnant woman. He slowly drew a finger across the bulges and crevices, much as he'd done long ago when he'd painted on cave walls.

Below a small knob for a head, two lumps resembling breasts sagged over a swollen belly. The figure transported Irik to a deeper place—a world within himself he had long abandoned. Here lay the act of creation, capturing the stuff of life so others could feel its spirit.

"Irik, are you all right?"

He shook out of his daze. "Where did Arol find this?"

"She made it. Gave it to me to help us have a child."

Irik was familiar with the beaded necklaces and bracelets Arol made for all the clansfolk, but this was different. It wasn't a cold object—here was a 'human' in your hand. He continued to examine the figure. The suggestion of arms and legs blended seamlessly into the sides and bottom of its central promise. He shook his head. Only a woman with the power of birth could create and communicate this. And, it took a compassionate woman to share it. Gently squeezing the figure, Irik felt Arol's spirit, and it recaptured him.

"Do you think it will work?" Nara asked.

"Aah... maybe."

Nara reached for him. "Let's try."

In the morning, as Irik turned over in bed, his knee fell on top of the pregnant figure. Hoping Arol's creation might work, he nudged it toward Nara's abdomen. Slipping out from their layers of caribou hides, he dressed in his warmest clothes, built up their fire, and edged farther into the cave to see if Arol was awake.

She was kneeling, tending her fire while Vir snored. She looked up and gave Irik her same radiant but now shy and womanly smile. She softly said, "Good morning."

Irik wanted to talk to her privately, but seeing her daughter standing next to her, he coughed and said, "I came to thank you."

She tapped the girl's head. "Keo, can you say hello to Chief Irik?" Keo smiled and buried her face in Arol's coat.

"She looks like you, dimples and all," Irik said with a small lump in his throat.

Arol added another log to the fire. "She's got Vir's long nose, though."

Irik shuffled his feet. "That figure you gave to Nara was quite striking. Thanks."

"You're welcome. I hope it can help you two."

"May I ask how you made it?"

"Sure. I was digging for tubers down by the pine grove in this thick, gray soil that clumped together. I took some home and rolled it into a ball for Keo. A few days later, I found it lying in the hot coals. Hard as a rock."

Keo tugged at her mother's arms. "Hold on, Keo," Arol said. "After that, I molded more of it into different shapes and heated them. I made that figure while I was pregnant." She laughed. "Never got that fat, though."

"No, guess it's what you thought might happen." He chuckled. "Nara believes the stone may have special powers."

"Do you?"

"I don't know, but if she thinks so, maybe it will."

Vir stirred.

Irik stood straighter. "Do you have a supply of already-made bracelets and necklaces?"

"I do. Make new ones all the time. Save them for gifts."

Vir sat up, rubbing his eyes. "Good morning, Chief. Anything we can do for you?"

"Nothing right now, Vir, but I have an idea. Later this morning, could you and Arol bring some beadwork to me? I'd like to meet with you and the men."

Vir nodded to Arol, and she scurried to the back of their chamber and returned with a handful of bone and stone necklaces.

"Perfect," Irik said, "let's gather Reto and Pral. Oh, and thank you, Arol, your art is beautiful."

Sitting at the community fire, Irik began, "I think I've found a way to hunt the mammoths. Vir? Show everybody Arol's impressive beadwork."

Confused, the men stared at Irik.

"Yesterday, we talked about persuading those other humans at Thumb Butte to join us in a big hunt. Together, we could better survive the winters ahead."

"An admirable goal, Chief," said Pral, "but just because their tracks look like ours doesn't mean they couldn't be more dangerous than the Lessors."

"We've feared that for too long," Irik said. "It's time to find out who these people are."

"Maybe so, but how do we approach them?" Pral crossed his arms.

Irik ran his hand under his wolf-fang necklace. "Forget you know me. If you met a man wearing this, what would you think?"

"That he was mighty powerful," said Vir.

"Deserving of respect," Reto added.

"Right," Irik pointed to his brother, "and if that man approached you surrounded by wolves he controlled?"

"You'll always be my little brother." Reto chuckled. "But strangers might be alarmed."

"I sure was," Vir said. "I feared at first your wolves would tear me apart."

"Of course, they'd be afraid," Irik said, smirking at Reto and reaching toward Vir's lap. "But if you approached them without threat and offered these beads—beautiful things they've never seen to decorate their bodies…"

"Aah…" The men nodded.

"These objects have meaning," Irik said, making them clack and tinkle together. "They can carry a message, like power. Or wealth. Or brotherhood." He looked into each man's face. "By giving them such gifts, we might gain trust."

"Maybe they'll return the favor," Vir's optimism made Pral, his father-in-law, grin.

"So, I hope," said Irik. "As soon as the skies clear, I will trek to Thumb Butte to meet these people." He swallowed and glanced at the men. "I need one other man to join me."

Pral raised his hand. "Chief, I've been doubtful, but I see what you see. May I go?"

From atop a rise overlooking the "new" united clan home, Irik admired the setting sun bathing his cave's entrance. He put his arms around his two new friends. "There's our home."

In only ten days, Irik and Pral had met, won over, and become impressed enough by the others near Thumb Butte to discuss uniting their people.

As was the strange custom of these others, they interlocked arms with Irik and did a little jig. Pral joined in, laughing.

"And look, there's my woman, Leta, going to the stream for water." Pral waved, but in the shadow of the failing light, she didn't see him.

"Lovelier than described," Boolip said, "and bigger than our cave. Right, Karango?"

Karango gave Irik a slight bow. "Yes, it was kind of you invite us to visit your clan."

Irik untied Deego and commanded, "Go home, pack!" The six hunting wolves raced down the hill, snow billowing behind them.

Hiking down to the cave in near-twilight dimness, Irik worried his clan might be startled by the strangers from Thumb Butte. The wolves had already alerted his family, but he ran ahead and found Reto and Vir guarding the cave entrance. As the wolves ran up to welcome their master, Reto and Vir rushed to greet their returning chief.

Still panting after hugging his brother and Vir, Irik said, "I have good news. The people at Thumb Butte are peaceful, friendly, and need meat."

"Good, good," Reto said, slapping his brother on the back. "How did you—?"

"The wolves," Irik answered. "Their clan's scouts had watched us work the wolves from afar for many moons. It was easy, Reto. When I approached Thumb Butte with open hands, they recognized my power."

"Great work, Brother."

Vir hugged Irik again. "Just like you imagined, Chief. Congratulations."

"Where's Pral?" Reto asked.

Irik turned and pointed. "On his way down with two men from the other clan."

"You brought them here? Now?"

"Yes. I thought the sooner our clan gets to know them, the sooner we can hunt together."

"Are they—?"

"Human? Yes, a bit different from us, but with much the same needs—food, shelter, family. They call themselves the Rhino Clan, after the woolly beast. Some strange ways, but they want to be friends."

"You understand when they speak?"

"Uh-huh. Their long-ago ancestors, like ours, traveled here from jungles and deserts. Our words are similar, and gestures help."

"Hello," Pral shouted down as he and the two strangers waved.

"Oh my." Vir ogled their tall silhouettes in the dying sun's glare.

"Don't worry," Irik said. "You'll like them."

As Pral and the Thumb Butte pair approached, Irik reached both arms out, interlocking them with the two visitors. Together, they whooped and danced.

Reto and Vir stood perplexed until Pral hugged them and said, "A harmless custom."

Holding out his hand, Irik said, "Reto, Vir, this is Boolip, Chief of the Rhino Clan from Thumb Butte. Karango is one of their best hunters."

Reto and Vir eyed the Rhino Clansmen's hair in large knots atop their heads, broad noses, darker skin, and cheeks painted with yellow stripes.

With wide grins, the Rhino men crooked their arms, halted a moment, then straightened them to grasp and shake Reto and Vir's hands. "Greelo."

Pral laughed. "They're saying hello." He showed how the Rhino Clan locked arms up to the elbows as a greeting.

"Hello," Reto and Vir said, locking arms with Boolip and Karango and laughing.

"Greelo," Vir added, earning a smile from both clan chiefs.

With everyone more comfortable, Irik turned to Vir. "Please run ahead and tell the rest of the clan the good news. Ask them to prepare a welcoming party with a feast. We'll be down shortly after I brief our new friends on our territory."

The savory smell of roasted meat and smoke poured out of the cave as Irik guided the Rhino men inside. The ten remaining adult members of the 'new' clan stood in front of the community fire.

The Rhino men's eyes bulged to gaze upon the rest of the old Valley and River Clans—nine women, some with small children.

All the "new" clan's women appeared shocked in kind. Molo, Mata, Leta, Tra, Arol, and Koto from the old Valley Clan plus Reen and Teela from the old River Clan averted their eyes. Only an occasional snap from the blazing fire broke the silence as the women stole furtive peeks at the stocky, hairy bodies and painted faces of the Rhino men.

Irik introduced Boolip and Karango and spoke of the friendship and kindness they and their whole clan had shown Pral and him. Locking arms with both men, he added, "We have great hope our clans can work and grow together."

Everyone clapped.

Irik introduced each of the women, starting with his mother.

Boolip approached Mata with a wide smile and warm eyes. He reached around her buttocks and squeezed them.

"Oh!" Mata cried and forced a crooked smile.

Karango followed his chief and attempted the same greeting.

Mata stiffened, backed up, and looked at her son. Not wanting to upset his diplomatic plans, she accepted the bizarre embrace.

Irik next introduced Nara and gave her a stern look. But when Boolip reached behind her, she cringed, took hold of his hands, and shook them.

"What wrong?" Boolip said, looking back and forth at Irik and Nara. "Not way you greet women?"

Seeing Boolip genuinely embarrassed and Nara equally angered, Irik put his arm around the man. "That's all right. People have different ways. In our clan, we approach women who aren't our own with handshakes or hugs." He gave Nara a quick hug to demonstrate and soothe her ire, but she remained stiff and flushed.

The introductions continued with polite handshakes, and when Boolip greeted Arol, Irik surged with pride.

Boolip touched the bead necklace on his neck. "Ahh! Arol. It was you made gift for me. Thank you. Our people never saw such beauty. You also lovely." She blushed and bowed.

Raising a finger in the air with a gasp, Boolip said, "Wait, I have more gifts," and turned to face Reto. He reached into a pouch and handed Reto a fist-sized, shiny black rock, already scarred by flaking. "Sido," the chief called it and searched another bag to produce an awl of the same stone.

Reto felt the tip. "What a sharp point."

Boolip said, "Sido good for carve wood and pierce holes in hides." He turned to Irik. "Which your women makes best clothes?"

"My mother," Irik answered. Given Nara's reaction, his innards clenched at what he'd let the Rhino men do to Mata.

"Can I give her?"

Irik nodded, checking to make sure his mother didn't object.

As Mata took it, a smile flashed over her still-reddened face.

Boolip spoke to Karango, who handed him a pouch of brown oval seeds. He sprinkled some into his hand and showed the women. With many gestures, he attempted to convey they could be planted and grown into knee-high stems topped with star-shaped flowers.

"Good to eat and help body." Boolip asked, "Can I give Molo?"

Irik asked, "How did you know our healer was Molo?"

Boolip smiled and held his nose. "She wear garlic around neck."

Everyone chuckled.

Molo raised her hand. "No, those would be for Arol. She is learning to become a healer from me."

"Let me show you." Karango handed him another pouch. "Once you grind seeds...," he said, making the motion in his hands. "... they make this," Boolip said as he gestured for everyone to put their hands together, palms up. He loosened the top of the sack and dribbled a yellow oil into everyone's hands. Pleasure lit their faces as they tasted the oil. Boolip held up his finger and made a sickly frown. He pretended to drink some of the oil, then rubbed his stomach, burped, and smiled.

"Aah," the clan responded as Boolip handed Arol the sack.

Boolip again raised his hand. "Not only make you feel better, you blend ochre with the oil and make beautiful paint for your faces." He pointed to the stripes on his cheeks, "...and color your hair." He smiled and pointed at Arol. "Or, even paint your beads."

Boolip spoke to Karango, who handed him a large sack. Going down the line to the rest of the women, he gave each a fistful of colorful feathers: striped brown from eagle tails, long black from vulture wings, short green and yellow from parrots, and fluffy white from auks. Finally, he delighted each of the children with a small wooden figure with arms, legs, and a head carved out of an aspen branch.

Noting the women of the clan had warmed to the Rhino men, Irik said, "Boolip and Karango, all your thoughtful gifts are appreciated. Let us salute our new friends for the many things already learned and shared."

Karango said, "May our clans become great allies," and hugged Irik. The men of both clans embraced while the women watched and snickered.

"All right," Irik announced, "we have a surprise for you. We've selected the best cuts of auroch meat—steaks and chops—from our frozen cache. While our women finish the cooking, I will take our Rhino brothers on a tour of our home."

Lighting their tallow lamps, the men walked past the family fires and explored the vast, empty chambers of the cave.

"Wonderful home," Boolip offered, "dry, level floor, and much space."

"More than we need," Irik said. "How many did you say were in your clan?"

"Forty-eight. Our small, carved-out rock ledges nothing compared to big cave."

Continuing into the farthest stony reaches, Karango asked, "Your women good?"

Irik stopped short. "What do you mean, *good?*"

"You know, open to men?"

Frowning, Irik replied, "They're good to the men they bond with."

"Hmm," the Rhino men grunted.

Looks were exchanged with no one knowing what to say.

Reaching the last tunnel, Irik said, "That's about it. Beyond here, the Lessors—you know, the broad, lumbering people with heavy brows—buried their dead."

"Oh?" Boolip's face lit with awe. "Can we see?"

"Why? We ought to get back."

"Those people our long-ago ancestors."

Irik froze. Up to now, he hadn't realized that Rhino men bore a small but sure resemblance to the Lessors. He coughed. "Let's get back to the feast."

At the community fire, the women were cutting up the chops. With the smell of roasted meat filling the air, the men ate with wolfish fury. After the meal, the women and children returned to their family fires, letting the men discuss the big hunt. Irik reviewed his plan and got input from the Rhino men on the mammoth herds and habits, as well as learning about the skills of their hunters. They decided they needed to bring more large sleds with them to carry the meat and hides back and charged Reto with building one for each man in two days when they'd return to Thumb Butte.

In the chief's quarters, Irik found Nara sewing him a rabbit-fur hat for the journey.

"How did it go?" she asked.

"Really well. If the hunt works out and they're interested, I'll invite them to move their clan and live with us."

"What?" Nara screeched. She threw the rabbit pelt to the ground, inhaling through her teeth and sucking on her bleeding finger.

He went to her side and took her hand. "Are you all right? Let me see." The needle prick had stopped bleeding. "It's not bad, but you look frightened."

"How can you talk about moving them in with us so quickly? I don't like those Rhino men. Where did you put them for the night?"

Irik leaned back. "That empty chamber beyond Vir's room. Why are you concerned?"

"You saw how they greeted us at first."

He scratched his head and sighed. "I know they do some odd things, but they are good men, and their clan seemed happy."

Nara's cold expression didn't change.

"What?" he said, narrowing his eyes at her.

"The other women didn't like them either."

Irik stood. "That's nonsense. These men will make our clan smarter, stronger, and more powerful."

She resignedly picked up the rabbit pelt and bone needle. "If you say so."

Chapter Thirteen

B Y LATE AFTERNOON FIVE DAYS later, the snow had stopped, and clouds lifted to reveal the outline of Thumb Butte. Boolip set down his sled. Irik, Pral, Vir, and Karango did the same, shaking the strain from their arms.

Gazing to the north, Boolip said, "Make home by nightfall." He pointed to the west. "There, narrow valley, ripe with greenery. When snow melt, mammoths move along to feed."

"Good," Irik said. "How far to the watering hole?"

"Close. You be there before I get home. Karango guide you to sheltered ridge above valley. Spend night."

"Think we'll spot a herd on the way?" Irik asked.

"Yes, maybe woolly rhinoceros too." Boolip said, as they locked arms, "I meet you there by midday."

"How many men will you bring?"

"Five hands worth."

"We'll need everyone," Irik said.

Boolip agreed and turned to leave.

Irik gathered his men and headed west up the valley. The light of the late-day sun reflected off the ankle-deep snow, making it difficult to take in the strange landscape. The valley looked more like a gorge, with high rims seemingly carved out by huge boulders piled on top of each other.

"Karango," Irik asked, "what is this place?"

"Ancestors tell me, long ago, big slow ice river push through mountains." He pulled his hands in toward his chest, then pushed out. "Melt, leave valley. Make water hole too." He pointed. "There."

As they approached the edge of the small lake, Karango gestured toward clumps of trampled willow reeds. Ahead, he stood with both feet in a depression.

Irik gasped at the many round, two-hands-wide, fresh prints in the snow. The wolves frantically sniffed the tracks, huffing and whining. "Mammoths were here?"

"Yes, rhinoceros too. Come most days." Karango signaled toward a trailhead. "Follow me to ledge where spend night."

Leaving the sleds on the valley floor, the men grabbed blankets and dried meat and settled on the rock ledge. Irik eyed his six best hunting wolves: Deego, Fola, Bika, Deela, and Cala. Curled up next to him, they looked harmless, but he trusted they would perform well, even against such large prey.

As the moon rose over the horizon, a distant wolf pack let out a woeful cry. He could tell by the tone, it was not a territorial warning. So, he kept the clan wolves from responding to the call of the wild ones, and everyone slept well.

"Greelo!" Boolip shouted from below, and his throng of Rhino hunters vocalized and shook their spears in the air. Irik and the men descended to greet them. Now dexterous at arm-locking, one by one, the men hailed each other in the shared conquest of the hunt.

With Boolip, Karango, Pral, Vir, and Irik squatting at the center, twenty-five Rhino men gathered around, waiting for their orders. Because of Irik's success with the hunting wolves, Chief Boolip had given him the lead in planning the hunt. After Boolip advised him on the mammoth herd movements, Irik drew out a two-team plan of attack. His clansmen, the wolves, and Boolip, with all but ten of his men, would move up the valley in search of the herd. In the event the lead team wounded but didn't kill a beast, the second group staying at the head of the valley could finish it off. Irik explained he'd direct his wolves to cull a single animal and surround it while the hunters formed a safer circle beyond them.

Boolip spoke up. "The beast will charge."

"Certainly," Irik said. "The wolves are quick and agile, so we must be too. As soon as the mammoth heads in one direction, we must rush from the rear and sides and throw spears. Like most prey, these animals will likely turn to defend themselves against the biting wolves, only to meet our weapons. With our men and wolves coming at it from every direction, the beast will be confused and slowly bleed to death from many wounds."

"Some spears not pierce thick hide," Karango said.

"True, my friend, but I see your men carry many spears."

"Three each," Boolip said proudly.

"Good. Some will stick." Irik stood. "Boolip, join me in the lead team. Karango, you command the down-valley team."

The two rose and shook Irik's hand.

"Yes, sir," Boolip said. "We with you and instruct our men."

The lead team edged west along the ridge of the valley while the wolves bounded ahead, following their noses. Progress was better than expected over the sloping, snow-covered ground, marked only with the tops of bushes and an occasional towering boulder. As the wind picked up and dark snow clouds formed on the horizon, they hurried.

Bureeah! A thundering roar shook the air.

The wolves barked wildly.

"Pack! Come!" Irik yelled, running toward what sounded like thunder. The wolves had heard him, but what they came upon drove their instincts, and the barking continued. They could ruin the hunt if he didn't get them under control. "Deego, come," he cried, hoping the self-designated pack father might turn the pack around.

Catching his breath at the top of a rise, Irik called again. Deego, finally hearing his master, stopped barking and ran to him. The rest of the pack, wild barking changing to excited yips, dashed after Deego.

In the distance, Irik squinted to see what appeared to be a scattering of hillocks covered in dry brown grass. But they moved. The mammoths grazed lazily, either not hearing or not feeling threatened by the wolves.

"There they are." Boolip and the men caught up to Irik.

"My, there must be four or five hands of them." Irik shook his head with a hanging jaw. "And they don't even run."

"Human never hunt," Boolip said. "They are biggest. Not afraid."

"How close can we get?"

"Can keep wolves quiet? Close."

Irik gestured to Pral and Vir. "Better tie them up for now. I'll take Deego and Cala in the lead. Chief Boolip, will you guide me?"

Boolip nodded, and they slowly made their way toward the gigantic prey. They approached the herd from the side and watched, staying some thirty body lengths away. The largest of the beasts raised its nose, grunted, and snorted.

Irik backstepped and said, "Quiet," as both Deego and Cala crouched and snarled.

"They fear wolves," Boolip said, "not us."

"Right, let's circle the herd so I can study them."

The woolly beasts, busy sweeping away snow with their long snouts to find clumps of grass, barely seemed to notice the men as they meandered nearer. Irik became transfixed by these strange creatures with impossibly long noses that foraged and fed, much like a hand. A just-born calf noisily suckled at its mother while she caressed it and flapped her long tail.

He marveled at their gorgeous white tusks. They didn't look as menacing as a boar's from a distance but must be deadly sharp. Irik's mind wandered back to the trophy room of their old Valley Clan cave. *How could I ever replicate the splendid sweep of that ivory on a cave wall?* He envied their thick winter coats—although dirty and matted—and wondered if they shed in summer.

Two adults, face to face, intertwined their trunks and seemed to embrace as they let out rumbling sounds from deep in their bodies. They silently scratched at the earth with their massive feet to find the tiniest of morsels. Irik could hardly believe such enormous beasts could be so graceful.

Coming full circle, Irik counted thirty-one animals huddled like a clan at a feast.

"Which one we kill, Irik?" Boolip asked.

Taken aback, Irik replied, "Are they all females?"

"Yes, bull only come to mate. Old mothers manage herd."

"Let's pick one without a calf."

When they reached the other men, all appeared anxious, spears gripped tightly in their hands. Irik took a deep breath to settle his nerves. "Men, as planned, we will start by sending the wolves in to separate one animal."

"Sure," Pral said, "but how do our chances look?"

Irik swallowed hard. "I'll send in our two bravest—Deego and Cala—to cull a female without a calf. She'll be less protective." Running his hand through his hair, he added, "Once they've driven her far enough from the herd, we'll move in, surround her, and throw our spears."

"That's all?" Vir asked and nodded quickly. "We'll be ready."

"What else do you need to know?" When no one replied, Irik took Deego and Cala's ropes and guided the men cautiously around the herd.

A second time. A third.

The wolves strained at their ropes. The beasts became agitated, sent their calves to the center of the herd, and faced the men. They raised their trunks high in the air and let out a mix of grunts, coughs, and snorts.

"That one," Irik said. He untied Deego and and pointed. "Go! Circle!"

The wolves charged.

The humongous beasts moved fast, forming a wall between the calves and the wolves. They stomped their feet, raising a cloud of dust, and together let out a horrendous roar.

The wolves recoiled, ears flat to their heads.

Some of the men yelped, turned, and ran.

Trembling, Irik whistled, and the wolves were at his heels.

With the men running far ahead, Irik had to regain control. He stopped. The screeching eased. "Hold it, men," he yelled and waved for them to come back.

This hunt would be like no other. The prey wouldn't scatter and bolt like caribou or bison, but the hunters might. Mammoths were not only bigger, unlike herds where each animal ran for its own life, but they also defended each other. When he had watched them earlier, he sensed they were different in a way he couldn't account for. *Have I misjudged their gentleness? They show the power of a united front. Can we overcome that along with their size and strength?*

As the men slowly, warily returned, Irik realized he needed to do more than regroup. He could no longer rely upon hunts he'd known. He must imagine, as his mother said he'd done when she told him stories, seeing endings others might not. He must dig deep into his mind and picture what could be, dream of possibilities. The clan needed food, and he had to find a way.

"What do we do now?" Boolip asked.

Irik stared after the lumbering herd moving east down the valley. Pral nudged his shoulder.

Shaking out of his imagination, Irik said, "Yes, sorry. Let's meet tomorrow morning..." He dreaded spending the night in the Rhino cave, hearing their questions. "...at the watering hole. Pral, Vir, and I will stay alone on the ledge." Without having any idea what he should do, he added, "Don't worry, I have a plan."

⸺✦⸺

The next morning, blue skies belied a bitter wind tearing up the valley to greet the hunters at the water hole. After everyone locked arms, Irik noted fewer Rhino hunters than before, but he chose not to question Boolip.

Squatting in a circle with Boolip, Karango, Pral, and Vir, Irik spoke with feigned conviction. "Our best chance is to hide in the rocks on either side of the watering hole and wait for more mammoths or other prey to come down the valley. With the wind blowing west, the scent markers left by the last herd might point the way for others, even predators such as big cats. Then, we ambush."

Boolip tugged at his beard. "Same as before?"

"No," Irik said, "only if we find a lone mammoth, a straggler."

Boolip turned to Karango, who nodded. "All right," Boolip said.

Irik shook his hand. "I will position Vir up the valley with my best tracking wolf, Fola. If they spot prey coming through, Vir will send Fola down to me, and we'll be ready."

123

Boolip sent Karango and half his men to the watering hole's other side to settle in.

———————◆———————

The day wore on, the only animal sighting being a soaring eagle scouring the valley floor. Every so often, upon Boolip and Karango's orders, their men poked out of the rocks and ran in place to warm themselves and stay awake.

By late afternoon, Cala, who rested at Irik's feet, shot up, nose twitching. She whined, and Irik spotted Fola scrambling down the valley, Vir not far behind. Not until Fola reached Irik could he make out anything up the valley. Squinting into the low sun, he struggled to fathom what he saw—a monster or a mirage?

Its hulking form rose from the valley floor like a bluff, only it swayed and lurched. The rays of the late-day sun cast a ring of fire around a creature much bigger than the mammoths by the pond. Ahead of it seemed to be brandished a long black club, waving back and forth. *Is it only the sun creating shifting shadows from my fear?*

A cloud blocked the blinding distortion to reveal an enormous male mammoth, drawn by the smells and sounds of females in heat. The wolves picked up its scent and whined, but it remained focused on mating and slaking its mighty thirst.

"A lone bull," Irik yelled to the men. "When it reaches the edge of the watering hole, attack to force it in."

As he drew nearer, Irik fought an urge to flee. The sight of a creature bigger than the huge females sparked terror in his gut, which traveled to the hand clutching the wolf ropes.

The mammoth bull stepped into the water to drink.

The wolves strained, whining in agitation.

Irik's need to feed the clan and prove himself reined in his fear.

"Go, pack!" he yelled, as he and Vir let the wolves loose. "Attack to the rear!" he shouted to the men.

The barking wolves frightened their quarry to turn and back up into the water. The men formed a semi-circle around it and threw spears—most bouncing off its thick, furry hide. The few which stuck enraged the bull to charge, but its heavy feet sank deeper into the mud, hobbling its movement. Blood stained the water, yet the beast showed no signs of weakening.

"Irik!" Boolip shouted, "the men have few spears left."

The furious behemoth gained ground.

Irik jumped into the center line of men, and the wolves lunged savagely at their target.

"Irik, what are you doing?" Pral shouted.

Holding a stick in his right hand, Irik notched a spear to the rear of his new wooden invention with his left. He pulled his arm back to throw, waited until the mammoth raised its head, and aimed for its neck.

Whoosh! The spear flew fast and hit its mark, sinking deep into the beast's flesh. It stumbled but roared and charged, raising its front legs to nearly crush Irik and the wolves.

Spear already loaded into the thrower, Irik launched again. The point landed deep inside the creature's open mouth, jutting far up into its massive head.

The monstrosity buckled and fell to its knees, causing a rumbling crash and sending a wave of blood-stained water splashing over the hunters. With the beast down and dying, Boolip shouted, "Men with spears, thrust."

Pral and Vir joined in, stabbing their spearheads into the bull's neck until it collapsed flat into the water. The tip of its long nose quivered and sank, red bubbles rising to the surface.

The wolves stopped barking. For several moments, Irik and the men stared breathlessly at their conquest, unsure something so tremendous could be dead.

Pral and Vir hugged Irik side by side. "You did it, Chief," Pral said.

"That spear-thrower works," Vir rejoiced.

Irik held the spear-thrower aloft to resounding cheers.

"Irik! Irik!" the Rhino men chanted.

After patting Irik on the back, Boolip and Karango took hold of the spear-thrower and examined it with wonder.

Whooping and hollering, the Rhino men climbed on the mammoth's body and began cutting into its head.

"The first piece to Irik," Boolip shouted.

A hunter held up a chunk of flesh carved out of the neck, then jumped to the ground. He bowed and handed the dark red, dripping meat to Irik.

"Eat," Boolip said. "You are master hunter."

Irik held the still-warm flesh in his hand. Although not hungry, he gnawed off a small chunk and chewed.

The men waited in silence.

Irik swallowed, and a smile spread over his face. He let out a little chuckle, dropped to the ground, and burst into laughter. "It's a little tough," he said.

The men roared with humor. After filling their stomachs with raw meat, Boolip ordered them to butcher enough to fill the five sleds and return to the Rhino cave. They covered the carcass with piles of snow, hoping to disguise the scent from scavengers. After a feast, they would return to the watering hole, butcher, and sled the hide and any remaining meat back to Irik's clan.

Following a feast of roast mammoth—much tenderer when cooked, Boolip stood and saluted Irik. "Thank you, Chief Irik, and your wolves for delicious food."

"You are welcome, Chief Boolip. All your hunters were brave and strong." They shook hands and sat down.

"My men follow you," Boolip said. "Best chief. Make new things happen. Me never think can train wolves, hunt mammoth. Kill big one, no hunter hurt."

Irik savored Boolip's praise. At twenty winters old, he haltingly conceded he may have become a better hunter than his father. Maybe he did have special powers. Boolip's admiration meant the Rhino Clan could help extend his influence too. "Thank you, Chief Boolip. I invite you and your clan to live with us in our cave."

"That another great gift, Chief Irik. We have little more to give, but work hard help you, and…" he grinned mischievously "…share our women. You pick tonight."

Irik ran his hand through his hair and bit his inner lip. "I have a woman, Nara. Our clan bonds with one woman, so men don't fight each other and can hunt as a team. If you live with us, you must follow that rule."

Boolip tugged at his beard, then let out a belly laugh. "Of course, but only if you become chief of all."

Any doubt in Irik's mind vanished as he imagined what he might accomplish with their help. "I would be honored."

Boolip locked arms with him, and they did a victory dance, all the others joining in.

"So be it," Boolip said and turned to his clansfolk. "Men and women of Rhino Clan." He waited for all to stand. "Irik invite us live with his clan in great new home."

Cheers and clapping rung out.

Boolip lifted Irik's arm in the air. "If Irik willing, I follow him as my new chief and chief of all our peoples. Irik, Chief of Wolf Clan."

Hearing his name chanted over and over, he let the pleasure of his earned accomplishments wash over him, become part of him. He felt sufficient at last and would never let it go.

Ten months later, all sixty-two members of the Wolf Clan crowded around the community fire, whispering and stretching their necks in anticipation. Chief Irik was flooded with steady applause as he parted the crowd. He waved it off, turned around, and waited, beaming.

A hush settled over the clan.

Irik swept his arm to make way for the hero of the day. Nara stepped into the firelight, and everyone gasped. Face radiant with joy, she gently raised the bundle and lifted an edge of the rabbit-fur blanket.

A sweet chorus of "aawws" rose as she turned in a circle so everyone could get a peek at the pink newborn. She handed the baby to Irik, and it began to wail. He awkwardly held the child and curled a helpless smile.

The crowd laughed.

"It's a boy," he said, straightening his shoulders. "I have named him Brul for my father."

Cheers rang out, and the clan rushed in to get a closer look. Irik handed him back to Nara and stepped away so the clan's women could congratulate her.

Irik, Boolip, and the men made small talk as they watched the procession "ooh" and "aah." Arol was the last to come up to Nara. Tears in their eyes, they embraced with the baby between them. As they finally broke off, Irik met Arol's eyes and mouthed to her, "Thank you."

Nara smiled at Irik, settling the sleeping baby between them, tenderly pulling up the blanket. "I'm sore and tired, Irik, but this has been the best day of my life. With Arol's help, you have your future chief."

Irik ran his hand over little Brul's head.

Nara wrinkled her brow. "You look more sad than happy. What's wrong?"

"Oh, um, the big clan, I guess. The squabbles. Complaints."

"You mean that business with Karango and Cret's widow, Koto?"

Startled, Irik barked, "He's been warned."

"Yes, they know they'll have to leave if you hear about any fights over women." She patted him on the knee. "You showed them absolute power, and they have respected that."

"I thought they had adjusted to our ways."

"Look at the important things, Irik. You've trained them on spear-throwers, and they bring back mammoth calf meat every moon. We give those Rhino people a better place to live and thrive."

He slowly nodded. "But they weren't happy when they learned about us stealing the home of their ancestors."

"Distant ancestors. They'll get over it." She reached and brushed the hair from his eyes. "Look, the whole clan adores you, Irik. You give us all a great life."

"I guess," he said, watching Nara's eyelids droop. "Goodnight and thank you for a perfect son."

Chapter Fourteen

THE NEXT DAY, WITH PLENTY of mammoth meat hanging low to dry on branches in the sun, the clansfolk enjoyed a pleasant summer afternoon around home. As Irik and Pral gathered firewood in the nearby timber, they heard Arol and Leta chatting while picking dandelions. Not far away, Vir practiced spear-throwing on partridge. Some of the Rhino men split rock faces on the hill above, looking for good blade material. Down at the creek, Tra watched over splashing children. The rest of the clan, including Nara and baby Brul, remained in the cave preparing dinner, sewing clothes, or doing other domestic chores.

"Did you feel that?" Irik asked Pral, dropping their bundles of kindling.

Pral looked to the ground, then the trees. "The earth is shaking, and it's not mammoths."

Irik shivered, inexplicably recalling cracks in the earth he'd seen moons ago seeping noxious vapors. He cocked his ear to the ground. "Listen." The rumble below became a growl, as if a fiendish beast lurked under their feet, ready to break soil and seize them with gaping jaws.

Boom! They lurched, an invisible wave shoving them backward. Clasping their hands over their ears, they reeled from the blast, a jabbing and ringing inside their heads.

Pral gasped, pointing to the distant north. "Look at that!"

An immense gray cloud billowed behind the mountain range and across the horizon. Red lightning flashed behind it, turning the sky pink. Irik stared in awe until an orange blaze parted the clouds and rose high in the sky. *Perhaps the subterranean beast has climbed out to roar fire.*

Another boom. They staggered, dumbstruck, engulfed by searing air. Before they realized the dark cloud had spread above their heads, Vir fled their way, screaming. Black rocks the size of walnuts fell from the sky, pelting them. Shielding their heads as best they could, they raced to find Arol and Leta.

They were gone.

"Head to the cave," Irik yelled as smaller, hot pebbles rained down, burning their hair and skin. The air, thick with falling ash and reeking of rotten eggs, scalded their throats and strangled their chests.

Vir wavered behind them, coughing as he ran. Irik grabbed his arm. "Put your hand over your mouth and nose." They stumbled on.

Nearing the cave, Irik blinked his scratchy eyes to see Arol and Leta dive into the entrance. Pral took Vir's other arm, and they dragged him the rest of the way.

Fits of coughing and crying filled the interior as doubled-over clan members struggled for a clear breath. The lucky ones who'd stayed home poured water over gray-dusted heads and bodies. Arol rushed to hug Pral, and he and Leta helped their daughter mix and distribute herbal ointments to soothe the burned and bruised.

Seeing Nara standing with Brul safely in her arms, Irik gratefully waved. "Bring hides to the entrance," he shouted down the cave. Hooded by a caribou blanket and gulping air, he ran out to the wolf pens, opened the gates, and herded the singed, yelping animals inside.

The men and women who'd hurried to the entrance with hides and furs started hanging them from stakes used for last winter's snowstorm. As the doorway closed off, Irik watched deer, rabbits, and squirrels collapse on the ground while trees changed from green to gray. Overcome by shock and loss, he retched.

Two months after the massive Campanian Ignimbrite eruption centered near present-day Naples, Italy

Irik opened grainy eyes. *Am I awake? Has the angry beast returned?* Deep inside, it haunted him—roaring, rumbling, then going quiet. Nara and baby Brul slept peacefully next to him, but the screams of the dying echoed within. The stench lingered and stung, grit clawing at his throat and peeling off his skin.

What was that beast? Nothing of the earth's surface. Somehow above and below it. More powerful than the man-beast. But it could not be of the living, although its giant hooves cracked the ground, and its fiery breath covered the heavens. It brought thunder and lightning but spit flurries of soot rather than rain. The days became so dark, he could not see his feet.

Irik jolted, hearing a distant scream, plus wheezing and choking. *What more can I do? Will it never end?* He'd told the clan to stop drinking from the stream. To dig for white snow under the thick crust. To stop eating poisoned plants. He should have known when they came back, eyes inflamed to blindness, throats wrenching for air. "Stay inside!" he cried.

Little Brul whimpered, and Nara stirred but relaxed, snoring softly. Irik gazed at the cracks in the ceiling. Now, after two full moons, the real beast had finally stopped roaring. But Irik knew the clan remained in peril. Sickness gripped bodies and minds, turning their warm refuge into a cold grave for too many. Hunting had long ago ceased, starvation showing its gaunt face. The stink of wet fur and smoke from fires used to burn off rotten meat gagged him. Reality and nightmare had merged, and he no longer knew which was worse.

Nara got up and began picking marrow out of a bone. Irik couldn't sleep or eat.

Plink, plink, plink... The relentless dripping of water from above dragged out time and drowned Irik's spirit. He desperately wanted to find deep sleep, get to a place where dreams would show him the way. Willing himself to rise, he peered at clusters of families huddled on the cave floor. His temples throbbed as he stretched his neck to glimpse light at the cave's entrance, but night still reigned.

He stood, layering a bison hide over his tunic and stuffing an unfinished mammoth chop into his pouch. Bending to kiss Nara, he told her he was going to say good morning to the families. With the weight of responsibility for over fourteen hands of clansfolk bearing down on him, he stepped forward. Slogging through the gauntlet of crying babies and pleading faces would only worsen his gloom, but he had to reach the outside. Only there might he find a glimmer of hope.

Families sat around their fires, shivering. Irik greeted them and asked if he could help in any way. Their eyes spoke of despair, but no one blamed him. Out of respect, none asked for anything. Irik knew having a home was far from enough, even if it had saved most of their lives.

Irik hugged a mother who had lost her baby. He handed her the chop from his pouch, and she and her husband bowed their thanks. The act of giving didn't lift Irik's mood, as he could not remember the woman's name. Too many people depended on him. *Am I losing touch? The faith of my clan? Belief in myself?*

Passing Reto's and Pral's families, he only waved and nodded, so eager to exit.

Barks and yips greeted him as he neared the cave entrance. His sadness lessened when he unlocked the pen he'd insisted on building inside to shelter the wolves. Joy crept into his heart when five hands' worth of wolves raced to greet him. His now-scrawny wolf family clamored for attention. Meeri, the first wolf, still had a visible streak on her chest despite her dirty coat. Deego, Fola, Bika, and Deela were the next oldest, her long-grown pups. Then there were their broods and those broods' litters. Four generations whose licking and whining might be contrived to beg food, but to Irik represented love.

"Go! Run! Play!" he said and watched them head into the black snow.

Outside, the frozen air rattled his bones and prickled his nostrils. As he gazed at the ash-laden snow, he recalled the time it had rained rock and dirt. Although most of the clan survived, some got too sick in their chests from the polluted air. Days later, eight men and seven wolves had died.

Fortunately, the sun had returned as a gray ball, yielding some warmth. Still, Irik had never felt so hopeless and powerless. It didn't help that his mother, Mata, had recently perished in her sleep, even if she did reach the old age of thirty-eight. Her death wounded Irik deeply, her faith in his ability to see ahead vanishing, which stripped his self-confidence. Never again could he go to her for advice or reassurance. Nor to his father or Uncle Orki. Like his old rival, Cret, he was an orphan now, beaten and bitter. *But I've had family and friends who care about me, so I have no right to dwell in despair.*

Irik watched the pups chase and nip at each other in the snow. He looked to the early-morning sky and saw a clear patch dotted with brilliant stars. An emotion he hadn't felt in two moons swept over him. Wiping ice crystals from his beard, he was astonished to find a smile on his face. His eyes flashed wider when he recognized the star cluster his father had called the hunter.

He remembered how he'd drawn a line with his finger between the stars that formed the hunter's spread-out arms and legs. The three stars closest to each other created the belt at his waist, and below it was the hunter's spear—the star that always pointed south.

At that moment, a distant wild wolf's howl rang out—a pack father, broadcasting his leadership strength. The wolf's noble call resonated deeply within Irik's spirit, and with a surge of hope, he darted back to the cave.

He knelt in front of his family. "I had a vision."

"Yes, I see the sparkle has returned to your eyes." Nara's lips curved expectantly.

"He stroked the baby's cheek. "There were stars out this morning."

"That's great, but I can tell there's more."

"You know my father taught me how to journey by stars, and Mother believed I could see what lies ahead." He took a deep breath. "Nara, the hunter's star spoke to me."

"Hmm," she muttered, moving little Brul to her other breast.

Irik grasped her by the shoulders. "We need to move the clan."

"What? To where?"

He rubbed his temples. "If we stay, many may not last the winter. The wolves are already skin over bones."

She nodded slowly. "We can eat the wolves if we have to."

He dropped his arms and gave her an angry stare. She kept her eyes on the baby.

"I can see a new home in the south toward the big blue water," Irik said, lifting his chin. "I will take a small group of men, leaving most to stay and protect the women and children."

"I can see you mean it. How far away?" Nara winced as Brul drank greedily.

"Maybe five, six days if we can find a pass through the mountains." She shook her head, eyes clouding.

"Trust me. The sun shines in the south. We'll find the herds and grow fat." Irik beamed.

Nara wiped the baby's chin. "But isn't that the territory of the fierce White Clan?"

"Nara, they are people like us, not Lessors."

"But aren't they savage warriors? Didn't Toor, the Rhino man who once lived with the Whites and escaped, say they are cruel? You told me he said they ate the meat of the people they defeated, and their leader took many women, even his own daughters." Nara cringed.

Irik exhaled slowly. "We can show them our ways. Share their large territory."

"What if they choose to fight?" She asked. "Aren't they many?"

He nodded. "Toor said they number twenty hands. But they have rough blade spears, not fine points like ours, and no spear-throwers. With our wolves and all, they'd see our power."

"Maybe," she acknowledged.

Irik stood akimbo. "I will summon the men and ask for support."

"Won't some be afraid of war?"

"Then I'll hear their concerns."

She looked over her shoulder and back at him. "You don't have to. You are chief." She pointed upward. "Tell them you received a message from the heavens, and all will die if they don't follow."

Irik scrubbed his forehead.

She touched the side of his face. "Look, if you want them to seek a new home in better territory, you have to show confidence."

Irik pulled another chop from the fire and gnawed at the bone.

*Passing through the Apennine Mountains near
present-day Cassino, Frosinone, Italy*

By dusk of the second day's journey, the scouting party of six men and
five wolves reached the deepening snow at the foothills. They unpacked
provisions and equipment to rest and prepare for the morning's climb.
Irik hoped, after this mountain range, he and the men would find a
pass leading to the big blue water.

Unstrapping their spears from bearskin backpacks, the men pulled
out parkas, mittens, and tall, fur-lined boots. It had taken their women
three days to sew the extra warm clothing, and the men laughed at
each other as they tried things on.

Irik worried about Nara, Arol, their babies, and the rest of the
women and children. But he'd left Reto and Boolip in charge as
co-leaders. He'd warned Reto to watch out for Koto, who did not want
any more advances from Karango.

Laden heavily with clothing and extra stone blades, the scouting
party had brought enough food for three days. That left plenty for the
women and children, and Irik was sure they'd find game on the trail.

Before eating, they gathered pine boughs, bending and tying them
with rawhide. This created large, flat shoes to wear over their regular
ones when crossing deep snow. After Irik dried his feet by the fire, the
wolves lined up to have ice removed from their paws. Starting with
Cala, then Deeto, Cho, Ory, and finally Koro, Irik finished with numb
fingers but warm feelings for his best-trained wolves.

After their light meal of dried deer meat and acorns, Irik surveyed the
men, glad he'd picked a strong, daring team. Vir—the only man from the
old Valley Tribe—was chosen for his grit and loyalty. From the Rhino
Clan, Nork impressed Irik with his hulking strength and bravery. Dar
possessed keen sight and agility, and Toor had lived with the Whites.
Old Perla knew some of the route and had climbed many a mountain.

―――――――――◆―――――――――

The next morning, Irik checked the route with Perla, making sure both
had the same memory of the mountain peak outlines for their return.

By late morning of the third day of climbing, the only animal they'd spotted was a lone, too-distant fox. Without a new supply of food, their lives would be at risk. Halting steps showed growing weakness from the climb and meager diet, although Irik never heard a complaint.

That evening brought a storm, winds howling and tearing at them. Snow stung their faces, and they fell against each other. Danger of injury forced them to seek shelter quickly.

Finding a deep, wide snowbank, Irik used his spear to draw what would become the entrance to their overnight snow cave. Digging with their mitten-covered hands, the men tunneled through the snowpack, creating a large cavern. After jabbing air shafts to the outside and closing the doorway with icy chunks, they settled in for the night. To prevent frostbite, the men lay head to toe with their hands in their groins—Irik pairing with Vir. Their four-legged travelers did something similar, sleeping tight together, heads curled under tails.

Before the men fell asleep, Vir began coughing.

"Are you all right?" Irik worried exposure to the ash-laden air might be causing it.

"Sorry, Chief," Vir replied. "I bother Arol at night too. She gives me water."

Irik relaxed. "Arol's a good woman, isn't she?"

"Yes, sir." Another cough. "You know that."

Irik nodded, exhaling against Vir's heavily wrapped feet. "Take some snow."

Vir melted a handful and drank, throat clearing.

Exhausted but insulated, they dozed off to the howling wind.

———◆———

Irik woke as morning light filtered through the snow. He cut a hole in the doorway, but the storm still raged, so he patched it up and nestled again with Vir. Sometime later, he felt an odd tickling sensation across his neck. Half-awake, he ignored it until he heard a scratching near his shoulder. The wolves didn't stir. He opened his eyes.

Burrowing into his parka was a tiny brown vole. Irik smiled, figuring the warmth of the men's bodies had brought the little creature out of his winter den. No longer than Irik's forefinger, the vole poked its pink nose into his fur—searching for a meal.

Irik watched with delight and woke Vir to enjoy their new companion.

Whump! Squeak! Vir grabbed and squeezed it into stillness, handing the limp body to Irik like a gift.

"No," Irik said with a grimace.

Famished, Vir bit off its head and chewed with joy. He elbowed Toor next to him and handed over the bloody rodent. Two more bites, and even the tail was gone.

When the sun lit up the snow cave, and the wind slowed, Irik roused the others. "Don your snowshoes. We can at least get a half-day closer." Without finding the pass, Irik had to push the men despite their hunger and weakness.

There were no complaints after a tough climb until they reached a plateau to rest.

"Maybe," said Dar, the youngest, "we should head back."

The men looked to Irik.

"I know this has been a difficult journey," he told them. "but without any stores of food, going back through the mountains would be even riskier."

Nork spoke up. "What about that mountain pass?"

Irik sighed and glanced at Perla. "Sorry. We haven't reached it yet, but we must continue. Will you trust me?"

Silence.

"We're with you, Irik," Vir said, glaring at the others.

Shouts and raised fists followed, and they moved out. As they veered toward the sunrise side of a sheer, snowless cliff, Cala began to whimper, ears fully erect and nose twitching.

A mountain goat. Munching on lichen that clung to a rocky ledge.

Irik shushed the men, "Don't frighten it off. He's faster and more sure-footed than us. We have to trap him." Gathering the men to form a circle, he drew in the snow. "I want three of us to climb high above the goat to form a line like this." He pointed to the ridge above the goat. "I need two men with spears to climb down, crawl along the ledge, and draw near the goat from both sides. The ones up top will shout and throw rocks to prevent it from escaping. The goat won't jump off the cliff to its death."

Everyone nodded, eyes shining at the prospect of so much meat.

"It will be a dangerous climb along that narrow ledge," Irik added, "so the two hunters must be good climbers and spear-throwers."

All five raised their hands.

Irik picked young and nimble Dar and sure-footed Perla. Pointing to where he wanted them to ascend, descend, and begin their approach, he said, "I will direct you from here with hand signals." He hugged the hunters and wished them success.

Not used to predators at these heights, the goat didn't notice the men until they got close enough to throw spears. The big-horned animal climbed toward Dar, back toward Perla, then looked up for an escape route. Irik gestured to close the gap, and they got ready to throw.

As the men advanced, the goat became increasingly agitated. Irik gave the upper team the signal to shout and keep the animal from climbing, followed by the slash of his arm to throw.

Whoosh! Whoosh!

One spear landed wide, the other high.

With only one spear left each, Dar threw and hit the goat in the flank, point lodged loosely in its flesh.

The goat clamored toward Perla. Standing tight to the ledge, Perla launched a good hit to its back, but the goat did not fall.

"Careful!" Irik shouted as Perla approached the goat from above, trying to grab and thrust the spear in deeper to make the kill.

The injured goat battled for its life, bucking its curved horns at Perla, who stretched closer. Irik gasped as Perla's right foot slipped on the edge. The older man began falling, but he caught the goat by the horns. His firm hold and their combined weight pulled them over the cliff.

"Perla!" the men yelled, watching his body tumble below and bounce off the rocks. They knew he would not survive, but once they climbed down, they would have food.

After everyone gorged on the roasted goat, Irik gave the scraps and bones to the wolves. He loaded the massive skull and horns onto his backpack and gathered the men around Perla's cairn. Standing above the piled rocks, he spoke with trembling lips, "Men of the Wolf Clan, let us thank Perla for giving his life and allowing us to live."

The men bowed their heads in deep appreciation and sorrow.

"That is not all Perla gave us." Irik pointed to a gap between the mountains lit by the setting sun. "This is the pass I hoped we'd find. Soon, we can reach the coast and have a decent passage for our return."

He placed his hand on the top gravestone. "We shall call it Perla's Pass."

The men cheered, and with pride filling his heart, Irik said, "Rest well tonight. Tomorrow we may find our new home."

Location: Heading toward the Tyrrhenian Sea, near present-day San Felice, Circeo, Italy

By midday, the Wolf Clan had descended to the tree line and entered a forest where they found boar tracks and scat. The wolves flushed out many plump, long-tailed birds, but the men didn't follow. Not needing to hunt, Irik pressed the marchers down through the pines and fog.

In the foothills, patches of blue brightened the gray sky, and the group quickened their pace. At the top of a bluff, the wind changed direction. The men rejoiced and ran toward a scent they hadn't encountered for many moons—the sweet bouquet of grass.

Irik grinned as they galloped through the tall hay, happy as horses. In the distance, surrounded by tree-covered hills, a grand, golden prairie unfolded. Squinting toward the south, he hoped what looked like ants might be grazing animals.

Making a mental map of the new territory, Irik stared at the southern horizon. Thin clouds scraped the sky, leaving a lighter blue void—a landscape he'd never experienced. *Could it be the sea Father told me about?*

By late in the day, sharp-eyed Dar pointed out what looked like thin plumes of smoke in the distance. Irik halted the men. "Those could be fires from the White village. We'll cross the grassland but stay alert."

Far into the prairie, Irik rejoiced at a welcome sight: aurochs— more than he could count. With Deela in the lead, the pack charged at the cows, culling head after head and circling them. The wolves stayed in position while keeping one eye out for Irik, awaiting a command.

"Down," Irik shouted, and the wolves rested in a circle, surrounding three petrified aurochs. He smiled and lifted his spear high in the air. "As long as there are aurochs, our wolf partners will bring us food."

"Ayaa!" the men shouted, jumping up and down.

"Pack! Come!" Irik called, and the wolves returned. "We'll hunt later." Turning to Dar, he asked whether he could make out the mounds in the distance.

"No, Chief, I first thought they were mammoths, but they don't move, and smoke seems to be coming out of them."

"I can smell the smoke," Irik said, "and salt in the air. Could be the White village." He turned around and called out, "Toor?"

"Yes, sir." Toor stood beside Irik. "That's their village for sure, and those are their huts."

"Huts?"

"Small caves made from tree trunks and branches. For each family."

Irik stared into the distance, stunned. He pointed and waved. "Let's move."

When they got close enough to see people milling about, Irik stopped again. "We must approach carefully. We don't want to scare them or cause them to attack. Keep your spears in the slings at your sides."

"But they are warriors," Nork said. "Aren't we taking a chance?"

"Yes," Irik confirmed everyone's fears. "But approaching them slowly in peace is best. Move ahead and load your spear-throwers only if I command."

Sheathing their spears but darting glances in every direction, the men crept through the grass toward the village.

"AaRoo!" An eerie sound shattered the silence.

"They've spotted us," Dar whispered.

"Steady," Irik said. "No spears unless I say." He gestured straight ahead. "We are not afraid, and we must show them that."

With Irik in the lead, wolves at his side, they marched across the rustling grasses. Irik knew the men's nerves were taut, so he must show steadiness.

Ory barked sharply.

The grasses parted as many fearsome white faces and bodies jumped out, spears drawn.

The wolves snarled.

"Down," Irik shouted.

The White warriors had them surrounded, jabbing their crude weapons in the air and whooping. As his men searched his face and fidgeted with their spear-throwers, Irik raised his open hands high in the air.

Chapter Fifteen

SURROUNDED BY SIX HANDS OF White warriors, Irik waved for his five men to halt. "Toor, come with me. The rest of you, stay here and stay calm." With Toor's knowledge of the Whites and the wolves at his side, Irik edged to within three body lengths of the front line of warriors. He held out his palms, hoping they'd see it as a gesture of peace and strength.

The warriors, dressed only in grassy loincloths over splotchy-white bodies, took a menacing step forward, pulling back on their spears.

"We are peaceful," Irik said, not knowing if they understood. "Toor, here…" he nodded toward him, "…speaks your language."

Toor translated.

"HeeKo!" shouted two White warriors, jumping in front of them. Irik didn't need Toor's help to know it meant stop. They fitfully pointed their spears between the two men and the wolves, which bared their fangs and growled.

Irik spun around. "Quiet!" The snarling stopped. "Sit! Lie down." He reached to pat their heads, and they panted contentedly.

When the warriors saw Irik's control of the animals, they greatly feared, their jaws dropped. Shuddering, they pulled back to regard each other with wide eyes.

Toor whispered, "Maku," to Irik.

Irik stared unblinking at the Whites and spoke in his lowest register. "I am Irik, Maku of the Wolf Clan. I wish to meet with your Maku."

Toor translated.

The warriors, seemingly dazed, grumbled between themselves.

"Caliss," one shouted and pointed up the trail.

"He wants us to follow," Toor said.

Irik waved his men forward and slapped his legs for the wolves. "Heel!" The Whites undoubtedly found his mastery over wild animals unearthly, so the wolves could be a lifeline.

Entering the village, they approached a large hut in the center. The two warriors stepped inside after ordering Irik and the men to kneel on the ground. Irik commanded the wolves to lie down behind them. Soon, a muscular young man wearing a headdress of reindeer antlers emerged from the hut. He carried a carved wooden spear and swaggered toward them. Standing above Irik, his eyes nervously darted between him and the wolves, who remained steady. *What did the warriors tell him about us?*

"Golo supit!" the muscular warrior shouted, pointing his spear at the wolves.

They bounded up as one, snarling with raised hackles.

The warrior flinched, holding tight to his spear.

"Down," Irik commanded and stroked the wolves' fur. They wagged their bushy tails.

The young warrior brooded, shaking as sweat beaded on his forehead.

Can this be the chief of the Whites? Surely not. "I want to see your Maku."

Toor translated.

The warrior stood motionless, a blank look on his face, then returned to the hut.

A hideous figure emerged—all white, like bones bleached from the sun. Although its legs looked and moved like a man's, long white feathers stretched from its arms and flapped as the body strutted toward them. Closer, Irik could make out a lumpy shroud covering its head and shoulders. Where a face should be, a yellow beak jutted, reminding Irik of an enormous sea bird.

As the birdman neared, he clacked and rattled. The shroud consisted of many interwoven strings of white beads made from shells.

Irik assumed the daunting creature must be the White's chief when he noticed tiny openings for eyes and mouth. Peering into the two top holes, he stifled a shiver as black eyes darted back and forth over his body, sizing him up.

"Wooso ay etay fom?"

Toor leaned toward Irik and whispered, "Who are you? Where do you come from?"

"I am Irik, Chief of the Wolf Clan." He made a sweeping gesture. "This is Toor, and these wolves are our clan brothers and sisters. We come in peace from over the mountains."

Toor translated to the Maku.

The White chief stepped closer, pulled a long knife blade out of his waistband, and pointed it toward Irik's chest.

The wolves growled and dropped into a crouch, ready to pounce.

"Back off!" Irik commanded, and the wolves settled down.

The Maku didn't flinch but chuckled. "Keerot haba mitee pows."

Toor whispered into Irik's ear. "He said he wanted to test your special powers."

"Tell him," Irik said, thinking he was a brave and worthy chief. "I can share my powers with him."

The White Clan leader lowered his knife, inched forward, and stared. He reached with both hands to trace the curved horns of the mountain goat headdress covering Irik's ears. Calmly meeting his sunken eyes, Irik let the chief caress and admire his wolf-fang necklace.

Toor translated the chief's next utterance. "He asked how you got the big horns. No one can hunt mountain goats."

Irik smiled to think the Maku admired their skill and bounty. "We did."

The birdman chief turned to his warriors and shouted a sharp command. *Is he telling his men, still aiming their spears, to attack?*

Before Toor could translate, the warriors lowered their weapons.

The chief threw his head back and pointed to his chest. "Kokor," he said and bowed.

Relieved, Irik returned the bow.

Kokor gestured toward the smoking huts and waved for Irik and his men to follow.

The chief put his arm around Irik's shoulders and said something to his warriors. They took his lead and befriended the Wolf Clansmen, staying a respectful distance behind their leader. Without Toor to translate, Irik tensed as they walked past the many huts. But soon, he marveled at the self-standing caves—hides stitched and wrapped over branches with poles set in the earth.

Irik ran his fingers over the hide. "Very stiff. Why is there no hair?"

Toor trotted over to resume interpreting.

"To make it waterproof," Kokor explained.

Irik turned to Toor, "Ask him how that's done."

"Once we scrape the meat and fat from the hide, we use ash and water to remove the hair." Shell beads clattering, Chief Kokor demonstrated kneading and washing the hide. "Then, we cook it slowly with animal brain to tan it. Finally," he pointed to a hide stretched on a frame, "we smoke it over a slow fire until it turns dark brown." He wiggled his fingers while dropping his hands. "Rain falls right off."

When they reached the largest hut, Kokor motioned for the rest of the men to stay behind. He conveyed through gestures that he wanted a chief-to-chief talk. Irik stiffened at losing Toor's assistance but followed Kokor as he lifted a flap of hide over the doorway. Two women, young and old, giggled and rushed out. The White chief smiled and welcomed Irik into his home.

A fire pit lined with stones wafted odd-smelling smoke over a hunk of meat hanging from a frame. The smoke trailed up to an opening between long, crisscrossed poles. Irik was amazed these people made homes they could move anywhere—one for each family. His clan could learn much from them.

They sat, and Kokor sliced off a chunk of meat, smiled, and handed it to Irik. The chew was soft and smoky but strange. Irik stifled a gag and swallowed hard. "What meat is this?"

The chief didn't answer.

Irik made a running gesture with his fingers. "What kind of beast?"

Kokor laughed, shook his head, and made a swerving motion with one hand.

Irik was puzzled.

The chief picked up a stick and drew in the sand. An image of a sleek, neckless creature with a tiny head, bird-like wings, and fan-shaped tail emerged.

Irik's eyes widened. Either Kokor drew badly, or it was an unfamiliar species.

The chief drew a wavy line underneath and said, "*Reela,*" picking up a strangely pointed spear. He stabbed it into the ground, lifted it, and wiggled the end.

Irik nodded without comprehending. *Must be a sea animal of some kind.* He held out both hands as a request to examine the spear. Unlike anything he'd ever seen, it had a straight piercing point and to the side a smaller point facing backward. *Maybe to keep the prey from escaping?* "*Reela,*" Irik said and wiped sweat from his forehead.

Kokor pointed to Irik's deerskin vest, looked up toward the sky, and fanned himself. Irik understood he meant clothing wasn't much needed in the warm climate. Irik took off his vest and handed it to the chief, who ran his hand along the grain appreciatively.

For the first time, Irik noticed a pinkish spot on the chief's white legs. He gestured toward it, wiggled his fingers, narrowed his brow, and pointed to the chief. "Do you paint yourself?"

Kokor laughed, slid his hands under his beaded shroud, and slowly lifted it over his head.

Irik gasped.

He was as human as Irik but paler and more wrinkled. Staring, Irik waved his hand over his face and chest and asked, "How… why do you paint your bodies?"

Kokor pointed again to the sky, wiped his brow, then blew on his skin. He glanced at Irik, standing and pointing to a pile of white objects. He grabbed a handful and dropped a thin "rock" into a stone bowl. Crushing, then grinding it, he handed the white powder to Irik.

Rubbing it between his coated fingers, Irik gestured upwards and said, "Aha, to protect your skin from the sun." Nearby on the ground, Irik noticed some tiny, conical, slotted shells with what resembled smiling mouths. *What beautiful beads for Arol.* Picking one up, he pointed to Kokor's shroud. "Same shell as in your headdress?" Kokor nodded, scooped up a bunch, and gave them to Irik.

The White chief gestured for a closer look at Irik's spear tip. Once he had it in hand, curiosity and admiration radiated from his face. He twisted and turned the sharp point, endlessly running his fingers up and down the flaked edges, murmuring and glancing at Irik in wonder.

Kokor took a few steps and picked up one of his spears to show Irik the point: a thick, roughly hewn triangle in the old Lessor style used for thrust hunting. The White chief seemed to recognize the superiority of the sharp Wolf Clan points, which could penetrate thick hides when thrown from a distance.

Irik wanted to share his know-how in making the finer points but hesitated to give another clan such a superior tool and weapon. Without Toor at his side, he remained unsure about how well he communicated. But thinking further, he knew he could gain knowledge in return and a new neighbor. He reached into his pouch.

Taking out a chunk of shale, he set it on the ground and handed the stone hammer and punch to the White chief. "Deer," he said as Kokor sniffed and fondled bumps on the antler.

Irik placed the point of the punch on an exact spot at the edge of the flint.

Whack! He hammered out a perfect long flake.

"Yiiee!" Kokor drew back.

Whack! Another perfect blade.

The White chief appeared eager to try, so Irik gave him the hammer and positioned the punch. "It must be angled like this and give it a hard blow right here."

Crack!

"Oww!" A small chip shot into Irik's arm. He pulled it out and tried to smile as blood oozed from the cut.

"Sopla!" Kokor cried and jumped over to a corner of the hut. He returned—regret on his face—holding a sprig of dried flowers. He rubbed them together, spit into his hands, and dabbed the paste on Irik's wound.

They smiled at each other when the bleeding stopped.

"Thank you," Irik said, "what is it?" *Arol might want some of that too.*

"*Oluu,*" the chief responded and retrieved a fresh bunch.

"*Oluu.*" Irik tried the unfamiliar word out on his tongue, nearly getting it right. "Very good. Thank you." He placed it in his pouch and waved toward the doorway. "It's late. I must gather my men."

Kokor held up his hand, rushed to the door, and shouted. The two women reappeared, and the chief spoke to them while they peered into the hut and smiled broadly. Kokor put his hand over his groin, thrust his hips back and forth, and nodded to Irik.

Irik stood, shaking his head. "No, but thanks." Inwardly he recoiled, suspecting they were the chief's wife and daughter. In any case, he'd wait for Nara, even if Arol showed up in his dreams again tonight. He exited and pointed to the eastern sky. "See you in the morning."

―――――◆―――――

For three days, the two peoples enjoyed learning about each other, eagerly sharing their lives and ways. The Wolf Clansmen had fun harpooning fish in the coastal waters. Struggling to crack open mussel shells, they slurped the gooey innards.

The Whites clambered to see how a spear-thrower worked. Irik allowed his men to demonstrate inserting a spear shaft into the notched end of the thrower. After two days of target practice, the White warriors grew sour at their limited progress with what they called an "*attul.*" Irik tried to explain how the weapon must be custom made and balanced to the body of each thrower. In the end, he suspected "*attul*" was an anger word in the White language and doubted they'd ever get the hang of it.

The women of the village were thrilled to learn Irik and Vir had, as youngsters, the chore of making sewing thread. The two demonstrated twisting and braiding flax fibers and left them with an antler sewing needle. In return, the women gave them a thin, hollowed-out leg bone with holes punched into its sides. A giggling girl blew a beautiful birdsong through it, but Vir's screeching attempt made Irik cover his ears. "Not sure Arol would like it," he warned Vir.

Later in the day, Irik and Wolt, one of the Rhino men, watched two White Clan members deconstruct a hut. The strapping, dexterous Wolt liked carving wood and weaving sticks or reeds, so he seemed perfect for the enterprise. The Wolf Clan pair took four hours longer than a single White would have to rebuild the hut. Clumsy and yelling in frustration, they acquired enough skill by the end to raise a village of huts for themselves someday.

Irik and the men grew restless to return to their families, so he informed Kokor they'd be leaving the next day. The White chief frowned, apparently saddened by their departure.

In the morning, Kokor invited Irik into his hut for a goodbye. When Irik pointed to Toor, asking if he could join them, the older chief scowled and gestured for just the two of them. Feeling his clan had gained the White people's trust and friendship, Irik explained as best he could their intention to come back to settle nearby. He opened his arms wide and pulled them to his chest. "Our families will come and join us here."

Kokor scratched his head.

Irik pantomimed the shape of a woman's breasts and various sizes of children. As the White chief nodded and smiled, Irik rejoiced he responded favorably.

When the morning sun peeked over the horizon, the Wolf Clan stood packed and ready. Kokor gave Irik a shell amulet carved with the image of a *reela*. Thankful for the welcome his clan had received and brimming with hope for their future, Irik put a hand under his wolf-fang necklace. He lifted the only treasure he had with him from his neck to give to the White chief.

Looking-back waves followed hearty hugs as the Wolf Clan headed up the trail toward Perla's Pass. They hiked in silence, mulling over the last three days until they reached the foothills and stopped to rest. Seated in a circle, they ate turtle eggs they'd gathered the night before from the beach sand.

Irik spoke. "With Perla's Pass ahead of us, we should be home within five days."

The men nodded merrily, enjoying their exotic fare.

"Once we share the good news with our women and children, we could prepare to return to our new home in as little as two moons. What are your thoughts?"

The clansmen looked at each other. Nork stood and waved his hand over the group. "Who is with our leader?"

All hands shot up, Vir's curling into a triumphant fist.

The usually-quiet Dar cleared his throat., "You proved your bravery again, Chief, but more…" He searched for words. "…you see ahead. A new way, better life for the clan."

The men stomped their feet on the ground and hooted.

Irik spoke with a quaver. "Thank you, Nork, Dar, all you men, for your faith in me. Do you think the White people would be good neighbors? Shall we move?"

"Yes!" the men shouted in unison. They jumped up and jostled to hug their leader.

After resting, the cheerful band started their hike toward Perla's Pass. The wolves yipped and frolicked ahead.

Vir walked alongside Irik. "I must tell you, Chief, some of the men do worry." Irik tugged Vir away from the line so no one would hear. "Why? They seemed so happy."

"They are. Full bellies and most of them had White women each night, but…"

"What?"

Vir glanced behind and murmured, "Some were concerned you gave away your wolf-fang necklace. They saw it as the chief's— something to keep. Symbol of the Wolf Tribe."

He froze. The weight of his spontaneous decision bore down on him. "Perhaps the goat horn headdress and trained wolves proved my power enough?"

Vir's young forehead creased. "Maybe, but I also need to tell you what the men found in many of the huts."

With a sinking feeling, Irik gestured for Vir to continue.

"Poles with human skulls perched on top of them. What could it mean?"

Irik could not bring himself to mention the man-beast and mumbled, "I'm not sure."

Chapter Sixteen

LIKE A WELCOMING FRIEND, THE sun emerged from cattail-fluff clouds to illuminate the travelers. Irik's face flushed with pride and happiness. Removing his vest to bathe in the warmth, he raised his arms in praise of the land. "This will be the new home of the Wolf Clan."

His people roared with joy, the children scampering downhill with screams of laughter as playful wolves nipped at their heels. Families rushed to stake out locations for their huts as the male wolves marked their territory by peeing and scratching at the earth. Because Wolt had learned from the Whites, Irik put him in charge of hut building, and his crew hurried to the woods to collect poles for the new homes.

The trek through the mountains had depleted food supplies. Irik knew spending nights out in the open with empty bellies would upset the clansfolk, so he formed a scouting party to learn about the surrounding land and plan a big hunt.

Irik guided the men on a circular route through the rugged hills and valleys, memorizing every vantage point and distance. The herd of aurochs remained a day's hike away on the plain, so he needed to find a way to get meat soon. It was nearing dusk when he spotted a narrow, short ravine that opened up to another valley. *Maybe we could drive and trap cows there.*

When Irik returned to the camp at nightfall, Nara ran to meet him. "Glad you're back," she said, hugging him. "Everyone's tired. Hope you found food."

"I think so. I'll speak with the men after we eat."

Following a meager meal of tubers and seeds the women had gathered, Irik called the men to the community fire. He added several logs to the embers to light the hopeful, if haggard, faces of his fellow hunters seated on a circle of flat rocks.

"Our stomachs will soon be full," Irik began, to the rapt attention of the still-hungry men. "A large herd of aurochs grazes on the southern plain." He stood for emphasis. "We can use the ways of the wolf pack to drive them to us." He raised a finger. "But unlike our four-legged brothers who work together to rush the herd and cut off one animal, we will split it. If we drive part of them north toward us, we can kill several at once."

The men leaned in as Irik picked up a branch and began to draw in the soft earth. "These dots are the herd of aurochs in the southern plain. These lines are men, here and there, who, with Deego's and Cala's hunting packs, will jump into the herd from two sides. Like this…" he drew two slashes "…and split off a section of the herd from the rear to drive them north toward us."

The men squirmed on their stone seats.

"We would run among them?" Nork asked. "They could scramble in any direction."

"They might easily trample us." Karango frowned.

Irik held up a hand. "You are strong, brave men. Your task is to run fast at them, shouting and waving your arms. With our barking, charging wolves, the beasts will panic and run ahead."

Karango spoke again. "Why don't we just spear one at the edge of the herd, butcher it in place, and sled back the meat?"

"Quiet!" Boolip glared at Karango. "Let Chief Irik describe his plan."

The men nodded and grunted. Irik shot grateful eyes toward Boolip.

"The problem is," Irik continued, "the herd is too far away from our village. It would take a day to bring the meat back, and the clan would eat it all in one day. Besides, we need lots of hides for the huts." He slapped his stick at the ground and jabbed it toward the men. "We must bring the herd *to* us."

They looked at each other and muttered.

"Once this part of the herd has moved north to here…" Irik drew an arrow in front of the men. "…my group will join the driving group from the south and push the herd east. We'll force the cows into the ravine where it opens up to a valley." He drew lines for a narrow ravine between two hills and Xs for men positioned at the end. "Our best spear-throwers will wait as the animals squeeze through and slay several at once."

The men looked uneasy about this new way of hunting. Karango shook his head and mumbled.

Irik scowled at Karango, waiting for the rest of the men to congratulate him on his strategy, but the only sound was the distant creaking of tree toads. He clenched his jaw. "Dar, you were in the scouting party and saw the ravine." Impatience clipped his words. "Tell them it will work."

Dar averted his eyes. "It could, but we'd have to watch out for the cliff that lies beyond the shrub." He pointed at the drawing. "It's a steep drop."

Irik sat heavily. "Thanks, Dar, we'll be careful. Tomorrow we'll prepare to drive cattle into the ravine, and I'll select teams. We hunt the day after. Are you with me?"

The hunters barely lifted their chins.

"What's the matter?" Boolip broke in. "Has Irik ever failed you?"

Nearly everyone said no, and some gave a muted cheer.

"Good," Irik said and raised a defiant fist. "I know you won't fail me either."

Retreating to his family's campfire, Irik found Nara, who'd sliced a roasted rabbit. "One of the women snared and gave it to us. Have some."

"Not hungry, Nara."

"What's wrong? You must be after such a long day."

"I can't eat." He waved her away. "Take it to Boolip's family. I need rest." He trudged to the fresh bed Nara had made from grass cuttings and sank into its rustling comfort. As he closed his eyes, he recalled the fear on the men's faces. They weren't ready to run at aurochs. If any of them balked during the hunt, injury or death could result. He'd be blamed and replaced as leader.

His eyes snapped open when Nara nestled into bed. "Irik, the men are afraid. They're telling their women it's a dangerous plan. Even Pral and Reto said so."

Irik's gut clenched, worry filling his throat. "I see. Need to sleep."

He tried to invoke the spirit of the wolf pack to guide him on how to hunt, but he could not sleep, let alone dream. As he mentally listed the risks, he realized shouting, barking, and running might not be enough to drive the beasts in the right direction.

Perhaps thanks to the dark of the moonless, open sky, Irik's mind wandered back to the painted walls of the old Valley Clan cave. He remembered a drawing done by a previous dweller of a herd of caribou and wondered why the other artist placed jagged lines behind the herd. He'd traced a finger along the marks, noticing remnants of red and yellow ochre in their depths.

As he drifted off, he pictured his rendition of the caribou buck he'd been so sad as a child to see killed. His empty stomach growled, and he smelled its fat sizzling in a long-ago fire with his father presiding as chief. "Survival means killing," he heard Chief Brul intone as he carved out the beast's heart to give to Reto, maimed by its antler. "We must take from nature or be taken by it. But never take too much or fail to honor the spirits of the animals who sustain us."

Irik tossed on the grass mattress. He heard his mother praising his caribou painting to his father while they thought he slept. "The boy sees things others can't." The wonder in her voice touched him even more as a struggling adult than it had as an insecure child. He missed Mata terribly and wished he could go to her for encouragement. She'd never failed to believe in him, to make him feel he could conquer anything. Losing her during the volcanic aftermath seemed especially cruel because he'd been too preoccupied with surviving to grieve properly.

As a tear escaped his closed eye, Irik's dream view wandered from his caribou and wolf pack paintings around the subterranean gallery. *Can the spirit of the wolf pack father show me the way?* The men of the clan always gathered to view the art by flickering firelight before a hunt, to glean wisdom or inspiration from the experiences of all who went before. He found himself transfixed again by that painting of a caribou herd with a strange orange residue. Wait! The lines weren't jagged but meant to be wavy, colored like flames. He shot up awake. It wasn't grass trailing the caribou—it was fire.

At daybreak, Irik circled the mostly sleeping clan to find Arol. She was at her family's fire, showing her daughter how to string painted wooden beads onto a strip of rawhide.

"Good morning, Arol."

"Irik, how are you?"

"Good. Where's Vir?"

"He's already out working on the huts."

"Good man. Could you do me a favor, please?"

She nodded. He fought not to get lost in her brightly beautiful eyes.

"Pull together a group of children to scour the woods and collect dry moss. Right away."

She wrinkled her brow. "What're you—?"

"It's important."

"Sure," she said. "Heard about your plan to drive the aurochs. Will it work?"

He rubbed his forehead, realizing even she thought it unwise.

She put her hand to her throat. "Sorry, I only wondered how you came up with it."

Unlike Nara, she always sees into my heart. He stood up. "I have a better way now. Can you get the moss?"

"The moms and kids will be happy to help."

"Thanks, Arol." He scooted off.

When he got to the pine woods, Wolt was directing his crew to cut poles and branches for the huts. Locking arms with the burly Rhino man, he said, "I hate to take you away from your work, but I have a special need."

Wolt nodded. "Of course."

I need you and your men to gather as much pine resin as quickly as you can and bring it to the community fire."

Letting go of a pine pole with surprised eyes, Wolt said, "Right away, Chief."

By mid-morning, Irik was pleased to find heaps of moss and clumps of sticky yellow resin waiting for him. Seeing Wolt bringing more, he thanked him. "That's enough for now. Will you gather the men and join me at the community fire?"

Last night's logs still smoldered as the men arrived, disquiet creasing their faces.

"Good men of the Wolf Clan," Irik boomed, "Tomorrow, we trek south for a great hunt and begin to conquer our new land." Their expressions remained glum. "I know some of you had concerns about facing and driving the aurochs."

The men nodded cautiously without speaking.

"I understand. We need to be sure they'll run from us, not turn on us."

"Yes, yes, true," the men murmured.

Irik reached behind him to pick up a long branch with a clump attached to the end.

He stuck it in the fire.

CRACK! With a flash, the stick leaped into flames.

As sparks flew, the men jerked back.

WHOOSH! Irik pulled the stick out, flaming and popping—black smoke billowing from the tip. He waved it back and forth, flame roaring.

Running around the circle of men, he jabbed the torch in the air, then toward them.

"AiiYee!" Some ducked, others crawled away.

Dar covered his head with one hand, his nose with the other.

Shrieks rose in the distance, and the women came running. The wolves cowered or fled toward the woods.

Irik stuck the torch in the earth and raised his hands toward the women. "Everyone is safe. I'm showing how to use pine resin torches to drive the aurochs. No need to worry."

Arol, Nara, and the other women grinned as the men laughed.

Wolt picked up the torch and waved it. "This will have the aurochs running." Chuckling and coughing from the thick smoke, the men patted Irik and each other on the backs.

"Brother," Reto jumped in, "elders Pral and I salute your plan."

"No animal will come at us if fire's in our hands," said Dar. "We're with you, Chief."

They chanted his name.

"Enough. We have to make the torches today." He pointed to the moss and resin. "Wolt, you collect the branches. Any volunteers to blacken their hands?" The men gathered and watched Irik mix a handful of moss with resin.

By day's end, they'd made two torches for each man. When they began to yawn and rub their hands with pine needles, Irik said, "Not done yet. Still need to make fireballs."

"Fireballs?"

"We won't throw stones as the Lessors did. Watch." Irik mixed moss with resin and rolled it into a sphere, adding a pointed tip. "Use these before running with your torches." He stuck the wick into the fire, then turned the ball over on itself until the flame leaped to one side.

As it ignited, Irik threw the ball over their heads. It blazed brightly with a long tail of fire and smoke.

"Aahh!" the men cried.

Dar lifted a torch and shouted. "This will be the greatest hunt ever."

Even Karango cracked a smile.

———————◆———————

By mid-afternoon, the two southern teams of hunters had positioned themselves, six men each, at the rear edge of the herd. Boolip was in charge with Deego's pack on the right side. Heading up the left was Karango with Cala's pack. Holding their unlit torches in the air, the teams lined up across from one another. With the wolves stalking at the men's sides, they stole closer toward a group of some fifty hands of aurochs.

Several body lengths away, the cows noticed the invaders but only snorted. The men knelt and struck their flint on the rock fire-starters. Sparks flew to the tinder, and with a blow, they had fire. As they stuck the balls' wicks into the flames, the rising smoke agitated the animals and signaled the hunters on the other side of the herd.

Whoosh, whoosh, whoosh! The fireballs sailed between the tightly packed aurochs.

Flame, smoke, and the acrid smell made them bolt, separating the cluster from the main herd.

As both teams, torches blazing and wolves charging, came together, the cows stampeded north. The thundering of their hooves echoed across the plain as dust blinded and choked their pursuers.

Farther north and west, Irik and his waiting team cheered when they saw the smoke and aurochs running north. The gap between the herd and the men widened, and from his higher perch, Irik could make out the line of men—their first torches burned out.

Irik squinted into the distance. "Dar, what's going on to the right of the men?" He pointed. "The line seems to be breaking."

"Not sure," Dar shielded his face from the blinding sunlight. "Oh, wait! Looks like some of our men are running west away from the herd."

"Why would they do that?" Irik turned to scan the horizon. "What is that farther east?"

Dar did a double-take. "Men, but not ours. Running on the other side of the herd."

"Who are they?" Every hair on Irik's body stood on end.

"They look... I think... it's the White warriors. With spears in the air."

"What?" Irik spat. "Are you sure? What're they doing?"

"Chasing us. Throwing spears." Dar's voice broke. "Some of our men are down."

Irik had no time to ponder why the Whites would attack his clan in this ample land, far away from their territory. He turned to the other men. "Kol and Chor, grab your spears and come with me. Our brothers are in trouble. Dar, stay with the rest of the men. I'll signal you when to push the aurochs east toward the ravine. Let's go!"

As he drew nearer, Irik counted only seven of the twelve Wolf Clansmen running toward them. In the distance, five bodies sprawled on the ground, spears in their backs. Irik could make out Nork's and Karango's panicked faces as they fled from the Whites in close pursuit. "Load your spear-throwers," Irik ordered his men.

He slowed, planted his legs, and notched a spear. "Now!"

Whoosh, whoosh, whoosh!

Two Whites fell. The others faltered.

Irik reloaded. "Launch again!"

Two more Whites went down. The rest turned and ran.

Still holding their unlit torches, the Wolf Clansmen reached Irik. Drained and struggling for breath, Karango moaned, "Why did you let them attack us, Irik? You said the Whites were our friends. They killed Boolip and four others."

Irik seethed at Karango's accusation, even if he was right, but this was no time for rivalry. He turned to see the aurochs had stopped moving. "Light your fireballs and torches."

With a wave, he yelled, "Throw!" They charged at the herd from their side.

Irik held up his torch and told everyone to light theirs. The west team spotted the signal, lit their torches and fireballs, and ran to the east.

"Throw your fireballs," Irik commanded.

Smelling the smoke, the small herd got skittish, and some of the animals switched direction toward the main herd heading north.

"Keep pushing them east," Irik yelled. *What were those Whites doing in the east? No time to figure it out now.*

Reaching the top of the rise, Irik saw what was too late to change. With the Whites pushing from the east and them from the west, the entire herd had shifted dead north—away from the ravine and toward the cliff.

Over the pounding of hooves, Irik shouted, "Pull back," before realizing the men already had. As he watched the inevitable unfold, his heart and time seemed to stop.

Row by row of animals disappeared over the horizon—flailing, bellowing as they soared off the end of the earth. The rumble of hooves mingled with thuds of countless bodies crashing at the same time, shaking the ground. A trembling in Irik's feet reached up into his throat, and he gasped for breath.

His men watched in stunned silence as the cows swept White warriors with them over the cliff. They could hear no screams, and no one budged until the last auroch plunged to its death. Only dust remained in the herd's wake.

The men crept to the edge of the cliff as more dust settled over the dead and dying beasts. The wolves sniffed and whined. Aghast, the men looked toward Irik.

This was not in keeping with respecting the spirit of the animals. But plenty more remained, so he didn't speak with too heavy of a heart. "Dar, take some men and bring the women and sleds for butchering. Wolt, find the best route to the bottom of the cliff."

"Ayaah! We'll soon eat," one of the younger men crowed.

Irik glared at him. "No celebrating. Too many men and animals are dead. Karango, go with Vir. Get men and sleds to bring back our dead."

Standing alone with the panting wolves. Irik lifted his eyes from the carnage and scanned the hills. He caught a white speck of movement against the distant pines. The painted body of a White warrior climbing fast—a lone survivor. *Is he one of Kokor's clan? If these were his warriors, it makes no sense. We left them on friendly terms—traded with them, learned from each other. I told Kokor we'd settle a distance away and be good neighbors. What happened?*

Irik's attention returned to the bottom of the cliff. Floating up the sheer walls were the final sounds of death. The gurgle of last breaths. The grunts of efforts to stand on injured legs. The faint bleats of calves who'd fallen on their mothers. *Will any live? What would my father think of me for causing such a calamity?* He covered his ears and closed his eyes.

A screech rang out.

He looked down.

Here and there, among the wide, deep piles of black and brown auroch bodies, rested a white arm, a twisted torso, or a bloody head. No human moved among the twitching cows with huge tongues hanging out, lapping for air.

The cry issued from a trio of big-winged, bald scavengers, descending in circles and calling to their kind to share a newfound meal. Until humans or hyenas ripped open the hides, they'd settle for feasting on the eyes. Easy pickings.

Irik dropped to his haunches in shame and regret. His hunting strategy would have worked if it weren't for the Whites. He'd tried to explain to Kokor they were coming to live nearby, but perhaps this was a different White Clan. Or maybe Uncle Orki had been right about their cruelty, and none of them could be trusted.

In the end, he reminded himself survival required killing. The wolf-pack father provides for his family. *Are we any different?* The wolves looked to Irik for a command.

Irik's weary eyes fixed on each of them. "I'm sorry," he said, sinking to the ground.

Body and mind drained, he waited for the women to come butcher the meat.

"Irik, are you all right?"

Hearing Nara's call, he stood shakily. She left her side of the drag sled and ran to him. The clan women dropped their sleds, rushed to the edge of the cliff, and gasped as one.

Nara threw her arms around him. "You're the great chief I always knew you'd be." She kissed his mouth, but he barely felt it. Dar says we have food for moons, and you defeated the Whites." She pointed to the chattering women. "They all honor you."

He took her hand, and they walked to the far edge of the cliff. The stench of expiring animal gases assaulted their noses. "But look at the cost," he said, waving his hand over the massive heap of tangled bodies. "Most of this food will rot. Five of our men are dead and half the White warriors."

Nara looked up at the vultures. "Other creatures will live from it." She touched his arm. "Don't be hard on yourself, Irik. Someday, you'll be chief of all the clans."

"Come on, everyone," Wolt called to the women. "This way down for butchering."

Nara kissed him again and joined the women on the steep path. Irik remained numb.

Arol appeared at the end of the line, and Irik motioned for her. She nudged her daughter and some other children toward another woman and walked to the edge of the cliff.

Looking down at the pile of dead aurochs, she cried out and put her hands over her trembling lips. Tears flooded her cheeks.

Even more distraught at seeing her weep, Irik tried to hold her.

She shook her head without looking at him and asked, "What have we done?" She turned to walk away.

"Arol?" He reached out.

Head down and softly sniffling, she returned to the children.

Chapter Seventeen

TWO YEARS LATER, IRIK AMBLED over to the cherished site in the foothills as the sun broke over the village. When he and the clan had first gazed at this open plain and crossed the creek, hope was all they possessed. Now, their sturdy huts teemed with growing families—the good people of the Wolf Clan. At twenty-two winters old, Irik came here to admire what he'd accomplished.

A proud smile lit his face as trails of smoke carried whiffs of roasted meat to his nostrils. The huts provided ideal shelter in the warm climate, and the clan was well-fed and safe. After the battle with the Whites—apparently resulting from his misunderstanding—Irik had retrained two hands of hunters into elite warriors. Day and night, they and the wolves kept vigil around the perimeter of the village, always alert for an attack from the south. Gorb, the defense-minded Rhino man Irik had appointed commander of the squad, had yet to report a sighting of a single White. Irik supposed whoever had attacked them on the day of the auroch massacre must have realized an abundance of resources made it wiser to share the land.

The clan's success at herd-hunting with wolves and the resulting bounty had transformed them into a respected regional power. Irik's belief in himself flourished, and he finally felt he had become a respected leader.

More and more humans were migrating and settling in small bands and clans to the east and west, but none approached the prowess of the Wolf hunters. During mass killings of game, the eastward clans stayed hidden but watched ravenously, not possessing the numbers or weaponry to attempt such feats themselves. Once the Wolf hunters sledded away what meat they needed, the others emerged like hyenas to happily scavenge the many leftovers.

Recently, herds had not only thinned but migrated more to the west. Most hunts centered there now, forcing Irik to consider expanding into that territory. If so, the eastern clans would lose a major source of food. One of their leaders had approached Irik to ask if their people could join the Wolf Clan, but Irik declined, focused on the promise of the west. The only downside in the west was a lack of high cliffs to force herds over. Instead, the Wolf hunters relied on a narrow, three-sided valley to drive animals into for slaughtering.

There too, they encountered other scattered clans of humans, some of whom also wished to join the Wolf Clan. Because they spoke a similar language and had familiar habits, Irik interviewed and invited some to become clan members as long as they brought tributes and tools with them. Otherwise, they were driven from the land.

With Chief Irik's growing success, the clan accorded his family many privileges. They built them a new hut, twice the size of the old one, including a playhouse for Brul. Receiving the best cuts of meat and already-sewn furs, Nara no longer had to butcher or work hides. New clan members, required to pay in gifts and work for joining, showered them with carved wooden bowls, reed baskets, and clever arts and crafts.

Irik had turned over wolf training to Soth, twenty winters old with no family but an innate talent with animals, with Brul as an understudy. Although revered by his clan as the father of herd-hunting that brought in copious food and hides, Irik relinquished leading hunts to Karango and his skillful Rhino crew. Nara told him it was a mistake to give up that role, but Irik didn't feel the thirst for the hunt like his father had. Increasingly, he felt uneasy, despite the laurels accorded him. *Why, with such success, is something gnawing at me, throwing me off balance?*

Irik's main activity as he delegated tasks was to walk among the villagers and oversee their work. At times he yearned to return to a simpler time when, playing with Arol, he didn't have responsibilities.

Back then, he was in harmony with the animals and could capture their spirits. But without stone walls to paint on or enough time between crises or disputes, he never got a chance.

One balmy day, when Irik, Vir, and other members of the clan were scouting out locations in the west to build a new village, screams rang across the plain.

"Sounds like Arol," Vir cried.

Irik's throat had clenched at the first hint of her raised voice.

Knowing she and Leta often searched for edible and medicinal plants, the men ran to a nearby meadow, only to find it empty. When they heard high voices echoing, they followed them into the valley where Karango and his men were finishing a hunt.

"Let the rest go!" Arol shrieked at Karango, whose men had boxed a large herd of red deer and were pushing them tighter.

The small, timid deer stood frozen as the men coldly speared them, some laughing at the ease and entertainment of it. The animals couldn't escape the line of zealous hunters and had no defense, only making mewling sounds while struck down to quiver and die.

"Call the wolves off," Arol shouted, seeing some charge at fawns, grab them by the necks, and drag them to their deaths.

Karango ignored her, so she turned her rage toward Irik and Vir, now close at hand.

"Stop this bloodshed," she demanded. "They're killing far more than we need, and the wolves are supposed to herd, not attack. Stop them!"

Karango kept his eyes peeled to Irik while his men continued the carnage.

"Arol, I know how you must feel, but Karango oversees hunting now."

Leta defended her daughter. "I agree. It's beyond cruel."

Vir's troubled expression sided with the women as he peered at Irik.

"Vir," Irik commanded, "take Leta with you. Tell Karango to call the wolves back. I'll talk with Arol."

"And stop the hunt?" Vir asked.

"I didn't say that." He pointed toward the hunters. "Go."

Glowering, Leta sauntered away. Vir approached Karango.

When they were alone, Irik scowled at Arol. "Are you finished screaming?"

"No! You can't let such brutality continue. What's the matter with you?"

"Nothing. I'm feeding my clan like any good chief would."

She shook her head, mortified eyes glowing like embers. "At what cost? How will you feed us when all the herds are gone?"

He smirked. "Oh, Arol, that's not—"

"Your father would be ashamed of you."

"For what?" Irik shouted, fists curled. "Succeeding where he failed?"

Arol punched him in the chest. "Your spirit is dying. You're a butcher, not a leader."

Before his hands, shaking with shock, could clutch at her, she ran away.

That night

Sitting at their fire roasting meat, Nara gave Irik a long look. "You're not hungry after that hard day in the west? Karango brought us the finest deer chops."

He twirled the skewered meat and sighed. "Some of the old clan think I'm overkilling."

"Who said that?"

"Vir, Leta, and Arol."

"Naaah! It's that nasty Karango. I told you, you shouldn't have given him that job. You're the leader, not him."

He glanced at her, forcing a smile.

She flicked her hand. "Arol's jealous at what I—we have. Look, if you weren't a wonderful chief, we wouldn't get all these gifts and respect."

Irik only sighed, feeling the unease return from yesterday when Arol had admonished him.

"Look at yourself," Nara barked. "Brooding like the timid boy you once were."

He drew back. "What did you say?"

"I said this is not the time to go soft, Irik. Look at all your triumphs. Your father would be so proud."

"I guess," he said and took a bite of the deer chop, relishing the taste.

Later that night

"There they are," Irik yelled as he reached the rise and spotted the horse herd. "Within driving distance of the cliff, resting."

"The men are exhausted, Chief," Vir said. "We've been chasing them since dawn."

"All right. Let's rest for a while, but nightfall will soon be upon us."

Vir lowered his hand, and he, the men, and the wolves sank to the ground. "Thanks, but how do we know they won't turn on us again in the opposite direction?"

"We can't let them," Irik answered, creeping slowly toward the herd. The horses were exhausted too, as attested by sweat drops clinging to their silky hides and glistening in the late-day sun. Much earlier, they'd run with the wind, long legs and hard hooves thundering on the earth—wispy manes and tails flowing behind.

The chestnut brown, midnight black, and dappled gray of their elegant, muscular bodies reminded Irik of watching his first caribou hunt. He wanted to feel the horse sinew, know the bone, maybe draw it.

With the sun setting and a full moon rising, Irik yelled, "Come on, men. Last chance to take them down, or we'll lose them." He pointed to Vir. "Quietly take three men and position them on either side of the herd with unlit torches. When I, the others, and the wolves start our approach, I'll give you the signal to light them. That'll keep the herd from turning left or right."

Soon, the men were in place. "Charge!" Irik commanded.

The wolves began howling.

"What?" Irik halted and pointed his arm forward. "Charge!"

Instead of running at the horses, the wolves ran around the herd.

Irik froze as the wolves moved in front of the horses, between them and the cliff. *What has gotten into the wolves? This is going to—*

With a jarring blare of neighing, the horses leaped toward the men, rumbling and tearing the earth into dust as they dashed together in panic.

"Run, men," Irik yelled, knowing they couldn't outdistance the stampede. His heart hammered against his ribs as hooves crushed heads and trampled bodies. A separate blow to his ribcage rocked him, and he turned to see the cause.

Arol? She looked at him scornfully, tears flooding her eyes.

"Irik! Wake up," Nara called, her hand on his palpitating chest. "Just a bad dream."

Next morning

Still haunted by the crazy nightmare, Irik fretted about what it meant. Was it that he had lost his hunting prowess or his way? He stepped out of the hut as the sun bathed the village. As flocks of children emerged to play, their bursts of laughter reminded him of how lighthearted he'd felt when small and free. *Why do I have this longing for the past? Why do I feel so out of balance?* He realized he was a different person before his father died, and he had to concern himself with all the killing.

Making his way among the villagers and greeting each warmly, he realized he missed the kinship he'd had with people in the tight-knit Valley Clan. Pral's death last year had not only devastated their daughter, Arol, but it also tore at him too. Indeed, the loss of elders left an aching void of knowledge and connection to the past.

With the Wolf Clan's numbers reaching twenty-two hands, it had become increasingly difficult to know everyone. Nara helped by staying close to all the women and listening for any whispers of discontent. She mentioned when jealousies arose between families about the amount of work or share of resources. Irik figured that might be expected in any large group of people.

Of more concern was her report of seeing Gorb spending more time with Karango. Irik had never liked or trusted Karango, but he admired his hunting expertise and tried to get along. If Cret had taught Irik anything, it was to keep the ill-tempered pacified while going about his business. Commander Gorb wasn't like Cret, Karango, or the other Rhino men. He'd always been loyal to Irik, even though he and his warriors had pushed to take out the Whites. To see a strategic soldier buddying up to a hotheaded hunter made Irik worry.

He knew Nara had a woman's insight about other people and their motivations, but was she only acting out of concern for holding on to power? To Irik, their privileges had begun to feel more like chains.

Even more broadly, he worried he was removed from his people, becoming aloof. Since he had little face-to-face contact with most members, he didn't know if they were happy with his leadership. As he passed the wolf pens, he reached over the fence and patted his eager, furry children. He somehow couldn't respond with an equal amount of joy. The sight of Deela—her streak as white as her mother's—made him only sad. He knew Meeri wasn't long for this world. *What has happened? Have I lost my spiritual connection to my four-legged animals as well as my own people?* He was more than out of touch. He was letting the spiritual bonds fracture.

Passing by Arol and Vir's hut, he felt a strange release. It came to him that he needed to lay down a new rule for the hunt. From now on, they would only kill what was needed. Herd-hunting would be restricted to winter when the extra meat could be kept cold and edible for many moons. The more prudent but dangerous cull hunting of individual animals would be required during the rest of the year.

He asked Vir to let every man know he wanted them to gather for a midday clan council. Vir also agreed to organize a crew to build enough raised logs around the community firepit to seat all nine hands of men. Irik needed to look each of them in the eyes.

A soft breeze wafted over the clansmen as they fidgeted, waiting for their chief.

"Thanks for coming," Irik said as he stepped nimbly around the circle, greeting those he could remember by name and shaking every hand. Standing at the center, he turned in a circle to catch the eyes of each man, worrying his new rule would not go over well with them. But he had to appear confident and began, "I brought you here today for a special announcement. I have new rules for the hunt, and I want to make sure everyone understands and agrees to abide by them."

No one spoke, but Karango seemed irritated, jabbing his spear in the ground with a huff.

"I want to first say that Karango and his men have done an excellent job in securing meat. The clan and I are incredibly grateful to you."

Karango grunted with a nod, and many of his Rhino men clapped.

"We will no longer herd-hunt in warm moons, only cull-hunt. Herd-hunting will be limited to winter when the cold can preserve extra meat."

Confused, the men looked at each other.

"Remember, the herds had stopped migrating north to us, so we had to move into the west to find them. I'm afraid we may soon no longer see them there either. If we continue to kill whole herds, including mothers and their young, leaving most to rot, they will disappear. We'll have nothing to eat."

The men muttered among themselves, disquieted.

Karango glared at Irik, his face turning red. "How do you know that?"

"Dead animals can't breed."

"Huh!" Karango scoffed, and the Rhino men chuckled.

Reto spoke up. "Irik sees things we can't, and he's right most of the time."

Vir joined in. "You need only look around our prosperous village for proof."

Karango's neck muscles bulged. "I want to herd-hunt all the time," he growled, spittle dripping off his lips. "Animals are still plentiful. It's easy and efficient."

The Rhino men chuffed in agreement.

Irik shook his head. "I know this will make hunts harder, but in warm moons, we'll only cull the herds for what we need, no more."

Karango snarled, "You no longer hunt or know. You put me in charge. I decide."

"You've had your say. The rules stand. I am chief, and unless the meat supply changes, you will follow my order."

A hand went up. Young Miis, a new clan member from the west, coughed then spoke. "Yes, we're supposed to all follow the rules of our chief, including about men and women—"

"Shut up, little man," Karango barked.

Irik gestured to Miis. "You have every right to speak."

"He...Karango, forced himself on my daughter, Bala. She's only ten winters old." His eyes burned with rage until his face crumpled in shame.

The crowd gasped. Some men nodded sadly.

"Is that true, Karango?" Irik croaked, his throat raw from rising bile.

"That girl wasn't anybody's woman."

Irik shot up. "Sit down, Karango! You knew the rules when you joined our clan. Fathers choose their daughters' mates. Boolip gave his word for all Rhino men."

Karango scoffed. "Boolip is dead. You got him killed by the Whites."

"Enough, Karango. You've been warned more than once about going after our women. How dare you assault a child?"

Karango kicked dirt in Irik's direction. "That's what I think about you and your clan."

"Get out! You're banished forever."

Karango lifted his spear in the air. "You get out. I am chief." He glanced at the Rhino men. "Right?"

They stood, all five hands worth. "Right, Chief Karango," they said and shook their spears." It seemed rehearsed, and Irik felt caught in one of his bad dreams. For a second, he felt like backing down and letting him become the chief.

"We never believed your foolish rule." Karango sneered. "Better women be for all men."

Vir rushed to Irik's side. "What do you mean, Karango?"

"At Rhino Tribe, men leave seeds in all the women. Women serve us. Children cared for by everyone. Men and women share, so our clan is one strong family. No little one-man, one-woman families for themselves."

Irik froze. He couldn't dream this. Why hadn't he guessed that the old Rhino traditions would someday flare up?

Commander Gorb spoke up. "It is true, Irik, what the Rhino Clan believed. When I was with them, I only took one woman, but I could have had any."

Irik looked stunned. No wonder he seemed different from the rest.

Gorb continued, "Boolip's gang stole me from my parents as a child, forced me into their ways." He turned to Karango. "It is not right what you did then and are doing now."

"Traitor!" Karango yelled. "Me and my men will fight to take over this clan."

"I don't think you will," Gorb said and turned to the Wolf men, who stood together and shouted, "We support Chief Irik."

Irik pressed toward Karango, standing in front of the man, a hand taller and two hands wider. He glared into his deep-set eyes. "Our men will not fight yours for leadership. I will fight you alone. To end this, now."

Karango scoffed and pointed his spear at Irik's chest.

Irik pulled a knife blade from his waist.

Men on both sides moved back.

Karango slashed his spear back and forth at Irik. With speed and agility on his side, Irik deftly dodged each swing. On the back strokes, Irik made swift, short jabs at Karango's big belly, further enraging him.

Irik momentarily lost his balance, tripping over a rock. Karango's spear blade landed low, slashing deeply across Irik's thighs. He fell to the ground, dazed as blood gushed from his legs.

Karango held his spear high with both hands. He leaned, aiming at Irik's chest.

Without knowing if he had muscle left in his legs, Irik rolled over and kicked at Karango's feet, catching his momentum and bringing him down. His spear landed past Irik and stuck deep in the ground.

Irik climbed on top of him and held the knife tight across his neck. "Take your men and leave, or I'll kill you." He pressed the knife deeper. "Which is it?"

Karango garbled, "We'll leave."

"Louder, so your men can hear it."

"I will leave!"

Irik inhaled deeply and stood up, wobbling, blood streaming down his legs. Pointing his knife at the Rhino men, he said, "You heard him. Go!"

"Irik!" Gorb shouted.

Irik crouched low and spun around, planting his blade in Karango's neck an instant before the treacherous enemy's spear came down.

Karango collapsed in a heap, blood gushing between his clasped fingers.

The men watched in horror as his cry became a gurgle, and he stilled.

With the Wolf men standing beside Irik, the Rhino men carried their chief's body away from the firepit. "Commander Gorb, you and your men follow them out of the village, making sure they take only their willing women."

Lightheaded and exhausted, Irik dropped onto a stone.

"Call the healer!" Vir shouted. "We need to stop the bleeding." He helped the delirious chief stretch out on the ground.

When Irik opened his eyes, Arol knelt at his side. Eating?

"Easy," she mumbled as he attempted to sit up. At the top of both legs, he felt a crushing pressure. Below, sharp pain.

"Hold still," she said as she let go a stream of saliva into his wound. "The rawhide around your legs has stopped most of the bleeding. This will help more."

He blinked to see through the darkness. She bit off a clump of small, star-shaped flowers from a long stem and chewed vigorously.

Speaking with her mouth full, she said, "We're lucky this flower grows in the cold." She spat into the other leg wound.

The sting jolted him to speak. "Where's Nara?"

"She stayed with you until I came but said she couldn't stomach watching my healing. Don't worry. Looks much better now. Here, drink this…" She held a gourd to his lips. "…to help you sleep. I cleaned the wounds, and now I'm going to add these squirrel-tail leaves to help the healing." Using her front teeth, she raked the tiny leaves off the stem and chewed.

Irik dropped his head into another stupor.

He woke to a jagged pain in his right leg. The sun was high above.

"Sorry," Arol said, as she pulled the flaps of skin together with her bone needle and flax thread. "After we close the wounds, we'll bandage them." She glanced toward a wooden bowl of soaking rabbit skins and stuck the needle back in.

He jolted.

Another pull.

Another jab.

Watching her, he felt tears streaming down his cheeks onto his neck.

Arol paused the stitching, reached up, and dabbed his face. "I'm sorry. I have to."

"It's all right," he said. "It's more than the pain." He took a deep breath. "I killed one of my own clan."

"I know," she said, "but you did it to save us."

"I'm not sure," he said as tears poured anew. "What will I do now? You know me."

She dabbed his cheeks again. "You have to see inside, not just ahead."

"What do you mean?"

"Find the scars that cover up your true self."

"Scars?"

"I don't know. Maybe power and pride."

Irik froze, then reached out to her.

She patted his hand. "You're healing now, Irik. I have to go. Vir is waiting for me."

Twenty days later

"You've hardly eaten anything." Nara pouted at his bowl of dried venison. "You need to keep up your strength."

"Just not hungry," Irik said through a frown.

Brul chipped in, "Father, the meat is spiced with onion and tender."

Irik caught his eye. "You want what's left of mine, Son?"

Brul looked at his mother.

"Certainly not, Brul," Nara said and pursed her lips.

"Here son." Irik handed him his food. "Finish it or take it to the wolves. They're already starting their nightly howling."

"I'll save it for Deela," Brul said in his most chipper voice. "She's been the best at tracking. The others follow her."

Irik managed a tight smile. "Just like her mother. How has Meeri been?"

"Not so good."

"Shush, Brul," Nara snapped. "Your father doesn't need to hear that."

Irik placed a firm hand on Nara's. "Tell me."

Brul gathered his thoughts. "She sleeps mostly. I have to lift her rear end and sort of drag her to eat and pee."

Irik bit his bottom lip, looking down.

Brul perked up again. "Oh! But she's always glad to see me and eagerly licks the pups when they come around."

"Good boy, Brul. Make sure you spend time soothing her. She's old, and her bones must hurt." Irik had learned more than he wanted to know about lingering pain thanks to Karango.

"I will. The other wolves—"

Nara interrupted, "Tell your father about your spear-throwing practice."

Brul looked to his father for a go-ahead.

The wolf calls hushed. Irik cocked an ear and fixated on a faint sound.

"Irik, your son was about to—"

Irik held up his hand, cocked his ear to the outside, and said, "I hear you."

Nara looked askance at Irik, who seemed to be in another world. "Brul, time for bed. Take the meat to Deela in the morning."

Brul gave his parents kisses, Irik hugging him especially tight, and headed off to bed.

"He's such a good boy," Irik said, "so caring about others and the wolves."

Nara lowered her voice. "Maybe too sensitive. He needs to toughen up like you did."

Irik scowled and stood, teetering.

"You shouldn't be on your feet," Nara scolded.

"I'm going out to check on the wolves," he said. "It's been almost a moon."

"What for? They're just making their usual racket."

Haltingly, he headed toward the door.

"Arol wouldn't approve."

"She would," he said and staggered out, certain he'd heard a cry amid the howls.

The wolves clamored when they caught the smell and sound of their human patriarch hobbling toward the pens. Wincing with each step, Irik made his way to Meeri's special area.

When he peeked over the fence, she whined but did not get up. "How are you doing, old girl?" he said and gingerly lowered himself next to her.

Her eyes brightened, and she answered with a twitch of her tail. He lay next to her and scratched behind her ears. She closed her eyes, letting out a low whimper. Irik's eyes welled up, thinking of the days he'd slept with her as a puppy, trying to keep her alive. He laid his hand on her streaked chest, and the steadiness of her heartbeat comforted him.

Soon he drifted to sleep and tumbled into dreams of his childhood. There he was, trying to squirt globs of mush into Meeri's tiny mouth—a bond forming between them. There she was, a full-grown wolf following his commands, earning him respect from his father. Together in the cave, he showed her the handprints of the Valley Clansfolk, telling her how much it meant to all. After he pointed out the animal drawings that gave courage to the hunters, they left the cave.

Heading toward the entrance, they saw a bright light glowing outside. It was the moon, rising to light the path he had forgotten. The Mother Moon had to take Meeri's spirit, but the wolf went willingly, casting a last, loving glance at Irik. Now the moonlight merged with his mother's face and shone upon him.

"Irik! Are you all right?" Nara asked as he fluttered open his eyes. "You've been out in the pens for a long time, you know."

He shook his head and looked toward Meeri.

"She's dead," said Nara.

Irik inhaled deeply and placed his hand on her cold head.

"I…" he choked "…I didn't say goodbye."

"You were with her, Irik."

He rubbed his eyes, sat up, and stroked her side in silence. "She, and the spirit between us, meant everything to me." He inhaled, eyes closed. "And still lives within me."

"Come to bed, now," Nara said as she reached for his arm.

Straining to his feet, he said, "I will bury her in the morning."

He leaned against Nara's side and limped away.

High in the sky hung the crescent of a waning moon as the wolves howled a mournful chorus.

Chapter Eighteen

"**C**OME ON, BRUL," IRIK GLEEFULLY shouted as he took Brul's hand, days later. "Let's go to the wolf pens."

Brul's eyes widened along with his smile. "You'll come with me, Father?" he asked, pointing at Irik's bandaged legs.

Irik reached down and pulled them off without a whimper, and pointed to the dry scars. "Arol has helped me to heal, see?" He jabbed at his chest. "Outside and in." He swung Brul's hand high in the air.

"Iyee!" Brul shrieked. "What are we going to do?"

"Aha," Irik said. "You know how we both feel close to our wolves?"

"Yes," Brul said, skipping to catch up to his father.

"More than guards and hunters, right? Well, Arol knew that all along."

Brul scrunched his nose. "What do you mean?"

Irik halted, knelt in front of him, and held his shoulders. "Wolves can be part of our family!"

Brul's face lit up. "They can?"

Irik nodded. "And more, you'll see. Come on."

Approaching the pens, the wolves yipped, barked, and howled. Irik put his hand on the gate. "We're going to get Deela and bring her home."

With Deela leaping at their sides, Brul asked, "Bringing her home to do what?"

"She's going to live with us from now on." Irik lifted Brul high in the air. "You and I have found the way."

As soon as they opened the door to their hut, Deela rushed to greet Nara and put her nose to everything within reach.

"Why are you bringing the wolf in here?"

"She's going to live with us, Mama," Brul offered. "We found the way."

She took Brul into her arms. "To where?"

Brul looked to his father.

"Deela is going to be our house wolf from now on, but it's bigger than that. I finally realized what Meeri had given me." He gestured to the outside. "And to the clan."

"What is that?" Nara asked.

"The way to grow the clan and make it a better one."

"But do we need a bigger clan?" She opened her palms. "You had a hard enough time managing the last one, and look what happened."

Deela began barking as Brul teased her with his clacking beads.

"Listen, Nara. There's a better way to replace the loss of the Rhino hunters. We have many mouths to feed, and we'd have strength in numbers."

"True enough," she agreed, "but how would we—?"

"We'd start with those people from the east that used to watch us herd-hunt with the wolves, then scavenge whatever we left behind. They seemed like peaceful people, like us."

"Why would they join us?"

"For starters, they're starving without our herd hunts. Moons ago, one of their people asked if they could join our clan. At the time, we had over a hundred members. Now we could use them." He was ready for Nara's next question.

"They would come and live with us?"

"No, but by living east of us, together with more settlements in the west, it would give us greater protection in case we're ever attacked."

Brul called out, "Father, can we take Deela down to the creek and give her a bath? She stinks."

"Yes, later son. Let me finish with your mother."

"Irik. You have an answer for everything, but how would they come to join us? How would you lead them?"

"Aha!" He raised a finger. It starts with the wolves. Those people are already in awe of our control over the wolves. To them, the Wolf

Clan is a legend. They see and respect our greater powers and want to have those powers themselves. Now, we just need to get them to worship us."

With an arched brow, Nara mouthed, 'Worship?'

"You see, our connection to the wolves goes beyond their powers as hunters, guards, and allies. We will build a connection between the spirit of the wolf pack and the spirit of the Wolf Clan."

"Look," she said with a shrug of her shoulders. "I too believe all animals, including us, have spirits, but how do we convince a different clan of people to connect to it in such an unnatural way?"

"I know it's hard for most to grasp, but the connection is real, and it comes from many places—like the stories we tell our children about ancestors, from the cave drawings that inspired our hunters. When you put these things together, they create beliefs. They tie people to each other. You can feel it..." he pointed to his chest "...in your heart."

Nara stared at her mate, then asked, "Is that where all this new energy comes from?"

"Yes, an energy I've had since childhood, believing that there must be a way for all people and animals to live in harmony." He nodded his head slowly. "Now, I can see it and make it real."

"Ho! As a child, you couldn't stomach killing or butchering, and you got over that." She squinted her eyes at him. "How do you come up with all this?"

He sighed. "Never mind. Once we unite with them, we'll have a bigger and better clan and call it the Wolf Tribe."

A nudge at Irik's shoulder interrupted his intensity. Brul stood next to him, his arm around Deela's neck. "Yes, Son, we'll leave shortly."

"Great," Brul exclaimed, "and how about giving a puppy to every child who joins the new tribe?"

Irik drew back. "Brul, you're a genius. You knew the way all along." He patted him on the head. "Give me a moment," he said and turned to Nara.

"I'm sorry," she said, "but I remain suspicious. You'll just have to show me."

"I will. Tomorrow I'm journeying east to meet their chief and offer to have his clan join us. Come on, Brul. Let's go bathe Deela, and you keep her clean until I get back home."

"Mother!" Brul yelled. "It's Keelo." Brul hugged the big, mangy male by the neck while Deelo licked his muzzle. "That means Father's home." Eight days had passed.

Nara emerged from the hut and caught sight of Irik and Vir walking through the village, waving.

"Welcome home," she said with open arms. Brul was already in Irik's, holding a hug.

"How did it go?" she asked.

Irik's smug expression gave it away. "They'll join our tribe like I said."

She kissed him. "I knew it."

He broke the hug. "You did?"

"Well," she smiled shyly, "knowing your stubbornness. What made them agree?"

"Hunger and hope, I'd say."

"How was their chief?"

"He was quite frail but still alert at an amazing age of thirty-five winters."

"What was his name?"

Irik pictured him in his chief's headdress. "Xanda."

"How many in his clan?"

"Ninety-six, and I met them all. Very nice people. Similar language and beliefs. They will more than double our size."

"What was the name of the tribe?"

"Nara. You ask too many questions. I am tired from the journey. And why does that matter?" He went inside to lie down.

As soon as Irik woke from his nap, Nara stood above him glaring. "You can't let that clan join ours."

He sat up and groaned. "That's not for you to decide. How did you—?"

"I asked Vir. Figured you were hiding something from me. You cannot let that vile Fox-tail clan in our midst. You know they stole my mother."

"Nara, listen."

"You listen," she snapped. "You can't trust those people. Just like you couldn't rely on the Rhinos. You're too gullible."

He stood and held her by the shoulders. "Nara, without trust, everyone would be alone. Look, I was shocked, at first, when I saw their chief's fox-tail headdress, but after two days of getting to know him and the history of their clan and meeting all their people, I am satisfied they would make good neighbors and clansfolk."

Nara grimaced. "How can you excuse their past?"

He rubbed his beard. "I can only conclude they were desperate at the time, and they never mentioned the Valley Clan."

She pointed an accusing finger. "Maybe they are hiding it from you."

"Look, Nara. Chief Xanda will soon be dead, and his son, Farl, will take over. He was too young to have been involved in your mother's capture."

Nara stared at Irik, tears flooding her face.

Irik hugged her, wanting to give her hope that her mother might still be alive and find new half-brothers and sisters, but he didn't dare. He held her chin and said, "You'll just have to trust me, Nara. Once these people pledge to join our tribe, they will be loyal to it."

A throng of men, women, and children, numbering one hundred twenty-six hands, stood surrounding a blazing bonfire one winter later. Four bodies thick, the crowd jostled and stretched to get a glimpse of the ceremony. As Irik waited for the next inductee, he recalled how his spiritual connection to Meeri—the first wolf—inspired him to follow this path. He was now the leader of a regional powerhouse of clans, known far and wide as the Wolf Tribe. How challenging, yet possible it was to peacefully leverage the power of wolves to bring large numbers of diverse peoples together.

Irik held up his hand. "For our final new tribe member, let us welcome Kipo." Irik turned and faced a boy about eight winters old, his parents and siblings standing behind him. "Kipo, which work have you chosen to do for the tribe? Hut-builder, tool-maker, hunter, warrior, or butcher?"

"Hunter, sir," he replied proudly.

"Great choice, young man. Do you know your local leader to whom you must bring forward any issues about your life with the tribe?"

"Yes, sir. My local leader is Werl."

"That is right. Now, if you're ready, by saying this pledge in front of all your Wolf Tribe brothers and sisters, you will be admitted as a full, lifetime member of the Wolf Tribe. Have you memorized the pledge, Kipo?"

"I have, Chief Irik."

"Great, now cross your hands over your heart and say the Wolf Tribe pledge."

Kipo nervously glanced at his parents, who gave him encouraging smiles.

He began,

"When the wolf bays at the moon
I will listen to its call
lighting the path for me

I journey with the Wolf Tribe
to follow their spirit
and become strong as one

When the tribe calls for the hunt
I am brave and able
to find and feed our own

When a wolf wails for a mate
I know there's one for me
to have and love for life…"

Kipo hesitated for a moment, looking at his parents. Getting a nod, he continued.

"The she-wolf sings to her pups
to teach and care for them
like mothers always do

As the wolf cries for her dead
I praise who've gone before
and stay bound to my tribe

When I see a new moon rise
I call for all on earth
to live and love in peace."

Irik shook Kipo's hand, and his parents hugged him.

The crowd roared.

Second Chief, Vir, handed Irik the Wolf Tribe medallion. Irik stole his way behind the boy and placed it around his neck. Kipo held the wood disc in his hands and smiled at the painted figure of Meeri.

As the cheers died down, Irik raised his hands. Young Brul approached with a squirming, gray-brown wolf puppy in his arms. Kipo bounced on his heels with excitement.

"Yes, Kipo," Irik said with a hand on his head. "Your own wolf puppy. A girl to raise and train."

Taking the pup into his arms, Kipo laughed as the little wolf licked his face.

"What will you name her?"

"Meerifor," he said, "after our Mother wolf."

"Good boy," Irik said, patting his head.

"Thank you, sir." Kipo waved to the crowd. "Thank you all."

As the clapping continued, Irik turned to see a radiant smile on Nara's face as he swayed arm in arm with her half-sisters. Arol gave him a smile and slight nod as if to say, 'you're on your path now.' He spoke to the crowd, "Thank you, everyone, for coming. That ends our new member swearing-in ceremony for the moon. Please come up, one at a time and personally welcome…" He turned and waved his hand over several families. "…our newest Wolf Tribe members."

Irik watched proudly until the last hug took place. Dropping Nara's sisters off at a nearby hut, Irik and his family returned to their hut.

"Good work today, Brul," Irik said. "How many pups do we have for next moon's ceremony."

"Only Cala's litter, Papa. Eight pups, one-and-a-half moons old."

"Fine. Take good care. We'll need them." He kissed Brul on the head. "Now off to bed." Nara took him by the hand.

Irik munched dried fruits one of the new families had brought him when Nara sat nearby.

"Another successful swearing-in," she patted his knee. "How many new tribe members have joined us so far?"

"Not sure," he answered, "maybe thirty-seven hands."

"Amazing what you've done in one year. The new clans seem so happy to be working together in the tribe."

"Thanks. Once I found inner harmony, I could see how to have harmony with others."

Nara shook her head. "I don't understand how you were able to do that, but—"

Irik wanted to explain to her how his need to prove himself as a better leader than his father made him lose sight of his dream of people and animals living together in peace. "We all want to belong, Nara. When I was little, I saw that humans are pack animals like the wolves. We are happiest when the group accepts and needs us."

She placed her hand on his cheek. "You've always been able to foresee ways and things others can't, and with your trickery—"

He drew back. "Trickery? That's not what it is."

"I'm sorry. What do you call it?" she lowered her head.

"I don't have a name for it. I only know it exists. It's beyond what you can see or touch. I felt it when the Valley Clan hunters took courage from my cave drawings but faltered when they lost the elk bone. I learned marks and tokens stood for something. I knew there was a spiritual bond."

"A spiritual bond?"

"Yes, something you can feel within you. And if you can give it to others, you can make it real."

"How do you come to feel it?" she asked.

Irik hesitated. It was the scars. How Arol knew and helped him. He said, "I think all humans have it, the ability to feel it, but they have to recognize it, then use it."

"I'm sorry, Irik. I don't think I can." She yawned. "I'm tired. Let's go to bed."

He nodded, and they slipped under the skins.

He put a finger to her chin. "Don't worry if you don't feel it, Nara. It'll come someday if you let it."

She closed her eyes.

As Irik lay there, he thought of Arol, who did know the spirit. As did young Brul.

Next morning

Hearing a faint cry, Irik opened his eyes. A patch of morning light shone through the hut's smoke shaft. *What made that sound?* He lifted his head and smiled. There was young Brul, playing with Deela and a puppy he'd sneaked into the hut against his mother's wishes.

The little wolf yipped. Brul looked in his father's direction. "Good morning, Papa."

"Good morning. Where's your mother?"

"She went to the creek to get water. Are you going to tell?"

"No, Brul. I'll say I let you." As he sat up, the cries grew louder. Coming from the outside. He threw on his vest, went to the door, and lifted the flap. Many human voices in the distance, screaming. He glanced to the south, where guards were always posted. There were none. "I'll be right back," he said and ran next door to second chief Vir's hut.

Arol huddled in a corner, holding herself, shaking.

"Arol, are you all right?"

She gave a troubled nod.

"Where's Vir? Your daughter?"

"He went looking for Shiri. She was playing with friends."

"Do you know what's going on?"

"No, it just happened, and the screams are getting louder."

"Stay put," he said, running out. "I'll find Vir and Shiri."

Returning to his hut, Irik told Brul, "I'm going to look for your mother. You stay here. Take care of your wolves. Don't leave until I return."

"I promise, Papa."

As he scrambled around the huts, north toward the foothills, the screams amplified.

Passing Reto's hut, he looked in. It was empty, the morning's porridge spilled on the floor.

Cly, Nork's woman, sprinted toward him, baby in her arms.

"Run, Chief," she gasped, "someone is hurling small spears at us from the foothills by the creek."

As he dashed north, more and more women and children brushed by him, screaming. Leta came at him, limping. Crying in fear and pain, she fell into his arms. Sticking out of her thigh was a three-hand long narrow spear, and blood was flowing down the back of her leg. "Who? What?" were the only words Irik could muster.

"The Whites!" she wailed, "coming down and shooting from the foothills. Look to the sky."

Irik glanced upward. White streaks flew then cut through the blue as short, slim spears rained down. *How could this be? Where are the warriors?*

Catching her breath, Leta said, "Reto may be dead. He and some of the men headed toward the creek. They didn't expect a surprise attack from there."

"Leta, can you make it back to your hut? Arol can help you."

"I think so," she said, stepping out of a pool of blood and limping away.

Nara?

Charging at full speed, Irik passed men, women, and children on the ground. Some dead, others writhing and grasping at the spears stuck in their backs. Deela ran up to each, then back to Irik, looking to him for a command. Reaching the creek, he saw many bodies scattered on the ground and in the water. A few Wolf men were chasing White warriors escaping into the hilly woods.

Irik recognized Nara right away by the yellow water skins she had painted, now at her feet. Spears jutted from her neck and chest. He knelt for a moment at her side, her blood-soaked body already turning cold. He could do nothing to save his woman. He kissed her forehead.

A scream nearby. Irik looked up to see a White impaled in the back by a spear thrown by Gorb, the head of their warrior team.

186

Around him, some women tended to their wounded men, while others lay over their bodies, wailing. "Oh no! There's Tra," he cried, seeing her sobbing and rocking over… it must be Reto. Irik hugged her convulsing body, feeling her pain.

She caught her breath. "Your brother is dead, Irik."

A shudder came to his gut and trailed up into his throat. "I am sorry, Tra. Is your son all right?"

"I think so," she nodded.

Irik brushed closed his brother's eyelids. Choking, he said, "Goodbye, brother," and kissed Tra.

A wail broke out nearby. A man moaned while he dug his fingers into the ground, trying to crawl away. Irik rushed to the man and turned him over. It was Vir, one spear sunk deep into his throat, another in his belly. Vir reached up and coughed, sending spurts of blood onto Irik's face.

Vir lifted his head, garbled, "Shiri," gasped, and fell back.

Dazed, Irik needed to find Arol's daughter. What if she, too, is dead? How can I tell Arol she's lost her man? What would I tell Brul about his mother? He bounded up.

"Chief?" a woman called, running toward him.

It was Cor, Mot's woman.

"Are you alright, Chief?"

"Yes, Cor."

"Nara?"

He shook his head. "I'm sorry. Did Mot survive?"

"Yes. He went into the huts and gathered women and children, and they ran south." Cor headed in that direction.

Gorb came running. "The Whites have all vanished into the hills. Many of our men are dead, sir."

"How many?" Irik asked, hating himself for being a blundering trusting fool.

"Too many to count, including your brother, sir. Here's the reason." He handed Irik a bent willow pole with a woven flax string tied tautly on either end. Deela sniffed the bow, and the hair on her back bristled.

Irik looked puzzled until Gorb gave him a small spear with two white and black seabird feathers fitted to the end.

Chapter Nineteen

IRIK SLUMPED AGAINST THE WALL of his rock ledge home and gazed at what remained of the Wolf Tribe. A thick mountain mist dampened the morning campfires into ghostly gray. Irik wished it could stifle the groans of the injured warriors and the wails of their women. His mind dragged back to the devastating White attack that forced the tribe to move east to the tree line of these craggy mountains, a location providing safety but little comfort. They lived off meager greens and the occasional rabbit or partridge that roamed the forest. The Whites had burned down the village huts, preventing re-building without hides from large hoofed animals.

Anger and shame consumed him. *What a fool to believe people could live together in harmony.* His blind trust had lost fourteen hands of men and almost ten hands of women, cutting the tribe to about half its size. In his eleven years as clan, then tribal chief, Irik had never lost a battle. Less than a new moon ago, he lost a war—vanquished by the Whites, people he once trusted. Maybe it wasn't Kokor's clan or his combative son who led the attack. Irik didn't understand why two groups of people couldn't live as neighbors. *We respected their way of life, offered them friendship, and left them alone. Why didn't they treat us the same? The Whites had vast land, so why would they need more?* Whatever the cause, he believed he'd failed his people, betraying their trust.

Deela barked a warning. Commander Gorb's taut figure slid from the mist toward Irik with a raised weapon. "May I report now, sir?"

Irik nodded and beckoned him under the ledge.

"Everything all right, sir?"

"I'm fine, Commander." He forced a smile. "Sit."

"It must be hard losing Nara." Gorb placed a hand on Irik's shoulder.

"Brother Reto, Vir, and many, many more, but thanks." Irik lowered his head. "At least I still have little Brul."

"He's a fine boy." Gorb nodded. "Someday, he'll be a chief like you and your father."

"Nara wanted that." Irik's voice dropped. "But I'm not sure…"

"He's very young."

Irik closed his eyes, picturing how he'd been at that age with *his* father.

"Chief?"

Startled, Irik straightened his back. "Commander, what is today's count?"

"Forty-three able-bodied warriors, sir." He hung his head. "We lost another man last night to old injuries—Sulo."

Irik swallowed hard. "I'll speak to Sulo's woman. How'd the hunt and search mission go?"

"No sign of the Whites, but the hunt was pretty meager. We speared a few rabbits and, with the wolves' help, scavenged a tusk pig away from a pack of wild ones."

Irik shook his head. "Fortunately, the women gathered lots of acorns. Anything else?"

"No sign of herds in that prairie, sir, but lots of grasses and stands of trees. We brought back a sled of grain grass to feed that injured cow."

"Good," Irik said, "maybe she'll keep giving milk for a few days."

"Near a streambed, we found gray willow trees, so we stripped the bark for the injured."

Irik smiled broadly. "That'll relieve some of their pain."

"They've already chewed most of the bark. And for the wounds, we collected lots of *oluu* flowers."

"Good work, Gorb."

"Thanks, and with sturdy willow branches, we made this." He held up a bent wooden pole strung end to end with braided flax and a small, notched spear. "It's rough, but look." He flexed the two ends of the bow between his muscular arms. "It has both spring and strength. Once we perfect the string, we can make hundreds of these new weapons." With a proud smile, he handed it to Irik.

Irik plucked at the fraying string. "It's not only the bow that matters, Gorb," he said without making eye contact. "Can we train the men for accuracy and distance?"

"I believe we can."

Irik shot back, "We must be superior. Those Whites are deft with these weapons, as our people so bitterly learned." He tossed the bow to the ground. "We lost many wolves too. I don't know how we can compete."

Gorb braced himself against his leader's dejection. "Do you want our homeland back?"

Irik narrowed his eyes and barked, "What do you think? I'm the one who lost it."

The commander's body stiffened, but he didn't speak.

Irik pointed to the surrounding campfires. "You think our people like living without decent cover over their heads in these woods?"

"No, sir." Gorb shifted his legs. "Are you still considering that dry prairie to the east?"

"With the lack of big game there, I'm not sure, but staying here is also risky."

"The herds are scarce everywhere, sir."

Fear, shame, and anger rose in Irik's chest as he contemplated the mass hunting practice he'd started. He kept running his hand through his hair, picturing the slaughter as his clan had wiped out many herds. He knew his father, let alone Mother Nature, looked down on the practice. Before he curtailed it, he kept telling himself it was necessary to feed the tribe, hoping the herds would replenish.

"Sir, we have to..." Seeing Irik bristle, Gorb softened his words. "In my mind, once we rebuild our army, we can launch a successful counterattack."

Irik searched Commander Gorb's face. "Are the men grumbling about my leadership?"

Gorb's face reddened. "No, sir."

"What are they saying, then?"

"They're... they're..." He rubbed his chin. "Cast down with defeat, sir."

"What do you mean?"

"Over their dead brothers. Their lost women and children."

A dull ache gripped Irik's chest and throat. "Do they blame me?"

Gorb averted his eyes. "No... not really."

Irik thrust a hand impatiently toward Gorb. "What then?"

"They want to take revenge on the Whites." He curled his fists, and a gleam stole into his eyes. "Surround them at night and burn them in their huts."

Irik cast both his hands wide open. "And you? Is that what you want me to order?"

"Yes, it is, sir."

Irik shuddered but stared steadily at Gorb. "You don't see any options?"

"No, sir."

Irik didn't raise the foolish possibility of making peace with the Whites. He tilted his head toward the outside. "Go now," he barked, "make your bows."

Watching Gorb triumphantly shake his bow in the air, Irik felt torn. He needed to take stock of the men and himself. He could no longer remain secluded on his rock ledge, keeping warm and dry while his people shivered under trees. The shame in his gut tortured him to act. Letting out a deep sigh, he decided to find his son.

Putting on the mountain goat headdress, he stepped briskly off the ledge, Deela at his side. At the first campfire, a young warrior lay on the ground, groaning as his woman dabbed wet leaves on his wounded thigh.

"Kolo," Irik called, "how are you doing?" The man opened his eyes and tried to prop himself up.

His woman, Zeel, said, "Not good, sir."

"Easy," Irik said, kneeling by his side. A putrid smell entered his nostrils. Deela slinked away. The blue-red veins jutting out of Kolo's swollen, blackened leg would soon send poison through the rest of his body. Irik wouldn't tell his woman there was no way to stop it. "I'm sorry, Kolo. Can you speak?"

Nodding through a deep cough, Kolo replied, "Yes, sir." He sat up, winced. "Do we need to prepare for battle?"

"No, not yet. I'll let you know."

Kolo fell back hard with a cry. "We'll be home soon, won't we, sir?"

Irik clutched at his throat. *Could the man bear the truth that the Whites had burned their huts? No, and no reason to hurt him more.* "Yes, Son," Irik answered, "rest now and feel the love of your woman." Choking at the sound and smell of death, he patted Zeel's shoulder and left.

As he approached shadows of men and women huddled around campfires, he girded himself for the next encounter.

A towering figure emerged from the mist. The big-bodied, wide-nosed Mot outstretched his arms for an embrace.

"Chief Irik. Good to see you, sir." He pounded Irik's back with massive hands.

Gratitude and guilt swept over Irik. Mot had saved him and many others from death by finding a path of retreat in the east.

"Mot, my good man," he said, slapping his shoulders. "I've come to see how you and the men are faring."

"Good. Let's talk." Mot gestured to his woman. "Come sit, Chief. You know Cor?"

"Yes." He took her hand. "A good friend of Nara's."

Irik turned to Mot. "I must thank you for your foresight. Finding that escape route saved many." He dropped his eyes.

Mot placed his hand on his heart. "But we failed you in battle, sir."

"No. I failed the tribe."

"Don't worry." Mot raised his fist in the air. "We will fight another day."

Cor nodded and smiled proudly at her man.

"The bow spears gave them a big advantage," Irik said.

"Yes, Commander Gorb is working on that."

Irik frowned.

"Sir?"

Irik exhaled loudly. "I'm not sure more weapons are the answer." He waved his hand over the campfires surrounded by wounded and grieving families. "Look what it cost us."

Silence fell between them.

Cor spoke up. "We had food, land, huts, and respect. Nara knew what mattered."

Irik drew back. *Is Cor saying Nara knew better than me?*

Cor added, "Irik, you were once a mighty chief—show us your strength."

"Shut up, woman," Mot yelled. "It's not your place to criticize Chief Irik."

Face burning, Irik stood. "I must go. I have many more to see."

Mot shook his hand. "I believe, sir, you will find every man, injured or not, wanting to once again hear your call to battle."

Irik nodded and stepped out among the fires, deep in thought. He no longer wanted to speak to the men who stiffly rose as he passed by. He could hear Nara's voice in his mind, *'They only respect power, Irik.'* Maybe she was right, but he no longer felt powerful in any way.

Heading toward the wolf pens, he passed a group of women shelling acorns and scanned ahead for Brul. Not far behind them frolicked the puppies, and Arol would be among the women helping Soth and Brul train young wolves. Deela whined for Irik to let her visit her kin. "Go," he said. As he approached the women, all but Arol stood and bowed. Shuffling his feet, he said, "I see you're all busy."

"Yes, sir," one woman answered.

"Are you well, Chief?" asked another.

"Fine, thanks," he said, hoping to engage Arol. As the pups yipped and tumbled over each other, he remembered how he and she, as children, had saved the orphaned wolves and tamed Meeri. He summoned his courage. "Arol, how are the pups?"

She only nodded, went to the pen, and opened the fence. Irik's heart sank. *She just lost her mate, idiot. So did I, for that matter. No need to hurry, and maybe she hates me anyway.* A squirming congregation of fur rushed to Irik's feet. He knelt, and they climbed on him, licking his face and sinking tiny teeth into his hands. Irik burst into laughter, having not felt such joy for what seemed like years. Deela heard the commotion and ran to watch, panting and bobbing like a youngster herself.

As he sat back, all nine pups jumped on him at once. He smacked to the ground.

"Help!" he cried melodramatically as they barked and pounced. He caught Arol's eyes, and in a flash of memory, she was with him. When she looked away, the distance ached. Once he'd been so close to her, but he buried the thought hastily. Over the years, herd-hunting and now warring had set them apart. She hadn't changed, but he seemed a stranger even to himself.

"Go, go, go." He rose and scooted the pups back into the pen. "Well-trained, I see."

"Your son is very good with them, sir," one of the women called out.

"So I hear. Anyone know where he might be? He left at daybreak."

The women looked at Arol. With her back turned, she pointed toward a hillock. "He's with that injured auroch and her calf."

"Thank you." For the first time since she healed his wounds, he tried to reconnect with her. Standing at the foot of the hillock, he turned, "Good to see you, Arol."

She didn't face him, but she murmured, "You too, Chief."

A gust of bitter northerly wind threw Irik off balance as he reached the top of the hillock. Another period of snow and ice loomed. He gazed down at Brul, trying to feed the calf a handful of grain. A few body lengths away, the calf's mother nervously lowed, struggling to rise on two broken legs.

Heading down the hill, he called to Brul, and Deela scrambled to greet the boy.

"Hello, Father." Brul dropped the grain and wiped his cheeks.

Irik assumed his son's tears were for his mother or his best friend, Jul, also killed in the fighting. Wanting Brul to be like the rest of the Wolf Tribe—strong amid loss—he said nothing.

"Good morning." He patted Brul's shoulder. "You must have gotten up early."

"At dawn. I came to see if Tuki—I mean, the calf—might eat grain today."

"She's still too young." At Brul's frown, Irik asked, "You're not letting her suckle at her mother, are you?"

Brul turned toward Tuki and snapped, "No, Father." The cow bellowed with concern.

As Brul tenderly stroked the young auroch's head, Irik knew he was lying, as he would have done at that age. His son must have let the calf nurse before the clan mothers milked the cow for their children in the morning.

"Don't let the calf at her mother's teats again. We have young to feed."

"But if Tuki doesn't eat, she'll slowly die."

"Maybe, but then she'd provide meat for us."

Brul gasped. "What about her mother?" He pointed to the pile of grain. "Commander Gorb brought lots of food for her—she's eating."

"That's good. We should keep her alive as long as she has milk. When it's cold, put a bison blanket on her." Irik bent down to his son and narrowed his eyes. "Have you eaten anything today?"

"No, sir, I'm not hungry."

"You're always hungry. What's going on?"

"Can…" Brul lowered his eyes. "Can I show you the puppies before we go home?"

"All right. Tie up Tuki, and let's go."

On the way to the wolf pen, Brul chattered about everything he and Arol had trained them to do. The excitement and pride in his son's voice tickled Irik's ears.

"Hi, Arol." Brul ran into her arms, and she held him with joy. Irik stared, awed by the affection he'd never witnessed between Nara and their son. Brul's mother always maintained an emotional distance, not wanting him to become too sensitive, imagining him as a chief someday. When she beat the child, Irik intervened, and she accused him of coddling.

"Watch, Father." Brul pulled Arol over to the wolf pen. The puppies jumped over one another, vying to be picked up. Their equally friendly mother jerked at her rope.

"Hmmm," Brul studied the pups. "How about you, Eely?" He reached down and lifted a scruffy, brown-black pup to his face. After licks and laughter, he held her up to his father. "Eely is the runt." He glanced over to Arol for reassurance. "From Melor's litter?"

"Tulu's," Arol said. "She's the guard wolf mother. Melor's a hunter, remember?"

"Oh, yes. Father, look." He set the wolf down several hand-lengths away.

Irik shook his head, amazed how his son took to the important task of training. The tribe needed these pups to grow up strong and competent. If it weren't for Soth's and Arol's care and foresight, their breeding as valuable hunting and security tools could have been lost.

"Staaaaaay!" Brul faced his palm to the pup. "No, no, no," he scolded as it ran to him.

"Say it louder in a sharp voice as soon as she moves," Arol said. "Like her mother would bark."

Brul put Eely on the ground and slowly backed up. Irik marveled at Arol's way with the wolves, even more intuitive than his own.

Turning his hand over, Brul patted his chest. "Come." The pup raced into his arms. "See, Father?"

"Good work."

Brul set the pup in the pen. "Now watch this."

Irik stepped beside Arol. "As chief…" He rubbed his forehead. "No, I want to thank you as myself, Arol, for what you've done. For our people… and my son."

She looked into his eyes for a moment, then smiled. "When I watch Brul, I see you."

He hung on her words. "What do you mean?"

"I mean, I see you in him… not Nara." She averted her eyes as if she had misspoken.

His heart fluttered, and he struggled to speak. "N-no, go ahead."

"I remember how you were."

"Father!" Brul yelled.

Irik turned. "Hold on, Son."

Arol's eyes, once again, saw inside him. He coughed to gain composure. "How was I?"

She glanced at Brul, then back at Irik. "Not like the others—you followed your heart."

"Yes, and it got Vir and half the tribe killed." He cringed at mentioning her man's name when she must still be raw from losing him and their daughter.

She measured her words. "You have to see past that. It doesn't mean you can't find another way."

He froze, stunned by her frank appraisal, recalling all that had separated them and made him what he'd become. *What do I still want and need to do?*

"Father, look how little Soro finds the squirrel tail. He'll be a good hunter." Brul beamed.

Arol tipped her head toward his son. "He can become a great chief."

"I'm not sure I want him to." Irik's mouth and shoulders drooped. "If you ask me..."

"What?"

"It wasn't might that made you a fine leader." She raised her honeyed eyes to his. "Like you, your son has a power. He can unite the head and heart, find better solutions."

Her words pierced through his numbness, raising goosebumps. She'd always known him best, and he longed to open up to her as he'd never done with anyone else.

Unsettled and spinning out of balance, Irik said, "Come on, Son, we need to go home. Thank you, Arol." He averted his eyes, took Brul by the hand, and walked away. Missing Deela's shadow at his side, he turned around to find her at Arol's feet. He caught a questioning or yearning look on Arol's face, but she switched to a neutral expression.

"Deela, come," he said, and they threaded their way around the campfires.

One at a time, the men stood and shouted, "We can beat the Whites!"

"Take back our home!"

"Our tribe is the chosen one!"

Irik only gave them nods.

Brul asked, "Do we have to fight again, Father?"

"Hope not."

Reaching the rock ledge, they found a pot of stewed mushrooms waiting for them, probably made by one of the widows. After eating, Irik let Brul go back to the wolves. He lay on his back, stared at the rock wall, and tried to make sense of everything. Slowly, a picture of himself as a young boy emerged. *What would my youthful heart have done?*

He would draw.

Picking up a stick of charcoal from the fire's edge, he held it against the wall.

His hand didn't move—his mind blank.

Once, he could draw sinewy horses, rhinos butting heads, and fleet-footed deer.

His hand froze and dropped to his side.

What happened to the animals? He used to honor them. Capture their spirits. Draw them every free moment he had. Then he gave life to the man-beast that killed his father and Orki. After that, he only scratched hunting plans in the dirt or combat plans in sand.

He held up the charcoal and drew a straight vertical line. Closing his eyes for a moment, he opened them to draw a small circle on top of the line. He added two horizontal lines jutting from both sides and two longer lines extending diagonally from the bottom of the first. His arm dropped again, touching the pouch at his side.

He felt the stone *reela* amulet from Kokor. A friendly gift from his White now-enemy.

He drew another human figure.

Another.

More. Drawing without knowing.

What are these?

Pressing the charcoal to the wall, he winced as it broke. What have I drawn? Warriors? Is that what I've created from another dark corner of my mind?

Picking up a broken piece, he pressed it even harder to the wall.

It shattered.

With his head in his hands, he slumped to the ground.

Chapter Twenty

IRIK HAD MET WITH ALMOST every Wolf Tribe member before sundown. As he asked them to attend what he called a tribal assembly, they listened intently but with mixed responses. Many seemed shocked or unsure of a new style of gathering to include women and invite everyone to participate. Some clansmen worried the assembly might replace the council, in which they and the chief decided rules and plans.

Women hesitated about speaking in front of men until Irik brought up Mata, how his mother's stories had touched everyone's heart. Her memory had popped into his mind earlier that day, giving him hope. Besides, the afternoon had turned warm, and a full moon promised a pleasant evening.

When Irik met with Cor and Mot, Mot expressed little interest until he learned the assembly wouldn't replace the tribal council. Cor, as Irik expected, loved the idea.

"Glad to hear it," Irik said, "but please understand the assembly's goal is to speak in a good way about the tribe."

She frowned and said, "Oh. All right."

Having clarified that, he focused ahead. "See you then. Do you know where Arol might be? I didn't find her at her campfire."

"She left early from gathering wood—off to find blueberries for her bead paints."

Doubling back only to find Arol's campfire dead, he called into the woods. "Arol! Arol!" Deela whined.

Alone in the woods at night. She should know better. He tapped Deela's nose and pointed into the trees. "Go. Find Arol."

Deela charged after a scent trail while Irik fought back low-hanging branches until his eyes adjusted to the dark. "Arol! Arol!" he yelled, watching Deela zig-zag through the brush.

Silence. Irik stopped to listen. "Deela?"

She whined.

Irik rushed toward the sound.

"Here." A faint voice.

"Arol, what in…" he paused, seeing she was holding her ankle "… are you all right?"

She let go and winced. "I know I shouldn't be out here, but I…I got turned around. She looked down. "Then tripped on the darn log."

"Let me see." He gestured toward her foot.

"No, no, it's…"

He reached down and felt her left ankle, then the right. She stiffened. "It's swollen, but I don't feel a break. Come on. I'll carry you."

"Glad you found me, but I'll be fine."

"Sure?"

"Yes, let's just sit here for a while. What brings you out here?"

He sat by her, and Deela settled at their feet. "I came to see you. After we talked…" He caught himself.

She arched her brow.

"I mean, I wanted to invite you to this evening's tribal assembly at the big fire."

"An assembly? Me?"

"You and all the women. Men too. It's not a tribal council but a way for everyone to share their stories and memories of belonging to the tribe." He spoke faster, breathlessly. "Tell stories that united us, made us become who we are."

"Wow." Surprise raised her pitch. "That's different. What made you think of this?"

"A lot of things at once." He sighed, eyes on the stars. "After Brul and I left you, everything hit me. I could no longer stand as the strong, in-control chief."

"How's that?" As Arol cocked her head, long hair fell against her shoulder.

"For the first time since the attack, I let myself mourn the loss of Nara, Reto, even Meeri. From there, I gained empathy with others who are grieving loved ones and realized I can't insist they be strong." As he turned to her, the moon reflected in a trickle on her cheek. His voice cracked. "I…I'm sorry I couldn't find Shiri."

She nodded, and they wiped their tears in shared silence.

Irik ached to hold her, comfort her as she once comforted him. But she was missing her daughter and Vir—losses he couldn't replace.

Arol forced a brave smile. "So, tell me about this assembly."

He grinned with pride. "Right. Once I grasped everyone's defeat and depression, I looked for something that could help relieve sadness."

"Hard to do." She dipped her head, hair falling forward loosely.

He sighed. "I know, but remember how I told you that my mother's stories used to lift me when I was down?"

"I do."

"Well, I'm hoping people will tell stories about what the clan means to them." He lifted his hand, sweeping it across the starscape. "Maybe by sharing, they'll feel pride as part of a bigger family, and…" he searched for words "…come to believe we're stronger together, can have better days." He looked to Arol for understanding.

"Sounds good, but don't you think all the stories will be from men about their hunting trophies and bravery in battle?"

He nodded. "Some, but you could tell others."

"Like what?"

He scratched his beard. "When your father returned to join us with the Rhino Clan."

"Maybe."

"Fun stories, like when you were a child, playing hide and find—anything. Will you come?"

"I'll think about it, but we'd better get back now."

"All right, let me help you." He stood, and as he did so often when they were children, reached down and took her hands. Deela bounded up, eager to join them.

Arol whimpered when her foot hit the ground. "I think I can walk now."

He slid his arm around her waist while she draped her arm over his shoulders, and they hobbled through the trees.

The touch of her, the smell of her, their closeness triggered memories of their childhood adventures. He wanted to hold her forever.

———◆———

"Go ahead." Irik watched Brul set a gourd bowl in front of Deela later that evening.

"Look, Papa, she likes it." Deela lapped up the remains of their wild turnip soup.

Irik chuckled. "More than I did, but don't tell Tra, or she won't bring us another meal."

"I won't." Brul winked. "Can I go to the assembly?"

"Sure, for a while, but it won't start until everyone finishes eating."

They laughed as Deela pawed at the bowl, flipping it over onto her nose.

"Brul, do you want to try and draw a picture of Deela on the wall?"

"Yeah. Will you show me?"

Irik picked up a piece of charcoal from the edge of the fire. "Come, Deela." He held her still in front of them.

Brul reached for the charcoal.

"Wait. First, you have to study her head. What do you see?"

"Her eyes—looking at me."

"Okay, but tell me about the shape."

"She's got a long nose, and below is her mouth."

"Good." Irik ran his finger along her nose. "Do you see how it slopes from here to the tip? What else?"

"Her ears."

"How do you want them to be in the picture?"

Brul lifted her ears. "Up, Papa."

"That's best. Now whistle."

At the sound, Deela's ears shot up, and Irik said, "See how they come to a point?"

Brul nodded.

"Now I want you to close your eyes and slowly run your hand from the tip of her nose down her chin, then up to the top of her head to her ears and remember how it felt." He waited. "Keep your eyes closed until you can picture exactly how she looks." He watched the boy concentrate.

Brul's eyes popped open. "I saw her in my mind."

Irik handed him the charcoal, said, "Great," and positioned him in front of the wall. "Picture her head in your mind and let that image flow down to your shoulder, through your arm, and into your fingers to make it appear on the wall."

Brul drew cautiously at first, but soon the lines started forming a good likeness. He often turned around to find Irik nodding encouragingly.

At the second ear, Irik said, "Draw it a little to the side of the first, so we can see both."

"How'd I do, Papa?"

Irik stood with open arms. "Perfect." They hugged.

"Did you used to draw?"

"Long ago, Son. Long ago. Okay, let's see if anyone has arrived at the assembly."

"Will Arol be there?"

"I hope so, but she hurt her ankle earlier, so I doubt it."

At the big fire, only a few folks had arrived. Mot and Cor sat near Nork and his woman, Cly. Maybe it was early, but Irik asked each couple to head off to the family fires and ask others to join them. Soon, more people staggered in and sat nervously around the fire.

Irik waited a bit, hoping Arol might show. "Thank you all for coming. Who would like to go first? Tell us about some event or person that made you feel good about our tribe."

Pral's grown son, Miko, raised his hand. Irik nodded. "My father told me he joined the Valley Clan because of Chief Brul's courage and strength. He said he used to wear a bear claw necklace because he killed a bear by himself in a cave while it was asleep."

"Ooh!" some in the group called. Eyes widened all around.

Young Brul tugged at Irik's arm and whispered, "Did he really, Papa?"

Irik nodded. "Good story, Miko. My father was a great leader."

Nork raised his hand. "I remember, too well, the time our hunting party had to ford a frozen river to reach caribou on the other side. It was early spring. I took the lead and, soon, a wrong step. I fell through the ice, pulled down by my heavy furs." He clawed in the air to demonstrate. "I tried to hoist myself up the edge, but the ice kept breaking. Dar, who's no longer with us, stretched out on the ice and reached for me, yelling at the others to pull his legs. Slowly they dragged me out. Built a fire right there." Nork reached out to the crackling flames, rubbing his hands together. "I sat naked until my furs dried out."

"A great tale, Nork," Irik said. "Shows the importance of working together." He looked around. "Do any of you women have a story to share?"

Reto's widow, Tra, raised her hand.

"Yes. You all know my son, Bir. He wouldn't be here today if it weren't for old Molo.

"Yes," Cor said, "she was a great gatherer of plant food. We miss her."

Irik pictured his grandmother's wrinkled face and bony hands as she tended seedlings.

"Also, very wise," Tra added, "and a hero to many of us. "When I was giving birth to Bir, she stayed at my side. I remember being in great pain all morning trying to push the baby out. Finally, his head peeked through, but he wouldn't move any farther. Molo saw the cord wrapped twice around his neck. He would have died if she hadn't cut it right then."

"Aah!" the women cried.

"A wonderful memory of a vital ancestor. Thanks, Tra. Does anyone have a fun story?"

Gorb burst out laughing. "Ha, I'm sure everybody remembers that wrestling match between big Mot and me."

The crowd sniggered.

"It was early summer when Mot threw me, and I landed in a big mud puddle. Everyone thought I was finished. But I was so slippery, Mot couldn't pin me, and I was declared the winner."

"You cheated!" Mot yelled.

The crowd nodded, some tittering along.

"Oh!" cried, Koto, "I've got a good one about you, Irik, when you were young."

Irik forced a smile. "Go ahead."

"Do you remember the bladder ball?"

He squirmed, face warming.

"Whenever we butchered a wild pig, the women always saved the bladder for the children. We'd clean it in the river, then blow it up with air and tie the tube at the top. They'd play catch and kick it around for days until it got busted. Well, one day, we set the pink bladder aside while we finished something else. Irik spotted it and started blowing into the tube. His mother yelled at him at the same moment he screamed. The urine hadn't been washed out yet."

The crowd burst out laughing, and Irik covered his face.

"Really, Papa?" Brul asked.

"Really. Now it's time for you to go to bed. I'll be by after we're done. Take Deela."

After that, everyone loosened, and the fun flowed. They remembered cow-pie-throwing contests that always followed the auroch herds. When Leta mentioned gathering leaves for the kids, Irik remembered diving into a big pile with Arol and hiding from each other.

Irik spoke in a lull between laughs. "This sharing has gone well. I hope this group spirit helps guide us into the future—wherever we go, whatever problems we face."

Out of the dark limped Arol. She waved and sat down across from him.

Tra, who'd known Arol since childhood, welcomed her. "Bet you have a good story to tell about our chief."

"No, no," she said, waving it off.

"Come on, Arol," Koto insisted, "we're all sharing."

Arol looked at Irik. "Do you mind?"

"No, please go ahead." He was so glad to see her he didn't care if she said something humiliating.

She'd tucked a daisy above one ear, and a strand of shells jingled on her wrist as she gestured fluidly. "Well, as you all know, Irik is the father of our Wolf Tribe, and it all began with Meeri, our mother wolf, whom he tamed and trained. But many of you don't know the very beginning." She took a deep breath. "I was there with him, both of us children, when he found Meeri, a just-born puppy."

When the "oohs" and "ahhs" died down, she continued.

"Not far from the old Valley Clan cave, we followed the blood trail of a wounded mother wolf. It ended at a crevice in the rocks where we heard the squeals of a litter of wolf puppies. Despite my warnings…" she glanced at Irik "…do you remember?"

He nodded sheepishly.

"I warned Irik the den mother would kill anything that harmed her pups, but Irik crawled on his belly into the den."

Gorb broke in, "A brave boy even then."

Nork added, "Maybe a little foolish." A few giggled.

"Well," Arol said, "the mother wolf was there but dead, and Irik hauled out six blind, helpless pups. One of them, a girl, peed all over him. She had a white streak on her chest."

Bir yelled out, "It was Meeri."

"It was," Arol said, "and Irik and I built a rock pen for them, hoping we could keep them alive." She paused. "We couldn't. One by one, they died without their mother's milk."

Silence fell over the tribe.

"With only Meeri left alive, Irik went to Molo, who told him about milkweed. Irik mashed it in his mouth together with meat and fed Meeri." Arol held and rocked an imaginary pup in her arms. Irik felt a quiver in his throat, thinking again of good old Molo. *Do I still have that pouch of seeds she gave me before she died?*

"Irik slept many nights in the pen with Meeri to keep her safe and warm. Finally, she started growing and opened her eyes to find—."

"Her ugly wolf father!" Bir said.

His mother shushed him, but the crowd laughed.

Tra spoke. "Arol, what did that tell you about our leader?"

Irik swallowed hard.

Arol looked toward him as he stared at the ground.

"I knew back then," she said, "Irik would be a strong leader. A chief who could see ahead what's best for his people, because…" she placed her hand over her heart "…of his big, open heart."

"Hear! Hear!" Gorb shouted.

Tra stood. "Arol. Give our leader a hug for all of us, would you?"

She approached, and they locked eyes shining with unshed tears. As they embraced, the crowd clapped and cheered.

Arol buried her face in Irik's neck, wet tears, and warm breath tickling and arousing a protective instinct within him. Barely aware of anyone else, he surrendered all emotions and senses, grateful to be wrapped in her arms. Only when other sounds faded as everyone left did the mingling of their heartbeats make him alert again.

He loosened his hold, gently nudging them apart. She was crying yet smiling—something he had never seen before. "What's wrong?"

She wiped her tears. "Just releasing sadness from the past. I'm happy now, Irik, happier than I've been in a long time."

"Me too." He wondered if he dared ask her.

Her eyes told him.

"Will you stay?"

She kissed his cheek and murmured in his ear, "I hoped you would ask."

He glanced around, confirming they were alone. "Come home with me?"

"Yes."

He took her hand, so different a sensation from during their youth. As they strolled in silence to his ledge, Deela sprang out, whining and greeting Arol first.

"Shh," Irik said, "you'll wake Brul." His son was fast asleep in his spot. Nearby, the flame of the tallow lamp flickered against stone.

Arol whispered, "I see you're drawing again."

"No, that's Brul's first drawing of Deela. I'm teaching him."

She squeezed his hand and pulled him closer.

He gazed into her amber eyes, and for the first time since childhood, he noticed the brown flecks and remembered. He kissed her rosebud mouth lightly. "Are you sure?"

"I am."

"Is it only loneliness?"

"No, I want to feel again." She traced her finger over his lips. "Your love was what I always wanted." She pulled him toward his bed and tugged his arm downward.

He sat entranced as she removed her fur cloak, exposing a soft leather vest. She brushed her hands under her hair, tucking it behind her neck. A tender smile warmed her face as she took off the vest, revealing full breasts. Desire awakened in his groin.

She untied the rawhide strip holding a leather wrap around her waist and thighs. It dropped. Beneath the slight belly of a woman who'd given birth lay the triangular patch he'd often dreamed of but never believed he'd see.

She knelt, removed his vest, and dragged the back of her fingers along his hairy chest and up to his neck. As she stood before him, he recognized her sweet fragrance, now lush as warm honey. She bent to kiss his forehead, breasts enticingly near his mouth. Gently kissing his eyes, cheeks, and nose, she brushed his open lips with hers. Irik couldn't hold back anymore. He reached hard for her, and their teeth clicked.

She pulled back.

"I'm sorry," he said, "I'm too—"

"No, no." She stroked his hair. "That will come."

His heartbeat slowed, and she nestled alongside him. He turned to her, and she took his hand, kissing his fingers. She placed it on her neck and drew it up to her chin, along her face, and to her ears, moaning faintly.

Ah, she wants me to start by caressing her. So different from Nara, always in a hurry.

Moving his hand down to her breasts, she showed him how to tenderly circle the tips. He slowly moved to her belly, pressing the jutting bones of her hips, then stroking her thighs up and down until she opened for him.

As his fingers met the wet warmth between her legs, she rose on one elbow and helped him remove his loincloth, releasing his eager shaft and beckoning him to rise above her. She guided him in, inhaling sharply. Holding his hips, she swayed them into a soft, slow rhythm.

When she stopped moaning and met his hips with a cry, he arched his back and pushed hard. He let go, his heart bursting along with hers.

They struggled to catch their breath, staring into each other's eyes.

Irik saw beyond the flecked amber, deep into her very being, surrendering to a force greater than himself, greater than anything.

Her powerful spirit connected with his in a spiraling journey that had to be shared. She had always seen into him. *Did she also see my undying love?*

"I love you, Irik," she whispered. "I always did."

"Me too. Why did I have to lose you for so long?"

"You've got me now." She chuckled.

Knowing his need for her would never cease, he kissed her once more, and they dropped off to sleep.

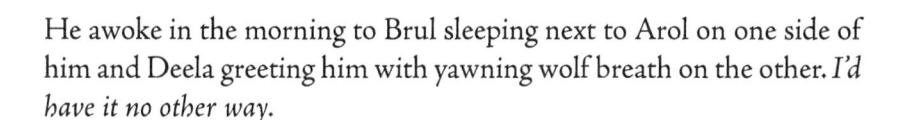

He awoke in the morning to Brul sleeping next to Arol on one side of him and Deela greeting him with yawning wolf breath on the other. *I'd have it no other way.*

Chapter Twenty-one

Near present-day Castelcivita, Campania

TWO YEARS LATER, MIDDAY SUN warmed Irik and Arol's skin as they strolled through the planting fields. Deela frolicked, chasing any varmints she found munching on young plants. The couple stopped, took off their wide-brimmed reed hats, and stared at the ground. Delicate blue flowers had blossomed overnight on tall, spindly seedlings. Helping Arol lower to her knees between the rows, Irik bowed his head in veneration of nature's gift.

With the tiny blooms nestled in their cupped hands, Irik reminisced. "Molo first showed me these flowers growing in the wild, and later I tasted the fruit."

"Nature keeps on giving," Arol said. "I used to hull brown seeds from the pods for my mother's thick soup. I liked the nutty taste, but it was filling and gave everyone wind."

"Ha! So true." He fingered the flower. "I hope these buds turn into pods."

She flashed a smile. "They will."

"Their beauty reminds me of you."

She cocked her head, the sun kindling the red in her hair. "What do you mean?"

"They grew from a small seed, and despite setbacks of drought and cold, they still bloom for us." He reached down and patted Arol's bulging tummy.

"Oh…" She puckered her lips, looking side to side, giggling just as she did as a girl.

"Let's call our planted fruit the mother bean. Once we harvest it, the tribe will grow fat." He bent over and kissed her belly. "By the looks of you, our baby will be born about the same time we pick the beans." He helped her up.

She groaned. "Thanks. Let's sit under the shade of that oak. I'm tired out."

"There," he said as he lowered her down and sat beside her. He waved a hand over the uneven rows of planted fields. "I never guessed Molo's seed pouch could produce such wonders. How fun to plant and watch what each seed grows into."

She patted his knee. "I look at them as living gifts. Funny how the old clan laughed at Molo for collecting wild seeds."

He nodded wistfully. "Once she saw the same grass the aurochs ate growing from the seeds in their dung, she realized we could grow plants, not only find them in the wild."

Arol chuckled. "And now the tribe puts their waste into the fields."

"Yeah, it still troubles me why dung doesn't help all plants. Sometimes the leaves brown and curl at the edges, and the plant dies."

"We're learning as we go along, aren't we?"

"Uh-huh, like with the fig trees. They didn't grow well until I planted them in spring facing south in sandy soil. They need lots of sun."

"Sunshine we wouldn't have if we hadn't followed your lead and moved. Seems there's a right time and place for every…" She stopped and glanced down the path. "Here comes Commander Gorb."

"Afternoon, Chief, Arol." Gorb waved and wiped his forehead. "Sir, our meat supplies are running low, so I formed a hunting party. This time last year, we found aurochs in the west."

"That's fine, Gorb. Make sure you try and capture a few calves. Maybe we can pen them up in the cul-de de-sac and tame them. Feed them with our stores of barley stalks."

"Of course, sir. We'll be heading out shortly."

"Good hunting, Commander." Irik waved and turned to Arol. "Let's check on Brul."

A sharp whistle and Deela was at their side, a rat's tail dangling from her mouth.

Walking toward the huts, they stopped to chat with Nork, head of the field crew.

"How's work going?" Irik asked, shaking his grubby hand.

"Getting it done, sir, but the crew does complain a bit."

"What about?"

"The weeding is back-breaking, and hauling water from the creek takes half a day. These plants are thirsty, but soon, the young children will be old enough to work."

Irik shook his head. "We need bigger containers than skins for the water." He ran his hand through his hair. Make sure you give them a rest break during the hottest part of the day."

"Will do, sir."

They found Brul sitting atop the boulders surrounding the community fire. Arol frowned as he furiously pounded with a rock.

"I sometimes think he's still angry about losing Tuki," Irik said. "Raising her and all, after her mother died."

"Can't blame him when he's like you. Always wanting to protect animals."

"As do you, my sweet." Irik squeezed her shoulders. "How's it going, Brul?"

"Oh, all right." He swept white powder off the boulder.

"What's that?" Irik narrowed his eyes.

"Nothing. Just playing around."

Irik licked his finger and picked up a touch of powder. "Tastes like barley."

"It is, Father. I'm making a powder to try mixing with water."

"Hmm, good idea," Arol said. "Maybe we can try cooking the paste."

"Why don't you two make a new tool to grind it?" Irik suggested.

Brul's face brightened. "That would help."

Irik took Arol's hand. "See you at supper, Son."

At a bellowing from a great distance the next afternoon, half the village gathered to welcome the hunting party back. The crowd gasped and cheered at two half-grown auroch calves pulled by ropes around their necks.

Irik pointed toward the narrow, three-sided valley and shouted, "Get the gates open." The excited crowd followed Brul and friends running to tear away wood poles jammed between boulders at the entrance.

Guiding the two young cows into the closed valley with steep, rock walls, the boys closed the gate. Brul returned with an armful of dried barley stalks, climbing over the rock fence to feed the jittery cows.

"Be careful, Brul," Irik yelled. "They're wild animals."

"Good work, Gorb," Irik said, patting the commander on the back. "A male and a female, perfect." They watched one cow nibble on what Brul had thrown to the ground. "My son will soon have pet names for them."

Two years later, standing at the edge of the vast, golden barley field, Irik and Nork faced a single, chest-high stalk and smiled at each other. Irik embraced the summer plant as though welcoming a friend. He pulled the stalk toward him for a better look at the rows of grain at the top. Plucking several, he handed a few to Nork, and they both set a hull between their front teeth and cracked it open to release the oval inner grain. Spitting out the tough chaff, they held the rest of the grain up to the sky and smiled before nibbling. As they watched each other chew, their eyes lit up, and Irik took Nork by the shoulders.

"You did it, my good man. It tastes nice and ripe and nutty."

"So it does," Nork concurred. "But, sir, I only supervised. We owe all our praise to the big spring rains and the field crew. Now comes the heavy work."

"Yes, and everyone will have to pitch in for the harvest. With our animal feed stores empty and two hungry, angry cows to feed, there's no time to lose." Exhilarated, Irik patted Nork on the shoulder. "Come on, Deela," he said, slapping his thigh, "let's take the good news to Arol and Brul."

Irik leaped into a sprint with Deela right at his side. About halfway to the hut, Irik slowed to a jog, then a walk, his legs tired and heart pounding. At twenty-six winters old and not having been on a hunt for years, Irik possessed more enthusiasm than stamina. Catching his breath, he welcomed the sight of his winter-and-a-half old daughter, Arolee, to energize him.

Her squealing greeted him before he opened the hut's flap door. Inside, Brul bounced her on his knee. Arolee looked up, shouted, "Papa," and toddled over.

Irik picked her up, blowing funny noises onto her tummy. Arolee issued a loop of laughter like her mother's.

Arol looked up from her beadwork. "You look happy."

"Always with this family," he said, "and I have some good news."

"Is the barley ready to harvest?" Brul asked. "Kiri and Rolo are getting leaner and meaner by the day. Rolo charges the gate whenever I come near. At the shoulders, that bull is taller than me, and with his big horns, he might break through the gate one day."

Irik let his son ramble, hiding a foxy smile. Arolee tugged his beard and giggled.

"It's Arolee's nap time," Arol said. "Come out with it, Irik."

He set Arolee down. "You got your wish, Brul. The cows will get their grass."

Brul jumped up. "Now, Papa?"

"Yes, grab a hand ax and go find Nork if you want to start cutting the stalks. Otherwise, tend to the puppies. I need a nap too."

Brul scurried out of the hut—without an ax.

Arol chuckled, "You can see where his heart lies."

Irik nodded and sat down. "Like father, like son."

She nodded. "Good to hear your news. Let me put Arolee down and tell me all about it."

"Sure," he said, lying down and closing his eyes.

"Wake up, Irik." Arol nudged his arm. "Nork stopped by saying something about a strange storm cloud."

Irik groaned and sat up. "Good, we need the rain." He gave her a quick kiss and headed out the door to hear a distant whir, unlike any wind he knew. Oddly, the air around him was still. Gorb and a group of tribesmen stared at the southern sky, so he looked up.

The black cloud surged toward them, a large mass with a tail stretching to the horizon.

"Looks like one of those flocks of blackbirds," Gorb said, "the kind that swerve as one."

"Could be birds," Nork said, "but I don't hear them squawking, only rattling."

"It's not a storm," Irik said. The cloud widened east to west, and gray shrouded the sky. He shuddered as tiny prickles broke out on his arms. Overhead, the clatter grew deafening.

The fluttering of an endless swarm of insects.

The hard-shelled bugs pelted and stung their faces. Deela barked wildly and jumped at them. Children screamed and ran.

Irik shouted, "Get the women and children into their huts," and spit out a squirming creature into his hand. Bigger than a finger, the stiff, spotted bug had long, jointed rear legs, broad, see-through wings, and big eyes. He threw it to the ground.

"To the fields, men!" Nork yelled.

Queasily, Irik turned as bugs alighted on the fields, thickly covering and squirming on every stalk in mere moments.

"Grab some hides, anything," Gorb shouted. "Chase them off the plants."

Irik ripped off his vest and swung it at a barley stalk. He gasped. The bugs fell off; the plant stripped bare. As the men screamed and frantically swung at the menace, Irik slumped, knowing it was useless.

He looked up when Nork nudged him. "They ate everything, sir."

"I know." He groaned and dropped his head into his hands. When the ravaging winds no longer blew, Irik became aware of a hand on his shoulder and a tiny voice.

"Papa?"

He kissed Arolee on the forehead and took her into his arms. Through the wispy strands of her hair, he saw the tribe wandering listlessly through the village. All was silent except the sickening crunch of dead bugs as they walked. Arol stood above him, looking back and forth from him to the sky.

"Are you okay?" she asked.

He nodded. "Are you? Where's Brul?"

"I'm all right. He's at the wolf pens, keeping the puppies from eating the bugs."

"Bad bugs," Arolee said.

Irik managed a tight smile. "Yes, my dear, they were." He stood shakily and handed Arolee over to her mother.

Nork stood a distance away, waiting, so he waved. "I must go check the fields." As soon as he joined him, the villagers descended upon them like the insects on the plants.

"Where did those bugs come from?" several shouted.

"Will they be back?" Wolt asked. "What are we going to do now?"

"How are we going to eat?" a girl Irik didn't recognize shrieked. "Why did they attack?"

"How are we going to feed the cows?" Brul's beloved murmur haunted Irik most. As the questions rang in his ears and echoed in his mind, Irik had no answers.

Commander Gorb parted the crowd and whispered to Irik. "Sir, maybe holding a tribal council later tonight will give you some time to recover."

Gorb's wise words broke through Irik's helplessness. He raised his hands with open palms. "Listen, people, I hear your concerns. We will get through this tragedy somehow. Let's catch our breath and go home to our families. Join me at tribal council tonight, men."

The crowd muttered and slowly dispersed, the unknown girl in tears.

As Irik and Arol neared their hut, Brul came running. "What are we going to do?"

Irik shook his head and gestured for him to come inside.

"We have to feed the cows, Father."

"I know."

"You'll have to order a crew to gather grass in the wild."

"It would take half the village days to gather enough to feed those beasts for one day."

"Rolo and Kiri will starve to death." Brul's anguished voice squeaked.

"So might our people."

Brul stared into his father's eyes. "The cows were part of your big dream. You're not thinking of…"

Irik stayed silent.

Brul stormed out the door.

"What's wrong, Mama?" Arolee asked.

"Nothing, Sweetie. Here. I'll let you play with the click beads. Will you go to your bed for a while so I can talk to Papa?"

Arol handed her daughter the loosely strung wooden beads. Irik smiled and nodded.

In a low, calm voice, Arol asked, "What *are* we going to do?"

He let out a long sigh. "For the future of the tribe, I honestly don't know. For tomorrow, we have to slaughter one of the cows."

She frowned. "I figured that."

Irik stared past her, deep in thought. "The cows never mated for a calf and milk. By not being free…" He shook his head.

"You tried, Irik. You saw a thing that could have been."

"Thanks," he said, bending to kiss her. "I have to clear my head." He stood. "Deela and I are going for a walk." He grabbed Molo's seed pouch, and they headed toward the wolf pens.

A chorus of whining broke out as Deela put her front paws along the fence line and reached to lick the noses of her extended family. Seeing their playful bonds gave Irik a short jolt of happiness. "Don't worry, Deela, they will all be fed. I promise."

Strolling around the perimeter of the village, he came across a young beech tree cut for a pole. He sat on a rock and noticed several leafy shoots branching out from the stump. He closed his eyes and pictured Chief Brul, Mata, Uncle Orki, Reto, and Molo until he felt their presence within him. With each breath, he grew stronger. More open to a path. More knowing.

Opening his eyes, he reached over and snapped off all the leafy branches and headed to the cow pen. Rolo and Kiri snorted as he approached. He climbed the fence and shook the leafy branches at them. Kiri cautiously hoofed over, smelled the greenery, and eagerly chewed. "That's all I've got," he told her, eyes welling up. "I'm sorry."

———————◆×———————

That night, Irik faced desperate and fearful men. He closed his eyes to invoke the spirit of his father. "Men of the Wolf Tribe, things seem hopeless right now, but I ask you to trust in me." He paused, throat tight as he swallowed. "The weight of this tribe is on my shoulders. If you let me carry you, as you carry your families, we will find our way out of this tragedy."

Gorb rose out of the silent crowd. "Sir, we love and respect you, but can we hear a plan?"

"Of course. Here's what I'm asking you to do. First, know that if we stay together as a tribe, we will not starve. Tomorrow we will butcher one cow, and with rationing, that will feed us for five or six days. During that time, we will return to our old skills and hunt in the wild for plants and animals. We can slaughter the second cow if we need to."

Gorb remained standing. "We expected that, sir. We're wondering what lies beyond."

"I understand. Our future will be up to each of you and Mother Nature."

The men looked at each other, mumbling. "What do you mean?" Nork asked.

Irik held up Molo's seed pouch. "Our tribe has proven we can use these seeds. With your hard work, we can grow food and not have to find it in the wild for long."

A man in the shadows called out, "Enough food? Since we've been settled, we have too many babies to feed."

"I know, but we'll plant more fields. We'll have brown bean plants and round yellow peas. Our trees may bear fruit again. We've got berries. Tubers that grow underground."

"But we need meat," Gorb thundered. "We never see big animal herds anymore."

"We can rely on small game until we bring in different, smaller animals to raise. Remember, everyone, we tamed wolves. How hard can squirrels or rabbits be?"

Many of the men grunted and nodded. A few snickered.

"We must build a new way of life, take care of ourselves in our own place. Far away from the Whites. No fighting over hunting."

"But, sir," Nork said, "how do we know bugs and drought won't happen again?"

Irik lowered his head. "We don't."

The men gasped.

"Nature gives, and nature takes away. It's a force bigger than us. All we can do is use what we have to learn and adapt. Like all animals, we'll do what we must to survive."

After a moment of quiet astonishment, Gorb spoke. "We're with you, Chief."

"Hear! Hear!" chanted the crowd.

Autumn, three years later

"Oooh!" Arolee cooed as she let go of Irik's hand and skipped into the flower fields. The short clumps of light purple flowers were due for harvesting. Irik remembered how he and Arol used to play with Meeri as he watched Arolee and her young wolf, Ror, dance between the rows. So named because of her squeaky bark, Ror was his daughter's constant companion. Along with Deela, they explored the fields together every day.

At four-and-a-half winters old, Arolee looked like her mother— auburn-tinged hair and tiny nose—and was just as spirited and good-hearted. Today, Irik wanted to give her a lesson along with play. "Don't step on them, sweetie. We need to collect their special crop."

"I know, Papa. Mama and I collected the bulbs, so we could grow them."

"That's right." He bent down and held a single six-petaled flower between his fingers. "Do you see in the center where the yellow flower was before? Now there are these red strings. Feel them."

"They tickle, Papa."

Chuckling, he asked, "What do we do with these little strings?"

"Cook them in stew, so it tastes sweet."

"Right. What else?"

She put a finger to her mouth. "Ah... ah, for Mama. When she has camps."

Irik laughed. "Yes, so her cramps, not camps, don't hurt so much. Let's pick a bunch."

After they filled Arolee's little pouch, Irik said, "How about some peas for lunch?"

"Yay, peas!" The little girl's eyes glowed.

"Hello, Arolee." Cor looked up from filling her reed basket with green pods. "What are you and your father picking today?"

"My favorite peas." She reached into the little bush, plucked a green pod, cracked it open, and popped a round, cream-colored pea into her mouth. "Yummy." She picked another.

"How's it going, Cor?" Irik asked.

"Very well, sir. This is the second harvest. We'll dry these in the sun for winter."

"Thanks for all your hard work."

"It is, sir, from dawn to dusk, but we all eat well and sleep well."

"How's the water channel working?"

"Oh, so glad you had the men dig that ditch from the creek. Saves us a lot of hauling. More time for planting and harvesting."

"Good," he said, "we'd better get picking ourselves." Seeing Arolee fill her face, he turned. "How much have you picked?"

She froze. "I forgot, Papa."

Cor laughed. "Here, take these. Saves me a few steps." She dumped her pickings into Irik's hat.

"Call Ror, Arolee." He took her little hand to head home. "Come, Deela." Along the way, Irik pointed and quizzed her as they passed plants.

"Radish?"

"Right."

"Flax?"

"No, millet."

"Grapes?"

"Good girl."

"Glad you could make it," Arol said as she and Brul looked up from chewing on meaty ribs. "Good job picking, Arolee," she added, looking at Irik's loaded hat. "You must have kept your father from talking with the villagers."

Arolee sheepishly looked at her father.

Irik winked and turned to Brul. "Been in the muddy pen with the piglets again, I can smell. Brul, you really need to wash in the creek before you come home."

"I have to go right back. Make sure Seely..." he interrupted himself, "...that new sow doesn't smother one of her babies."

"Okay," Irik said, but you know I don't want you giving names to the boars. They're bacon, not companions."

"I know, Papa." He got up, grabbed a handful of peas and limped toward the door.

"Brul." Irik stopped him. "How's your leg?"

"Better. Arol put *oluu* on it."

"Good. Which wolves are guarding the pen tonight?"

"Bira and Nolo."

"Good wolves. Make sure they have some exercise before you tie them up out there."

Brul waved, hitching on.

Arol asked Arolee to shuck the peas and turned to Irik. "Don't be so tough on him, Irik."

He considered what she said. "I try not to be any harder than my father was on me."

"Times are different, and he's done so well with the boars. If it weren't for his building that separate stone corral for the piglets, we might have lost our stock to that cave lion."

"I know. He was extra smart adding that pole roof. He's a hard worker and brave besides. I should never have let Brul in the main pen with that big boar. The rutting male weighed twice as much as him and gored him pretty badly." Irik thought back to a caribou hunt with the brother he'd envied, treasured, and lost too young. Brul grew up sheltered compared to the two of them, not having to hunt dangerous animals or confront scavengers often. Still, the new way of life had its hazards and required long hours of labor.

Arol nodded. "At fourteen winters, I think we ought to be very proud of our..." she caught herself "...your son."

Irik laid his hand on hers. "You've been wonderful for him. I think your nurturing ways have helped him mature into a man already."

She kissed him. "Thanks. When I think of what he's done with the boars and providing meat for the tribe, it's amazing. The understanding of animals comes from you."

He shrugged. "However he got it, the fourth generation of pigs is almost tamed. I only wish he'd bathe more often."

A muffled shout woke Irik at dawn.

"Chief, it's Gorb. Our boar pen has been attacked."

"Hold on." Irik rose and dressed. *Another lion? Why didn't the wolves warn us?*

Arol stirred.

"Go back to sleep. I'll be right back."

Gorb's somber face and rapid breathing spoke of disaster. "Four adult boars missing. Gate broken. Blood everywhere."

"Didn't the guard wolves warn us?" Irik asked.

"Afraid not. They were killed."

Irik stood stunned. "The piglet pen?"

"Saved, sir."

"What was it?"

"*Who*, sir." Gorb lifted his right arm and handed an arrow to his chief.

Irik ran his fingers along the shaft until he came to the two feathers. "White and black seabird feathers like the—" He looked to Gorb for confirmation.

"Yes, sir, the Whites." They silenced the wolves, then killed and dragged off the boars."

Irik fixed his eyes on Gorb's, silently begging for a solution.

Gorb lifted his left arm to hand him a longer arrow with three gray feathers at the end. "The way we mount these owl feathers makes ours more accurate at long range, sir."

Gorb's words might as well have been an arrow piercing Irik's heart.

"Papa." Brul stuck his head out the door. "What's going on?"

"The boar pen has been attacked," Gorb said, sparing Irik a grim duty.

Brul bolted toward the pens.

Irik didn't have the heart to tell him.

Chapter Twenty-two

APPROACHING THE MIDNIGHT SHADOWS OF hills that formed the serpentine path to the White people's village, Irik stopped. He turned and straightened his aching back to face the small escort of Wolf Tribesmen. Raising his hand, he bent his tired legs to the ground and sat. The men and guard wolves, Deela and Ory, did the same. Seven months had passed since the attack on the boars, but the pain and disappointment lingered in all of them.

After three days of hiking, the time had come. Sighing, Irik regarded his son, then his warriors. "This is where we part, men." He pointed to a rock outcropping. "A good spot for you to wait for my return."

"Let me come with you, Father," Brul pled.

Irik's heart told him he alone held the best hope for peace. Kokor and the Whites still feared his unearthly powers. Even Arol, terrified she'd lose him, said he had to try.

"No, Son. Take care of your wife and baby…" he swallowed hard "…and the tribe. I should make the White village by dawn. If Chief Kokor accepts our truce offer, I'll return by dusk tomorrow. Hand me my goat horn headdress."

He took a deep breath, turning to the whole group. "If I do not return, head back to our village and decide on an alternate plan."

"How will we know if…" Gorb started to say, but dropped his head "…if you are not coming back?"

Irik feigned a chuckle. "I've lived almost thirty winters and am in bad health. My time's already up."

"But the wolf pack that's been trailing us…" Brul pleaded. "Lions could be anywhere."

Irik patted Deela and Ory and smiled. "My best guard wolves will protect me."

He groaned and pushed himself up, hands on creaking knees. "I'll be off, now. Meet me at dusk." Not to appear troubled, he gave his son a short hug. Irik hoped his actions would inspire Brul. Only fourteen winters old, the boy sometimes acted glum or touchy. Whatever happened, Arol would help Brul become a better chief than he had been.

"Father, at least take a knife blade," Brul said, worry etched on his face.

"No, Son, I must go unarmed." He waved and set off as briskly as he could toward the hills.

The night hike was slow, as Irik had to stop and rest without sleeping. The low-lying shrubs and rocks made him stumble, and once he fell facedown. Deela leaped to his side and licked his face to recuperate him.

He pulled himself up. He must be strong. If he didn't reach the Whites and secure peace, his tribe would have to flee or fight again. Since the wild herds had mostly disappeared, White warriors came a long distance to raid their boars. There had to be another way. *Can't we coexist?*

Unsteady but marching on, Irik approached the last valley before the White village. The wild wolf pack trailing him must have found other prey, or at least he didn't hear them anymore. Dawn would present another challenge.

Deela and Ory's growls and a rustle in the bushes stopped Irik cold. He raised his hands in the air.

"HeeKo!" shouted two White warriors as they jumped in front of him. Deela bared her teeth and snarled. Their bows were pulled tight as they aimed fearfully back and forth between Irik's chest and the wolves. Irik recognized the White word for "halt" and hoped to remember other words he learned years ago when he stayed with them.

"Back! Sit!" Irik yelled at the wolves. Like other White warriors before them, the men's jaws dropped at Irik's control of the wolves. But fear of the vicious animals and suspicion of Irik's mastery made these warriors even more nervous and likely to launch their arrows.

"I mean no harm," he said calmly, "and I have no weapons. I only want to meet with your chief, Kokor."

Confusion crossed the warriors' faces, their bowstrings held taut.

Watching their reactions, Irik slowly reached into his pouch. He grabbed the *reela* amulet Kokor had given him and held it out. "Chief Kokor gave this to me."

The warriors stared at the amulet, looked at each other, and slowly relaxed the pull on their bows. "Caliss!" one warrior shouted and pointed up the trail.

Irik ordered Deela to his front and Ory to the rear to watch the bowmen as he stepped forth. By mid-morning, they approached the narrow ravine Irik remembered as close to the White's village.

"Aayee!" dozens of bowmen yelled from above and aimed their arrows.

One older warrior, who wore a white feather necklace, may have recognized Irik from years ago. He ran down the side of the ravine toward the village.

"Caliss," the other warriors ordered, jabbing their bows to keep moving.

On the village outskirts loomed a gateway new to Irik. Squinting, he made out two rows of tall spikes mounted with… yes, human skulls, feathers fluttering along the base. Fresher heads severed at the neck regarded him with sockets pecked free of eyeballs and maggoty flesh rotting in the sun. He shuddered. *Have the Whites become more violent?*

Through the gruesome, reeking gateway, huts filled the entire valley floor—women and children clustered around them in the hot sun. Bow and spear-carrying warriors hastened to gather around— the clamor of their voices making the wolves tense. Irik wondered if anyone recognized his headdress and remembered him as chief of the smaller Wolf Clan they defeated years ago. Many of the warriors appeared underfed, skin pulled taut over their ribs.

Nearing a large hut in the middle of the village, Irik remembered it as the chief's. The old, feathered warrior commanded Irik to kneel on the ground. Out came a young, muscular man in an antler headdress:

Kokor's son. Carrying a carved wooden spear, he swaggered toward Irik, but his eyes darted nervously between him and the snarling wolves. *Which does he fear more—a fierce predator or a once-powerful chief?*

Pointing his spear at the wolves, the young White warrior shouted, "Golo supit!"

"Down," Irik commanded and patted the wolves' heads.

Is he the new chief of the Whites? Irik recalled him as arrogant and dreadful. Although worried, he confidently said, "I want to see Chief Kokor."

The warrior stood motionless, darting black eyes conveying hatred and fear.

Irik held out the *reela* amulet. "Kokor gave me this in respect. I wish to meet with him."

The warrior took the amulet, grunted, and walked back into the hut. Moments later, a head peeked out, hair as white as his painted face. When he stood, the wolf-fang necklace Irik had given him dangled on top of Kokor's round belly. Although Irik assumed the White chief to be about his age, he hobbled toward him with difficulty. His steady eyes glittered with hate.

As he neared, the wolves snarled, saliva dripping off their bared teeth. Chief Kokor, familiar with Irik and his wolves, boldly faced him. His penetrating stare chilled Irik, so he showed deference by crossing his hands over his chest and bowing.

Kokor pulled a long knife blade from his waist and pointed it toward Irik's chest.

"What are you doing here? I should kill you."

Irik bristled at the rage-filled tone and threat.

The wolves growled and dropped into a crouch, ready to pounce.

The crowd of warriors blurted, "Ohhh," and drew their bows.

"Back off," Irik said, and the wolves settled down.

Kokor didn't flinch. "I see you're up to your same tricks but powerless now. I should cut out your heart for my people to eat."

"I come in peace, Chief Kokor, to renew our friendship."

Kokor narrowed his eyes. "Peace, what is that?"

"A way our tribes can live together."

"Ha!" His plump, pale belly jiggled. "After you killed many of my people and almost starved us out?"

Irik steadied himself. *How dare he gain weight while his people waste away?* "We never meant the White Clan any harm. Our old Valley Clan came to you as friends. I told you at the end of our visit we'd move our clan north of you. Don't you remember?"

Kokor donned his beaked and beaded headdress, and it clattered as he vehemently shook his head. "No, you never said you were coming to our territory."

Irik felt as shocked as Kokor had looked before covering his face. Wondering if the chief did so out of disadvantage, Irik pressed on. "My interpreter wasn't there, but I showed you how our women and children would settle nearby." He pointed into the distance.

"No," Kokor growled. "We would never let you live near us. This is our place."

Irik grasped for a way to calm him. "We didn't mean for your men to get caught and killed in that auroch stampede."

Kokor would hear none of it. "You hunted in our territory. That's why we drove you out with our arrows."

Irik struggled to diffuse rising anger. *Why did they take our boars? Are there no more animals to hunt?* He fixed his eyes on the White chief in his clinking, curiously intimidating regalia. "So now, you come into *our* territory, kill our brother wolves, and steal our boars."

Kokor flinched and went silent.

Irik saw an opening and raised his palms. "Chief Kokor, we don't have to fight over hunting. I have a new way."

Kokor jabbed his blade toward Irik. "You lie. There is no other way."

Irik struggled to stand. "Let me..."

"Stay on your knees, trickster. How do I know your warriors and wolves aren't surrounding us right now?"

Irik put a hand to his chest. "There's no trick, but I have powers greater than killing to share with you."

Kokor tilted his head and grunted, eyes veiled by the swaying white.

"Remember when our tribes met? Traded tools, knowledge, even gifts?"

Kokor placed a hand on the wolf-fang necklace Irik had given him.

"You seemed to appreciate how we could help each other—in peace."
The White chief lowered the knife to his side.

Irik patted the wolves and received tail wags in return. "You saw how I rule these fierce wolves with my voice alone. We train them to be living tools, in this case, guard wolves. They'd give their lives to protect me, as though I were their pack leader. If you let me, I can show you how to have such power."

Irik pointed a finger at his wolves. "Speak!"

Both Deela and Ory let out a single bark.

"Lay down."

The wolves obeyed.

Kokor's eyes widened inside the headdress.

Irik touched his temple. "Once you learn how to tame them, they won't harm you. Wolves can protect your tribe from marauding hyenas, even lions. At night, they'll warn you of any attack."

Kokor said nothing. His men had managed to kill guard wolves before the boars.

"If you don't believe me..." he pointed to Ory "...I could give this one to your tribe."

"A wolf in our village? It would eat our children." Kokor huffed.

Irik shook his head. "Not if accepted into a human pack, trained, and treated with love."

"Love?" Kokor laughed. "A wolf?" The White warriors chortled along.

Irik gestured to his wolves, himself, and then Kokor. "Let me show you."

Kokor hesitantly nodded, picking his teeth behind the beads.

Irik scanned the crowd of warriors with scrawny, underfed bodies. He stretched out his arm. "Which of you men will lay down your bow?"

Either no one volunteered, or no one understood,

"I can show you how Ory will walk with you, do as you say, and be your friend."

The warriors muttered, shook their heads, and shared smirks.

Kokor waved his hand over them, speaking at length, ending by gesturing for a volunteer to come forward.

The youngest-looking man raised his hand.

Irik motioned him to come closer and set down his bow and spear. "What's your name?"

"Kela." He nervously rubbed the downy stubble on his chin.

"Glad to meet you, Kela. Kneel down like me in front of Ory here. Without looking her in the eyes, say, 'Ory. Good girl, Ory.'"

The man spoke with a tremble, but Ory twitched her tail.

"Good start, Kela. Once Ory sees you're not a threat and she can trust you, she'll listen to anything you ask." He handed Kela a piece of dried meat from his pouch and demonstrated how to put it in the palm of his hand and say, "Come, Ory."

Kela did as shown. Ory's nose quivered, but she waited, looking at Irik.

Irik patted her back. "It's okay, Ory." He nodded and pointed to Kela. "Go. Go to Kela."

Slowly, the wolf crawled toward the man. Kela stiffened.

"Steady, Kela. She won't bite you."

"Ahhhh!" gasped the warriors.

Ory gently took the food and backed up.

Irik thought he saw Kokor smile behind the beads.

"Now, Kela, once she's done eating, slowly reach over and pet her on the head like this."

"Good girl." Kela grinned as Ory wagged her tail and nuzzled him, smelling for more.

"Kela," Irik said, "you're very brave, and if you always treated Ory as you would a member of your family, she'd come to guard you with her life." Irik glanced over to Kokor. "Will you take Ory as a gift to your tribe?"

Kokor narrowed his eyes. "What trick is this?"

Irik stood. "Not a trick, Kokor, trust. Ory is just a start. If you let me, I'll share much more with you."

Kokor's curtained eyes narrowed.

"Watch." Irik looked at Kela, shocked how his ribs protruded over his sunken stomach. "Now, Kela, stand and pat your legs like this and say, 'Come, Ory, come.'"

Kela did, but Ory turned again to look at Irik.

Irik nodded, and Ory went to the man.

"Good, now walk to your hut."

Kela beamed. "Come, Ory." She followed, looking back at Irik only once.

The crowd of warriors jumped up and down and cheered.

Kokor scowled and spoke rapidly in his language so Irik would be unlikely to understand. He asked Irik, "What is it you would ask of us in trade for your supposed gifts?"

"I didn't wish to be your enemy, Kokor, nor do I seek revenge for your attacks." He swept his hand in front of him. "I ask nothing. Our tribe only wants to live in peace with yours."

"I do not believe you."

"You will when I bring more gifts. We will teach you how to tame and train your own wolves. We can help you feed your families. You will no longer need to hunt or fight."

Kokor spit at the ground.

In the distance, a high-pitched squeal echoed down from the huts. A mournful animal cry Irik knew too well. Deela's ears pinned back as she whined. The White Tribe direly needed food. They'd killed Ory. Pain pierced Irik's heart, but he must recover. He bit down hard on his lip.

Kokor tipped his head in the direction of the sound. "*That* is who we are."

Despite the power Irik had shown them could be theirs, hunger and distrust triumphed. Even more than the wolves, however, their starvation might give Irik an advantage. "You and your people can do better, Kokor."

"How?"

"Put down your weapons."

Kokor pulled his knife back out. "Ha! Give up our way of protecting ourselves?"

Are the Whites destined to only be killers? Holding onto hope, Irik said, "Yes."

"You fool," Kokor sneered and lurched.

The warriors moved in, spears drawn.

Deela snarled.

Raising his knife, Kokor swung it toward Irik, throwing himself against him.

Deela lunged at the attacker.

"Ayee!" Kokor screamed.

Deela sunk her jaws into the White chief's forearm as he fell on top of Irik. She kept the knife from plunging into her master's chest.

Kokor put his considerable weight behind the knife, but Deela shook his arm back and forth. It fell to the ground as blood flew, both men and the wolf growling.

Irik shouted, "Deela, off!"

She let go of Kokor's arm, but to Irik's surprise, jumped on his back. She tried to bite his neck through the beaded headdress.

Both men eyed the knife.

"No!" Irik yelled, trying to tame the beast within himself. "Off! Deela!"

Kokor picked up the knife and sunk it deep into Irik's shoulder.

Deela lifted her head, and Kokor turned and plunged the blade into her chest. She collapsed, aortic blood flooding the ground.

Kokor held the knife above Irik's throat, staring at him. *Does Kokor understand I tried to save him from the jaws of the wolf? Will it matter?*

Kokor, catching his breath, croaked, "I should kill you."

Irik nodded. "You could, or you could save your people. Let me go, so I can return with food and gifts. You'll be able to feed your clan and become more powerful than ever before."

Kokor grasped the knife harder, his hand shaking. "Grrr! Get up." The White chief stood and slid his knife back from where it came. "Go. Bring back your gifts. No tricks."

Irik staggered up, clutching his wound, blood dripping down his side. He gave Kokor a slight bow. "I'll return at new moon." Relieved, he stumbled toward the village gateway.

As he passed underneath the spikes mounted with skulls, Irik rejoiced at being alive and the first part of his mission succeeding. Now, to make it back by dusk and tell his men to return with food and gifts. He'd earned his Wolf Tribe a chance of preventing war.

Checking the waning afternoon sun to gauge how much time he had, he stumbled on a loose rock and fell to his knees. The knife wound began oozing. Irik clawed the earth and forced a handful of sand into the gash. He cried out as grit scratched every exposed nerve.

Ahead, two White warriors turned and looked at him. He could only hope Kokor sent them to tell the mountain guards to let him pass unharmed. *But injured, can I make it?* He felt so alone without Deela and Ory, trusted wolves who gave their lives for him.

Wincing, he staggered to his feet. He would take one step followed by another until he reached Brul and the men. If they weren't there waiting, how would they know what he'd done? He picked up his pace, and the pair of warriors faced forward and trotted ahead.

With the sun nearing the horizon, light-headedness and weak legs plagued Irik. He must regain strength, not just to rule or to fight. He needed the deeper resolve he'd felt as a youth. Mata and Arol knew he had a special ability. Whether drawing animals or training wolves, he'd hear them say, *"See it in your mind, Irik."* He must picture the outcome as it could be.

He stared at the narrow ravine into the distance. His home lay beyond. He could visualize the prairie, the animals, and his families working in the fields and playing with their children. Pressing his hand on the stinging wound, he began to run—one footfall after another.

Exhausted by the time he passed through the last set of hills, he noticed the White guards stop and take their positions. The low sun had given up its warmth, and the sweat on his arms chilled him. With darkness setting in, he remained far from the meeting place.

The howl of a lone wolf drifted eerily over the valley. Irik froze. He could tell by the urgency of the call and the response, the pack was going on a night hunt. Without his wolf guards at his side, he'd be vulnerable. The wild cousins to his loyal wolves must have picked up his scent, so he tore the blood-soaked vest from his body. Grabbing a handful of sagebrush leaves, he rubbed the blood off his shoulder and arm and ran for his life, fear and brisk air renewing his energy.

Thirst seized his throat. *See it in your mind, Irik.* A few more steps, and there it was—a meandering outline of trees growing along the sides of a creek bed.

Moonlight danced off a mere trickle between the rocks. He dropped to his battered knees and heaved out a boulder to form a small pool. As he scooped a palmful of water into his mouth, a spike of terror shot through him.

What was that? A rustle above and to his side. *Wolves? A lion?*

He picked up a rock and threw it in that direction.

More rustling. Louder.

He threw another rock.

A thud.

A snort.

A boar.

He sighed and turned back to what had become a small pool. He quickly dunked his face in and drank like an animal. He looked up and listened—nothing.

The pool re-filled, and the moon lit his reflection as tears mingled with the water. Had it been a lion, he'd already be dead. A quick bite to the neck—just as his father had gone. Wiping his face, Irik realized Chief Brul had given him strength, something he'd misused by over-hunting and seeking power. *What will I give my son? What if young Brul unleashes his own inner beast?* He must remind him of the power and purity of the moon—how it illuminates the truth and shines the way for the living.

See it in your mind, Irik.

He pictured Arol watching over him. He saw his son with Chocho and their baby.

As he struggled to get up, his head swam. He stumbled to one knee, hauling in deep breaths. Pulling himself to stand, he barely trusted his senses. Behind his closed eyes danced his father, mother, so many of the tribe. He blinked. *Do I see the rock outcropping and the men waiting for me? Do I hear Brul calling?* Reeling, he fell backward, hard to the ground.

Chapter Twenty-three

THE WOLF TRIBE HUSHED AS young Chief Brul stood. At only fourteen winters old—no whiskers and a hooked nose like his father's—Brul gathered his thoughts. He ran his hand through his bushy hair in a manner familiar to all.

"Good people of the Wolf Tribe, tomorrow we leave on a journey dangerous for those who join me and for those who guard our home. I believe, as my father did, the venture holds promise. If we share our wealth by teaching the Whites to raise animals and grow plants, they'll have no reason to take our food by force." He scanned the crowd. "My father asked me to see this through and to make sure the entire clan supports the effort. Does anyone have concerns?"

Commander Gorb raised his hand. "Sir, we all agree with the goal, but what if the Whites don't believe us or accept our gifts?"

"Yeah!" shouted Tolo. "We know they're killers."

"They have been, and we can't be sure how they may react to a new way of life. The Whites could attack us again, but our great chief Irik met with them and came back with hope. In the past, you all have trusted him with your lives, as have I." He placed his hand on his heart. "I ask you now to trust me to bring you peace."

The crowd stayed silent and motionless until a young mother with red hair falling to her waist and an infant in her arms stood up. "No more war. We must have peace. I want my children to grow up safe."

"Yes, peace," said her husband, standing with their freckled boy at her side.

"Peace! Peace! Peace!" rang out. One by one, the tribe members stood, waving hands.

"Thank you, Woto." Brul hugged the woman. "Thank you all. We depart at sunrise."

Dawn did not break quietly over the Wolf Tribe. Most of the villagers left their huts and gathered around the band of travelers to bid farewell. As the bow of the new moon hung in the eastern sky, the tribe waited on edge for their new chief to lead the march into White territory. With memories of Irik's loss still fresh, grieving sobs and talk of danger filled the cool air. Every time the boars snorted, the wolves barked, and the boars squealed anew. But their clamor did nothing to muffle cries from the hut where Brul, his woman, and their baby remained.

"Please, Chocho, stop crying," Brul pleaded within clinging arms. "Come out and wish the journey well."

Chocho pulled away, clutching their infant to her chest. "Don't go!"

He inched closer, already missing the comfort of her touch. "I'm chief now and must do this for little Irik." He rubbed the baby's shoulder. "Father never showed fear. Neither can we."

She wailed and slumped to the ground. The baby whimpered.

Brul knelt and wiped her tears. "Please, Chocho, I must honor my father and the people's faith in me." He patted little Irik's dark hair. "Father died in my arms, his last wish being peace."

She grasped his hand. "But what if you don't return?"

Brul pulled his family into a hug. "Come out and say goodbye to the marchers."

Tears dripped off Chocho's chin. "I can't..."

He hugged her fiercely and whispered. "I understand, but I have to leave. Try and be strong, Chocho—for the baby." He turned and trudged from the hut.

Chief Brul reached the front of the throng to muted cheers. He waved bravely and consulted Commander Gorb for a final provision check.

"Brul," a squeaky voice called.

Arolee ran to him, followed by two wolf pups and her mother, Arol. Reaching to catch her, he brought her up into his arms while the pups nipped at his feet.

"Can I come with you, Brul?"

He tapped her tiny nose. "No, little sister."

Arolee wiped her tears, looking at the pups. "Why do you have to take Heelo and Riit?"

Brul held her petal-soft chin. "Listen, Arolee. I have Keelo with me to help protect them. If we make peace with the Whites, you can see them grow into great workers, companions, and neighbors."

"Give your brother a kiss now," Arol said, reaching for her daughter. "Brul has to go."

Arolee sniffled as her mother pried her from her brother's arms.

Brul picked up the pups. "I'll take good care of them, Arolee. Go back now and mind the other puppies. Promise me?"

"I will." She waved goodbye.

As she ran off to the wolf pen, Brul shuddered, recalling what his father said the Whites did with Ory. His lead guard dog on the journey, Keelo, happened to be Ory's son.

As the rising sun lit tense faces, Brul spotted Soth, the wolf trainer going along, and handed the pups over. He pulled Arol a few feet away from the crowd for privacy. "You've done a great job raising Arolee. Sad she has to worry."

"She fears you'll never come back like her father. Please prove her wrong."

Brul looked down, choking back a sob. "I'm sorry, Arol. I wish I could have saved him."

"If you hadn't waited for Irik into the night, you wouldn't have learned of Kokor's openness to gifts, maybe peace." She patted his upper arms. "Now, you're chief, and you can save your Chocho, your baby, and the rest of the tribe."

Brul gazed into her misty eyes and shook his head. "I don't know..." He gestured toward the gathering. "...if I can do this."

"You can." She took a deep breath. "I know you, Brul, like my own son." She placed her palm on his chest. "Your heart beats from his blood, but you didn't have to fight, like he did, to survive. You don't carry the same scars." She put her finger to his chin. "You told me when he spoke his last breath…" Her voice wavered as she teared up, but she pushed on, "He said you also see a better way and must lead this march."

Brul closed his eyes and nodded. "He did."

Keelo came to his side and nudged him. Irik gave him a pat. "As the hour nears, these wolves remind me. Irik taught me everything I know about them, even why they howl."

"I know, and they will keep you strong." She opened her arms.

Hugging her, Brul recalled how warmly Arol took him in after the terse Nara died. "Thank you for your faith in me, Mother."

She held his shoulders. "The same belief I always had in your father goes with you." She smiled. "Go now. Lead the people. See a good ending in your mind."

***

By late morning of the journey's second day, the band of men, women, children, wolves, boars, and sleds piled high with provisions and gifts reached the edge of White territory.

Brul turned to Commander Gorb. "Let's rest before we enter the valley. These tree-covered hills may hide many warriors." He faced the tribe, raised his hand, and lowered it. Grateful cheers went out as everyone, including the wolves, sprawled on the ground.

He turned back to Gorb. "Once we enter the valley, it will be hard to return."

Gorb sighed. "I know."

Brul patted him on the back. "Go tell everyone I'll soon speak to them."

When Gorb returned from the back of the line, he found Brul sitting on a rock, eyes closed but back held straight. Keelo barked as Gorb approached. "Chief?"

Brul blinked and forced a smile. "Yes, Commander?"

"The men want to know if they should ready their bows and spears for an attack."

"No, I want them to stay at the rear of the march, as planned, weapons to their backs."

"If the Whites attack, Chief?"

Brul shot upright. "We'll be forced to defend ourselves. But our approach is not to look warlike. Let's hope his warriors know we're bearing gifts in peace."

Worry creased Gorb's face.

"Stay strong, Commander. My father believed the White chief to be trusting when not feeling threatened."

"You're right, Chief. Just feels like we're delivering ourselves along with the goods."

After a short rest, Brul meandered into the crowd. He turned slowly in a circle, gazing into every face. He cleared his throat and spoke in as booming a voice as his age could muster. "Good men and women of the Wolf Tribe, we have reached a turning point."

He gestured toward the valley. "Past those hills lies the White Clan and much danger. Are we ready?"

They stood as one. "Yes, sir!"

Brul's heart warmed at their loyalty and bravery. "Thank you all for having the courage to follow me on this vital quest. My father would be proud of each of you." He raised his palm. "We need to get there before nightfall. Let's march."

<hr />

The late-day sun cast long shadows over the tribe as they entered the ravine. All eyes shot upward. The ridgelines on both sides filled with ghostly White bowmen—arrows strung and pointed downward.

Commander Gorb broke through the crowd and rushed to Brul's side. "The Whites moved fast and closed off our rear."

"That was to be expected, Gorb. I know it's terrifying, but they're not attacking. Keep the men steady, and we'll soon be at their village." He raised his arm and motioned for the marchers to pick up the pace. Slapping his thigh, he kept Keelo close.

As the band approached the village gateway, White warriors jumped from behind rocks to face them. The tribe's wolf guards barked wildly, and the agitated boars snorted and pulled at their ropes. Staring down arrow shafts, the warriors' black eyes burned within white-painted faces. Their muscles bulged with tension, holding the bows taut, but their ribs rippled over empty stomachs. The Wolf Tribe was surrounded.

Brul turned to the marchers, fear gripping their faces. "Everyone, stay calm. If you're not tending animals, sit down. I know you're scared, but they're not attacking, showing they're willing to listen." He tapped his chest with his fist. "I will talk with their chief."

Gorb returned. "The men are as jittery as pigs but staying in line, weapons at rest."

"Good work, Commander. Hand me the goat horn headdress."

Adjusting it, Brul told Keelo and the other wolves to sit and stay. Holding his hands in the air, he stepped out toward the line of White warriors. When he came within two body lengths of them, an eerie, low-pitched growl issued from the warrior's closed mouths. He stopped.

"I am Brul, Chief of the Wolf Tribe. We come with gifts and in peace."

Speaking among themselves, the Whites sent one of their men scurrying into the village.

Shortly, a young White warrior wearing a deer antler headdress ran to face Brul. "Who are you?" he shouted, pointing his spear. Keelo and the rest of the guard wolves snarled, and the White warrior said, "Keep those beasts away from me, or I will kill them all."

"I am Brul, son of Irik and new chief of the Wolf Tribe. May I speak with Chief Kokor?"

"No Kokor. I am Holor." He puffed up his chest. "I am in command. Where is Irik?"

"My father is dead." He pointed to his headdress. "I am chief now."

Holor narrowed his eyes. "How I know not trick? Maybe Irik lead more warriors to attack."

"No trick. We left our warriors in our village to protect the women and children who stayed behind." He gestured toward the back of the crowd. "There are only a few warriors here. We want to be your friends and share our bounty."

Holor glared at Irik and walked slowly back and forth in front of the women, children, and snarling wolves.

"Lay down your weapons," he commanded, shoving his spear toward the tribesmen.

Gorb broke in. "Sir, we have no defenses. He could easily kill us all."

Brul patted Gorb on the shoulder. "He could, but support me, Gorb. Tell the men to drop their weapons slowly. Another sign of peace."

Nervously, the Wolf Tribe warriors set down their bows and spears.

The White warriors gathered them and returned to their defensive positions.

"You see, Holor, we are not here to fight," Brul said. "My father made a pact with Kokor for the gifts we bring."

Holor smiled and grunted. "I could kill your men and all your animals. Take your women and children as slaves."

"Not without Kokor's say."

Gorb glanced at Brul with fear in his eyes.

Holor looked up at the surrounding warriors and raised his hand high in the air. The warriors aimed and drew back their arrows and spears.

Cries broke out from the Wolf Tribe.

Brul shouted over them. "I want to see Kokor now!"

Holor stared at Brul for a moment, then raised his hand still higher for a signal.

Brul gasped.

Instead of a sharp downward strike, meaning 'shoot,' Holor turned his palm up and slowly brought down his arm.

The warriors lowered their weapons.

"Whew!" Gorb exhaled and laid a hand on Brul's shoulder. "My heart was in my throat."

Brul nodded and swallowed hard. "As was mine."

Holor headed back into the village.

"How did you know, Chief?" Gorb asked.

"I didn't. Only I suspected Holor *wants* to be chief. At his core, he's a coward. I took the risk Kokor remains in charge."

Gorb shook Brul's hand. "Like your father, you see things most of us can't."

"I saw it in Holor's body, eyes, and voice." He let go of Gorb's hand. "Go now and check with the tribe and reassure them."

Two White warriors tramped through the village gate, pulling a sled piled high with seal skins. In the low sunlight, Brul made out red blotches on a gaunt face with a few white wisps of hair. Although not in the beaded headdress Brul's father had told him about, the figure wore the wolf-fang necklace Irik gave him. It had to be Kokor, as Holor did not return.

The warriors propped the sled upon a rock, and Kokor beckoned Brul closer. He coughed, spit to the ground, and spoke. "My son, Holor, tells me you are Irik's son. You are very brave to come here. What happened to your father?"

"He died on the return from your village."

Kokor jabbed at his chest. "Old like me."

"Almost thirty." Brul took a deep breath. "I come with the gifts Father promised." He gestured for Soth to bring the boars forward.

Soth switched their rear ends, and the pigs launched into squealing madness.

Kokor cringed. "How you have boars? They are tough, wild beasts."

"Not anymore. Long ago, we captured young ones and raised many more from birth."

Kokor's eyes narrowed. "How they so fat?"

"We feed them."

Brul yelled to the back of his tribe. "Bring a sled of grain."

When it arrived, Brul grabbed a handful of grain and handed it to Kokor. The White chief smelled it, put his tongue to it, and spat it out. "Where you find this?"

"We grow it—big fields of grain, beans, and peas from seeds. We harvest them for our tribe's food and give the rest to the boars. When most of the males get big and fat, we eat their meat." He pointed to the swine. "Chief, we are giving these pigs to you. Three sows and one boar. If you build a pen like ours, you can raise more and have a steady supply of meat."

Kokor shook his head. "How do we grow food?"

Brul grabbed a pouch off his waist and handed it to the chief. "Look inside. You can grow many plants for your clan and pigs; we will show you."

As Kokor examined the seeds, Arolee's black and tan puppies, Heelo and Riit, broke from behind Soth and charged at the pigs, yipping.

Brul picked up the squirming pups by the scruffs of their necks and held them up toward Kokor. "And these are the greatest gifts of all." The pups whined and licked Brul's face. He held them toward Kokor. "These two wolf puppies, with more training, will help you hunt game and be guards to warn and protect your tribe from wild wolves, even lions." He gestured to Keelo. "Like Keelo, here, does."

"Thank you," Kokor said, holding up his hands and gesturing to a warrior to take the pups. He rubbed his chin in silence. "But we don't know these ways, nothing about training."

"We can teach you," Brul said, "and anybody can do it with love and patience."

Distant squeals of laughter broke through the quiet.

"Hear your children?" Brul pointed toward the village. "Ours sound and play the same when caring for pups."

Kokor grunted, but a smile teased the corners of his sunken mouth.

Brul waved behind him and called, "Woto, bring your children here." As the family came forward, he turned to Kokor. "Ask some of your children to come meet ours." He motioned toward the village.

Kokor spoke to his warriors, and soon one returned with a young boy and girl. Both naked, thin, and scared. Woto, with her baby and boy of eight winters, smiled encouragingly at the other family.

Brul asked Woto, "What is your son's name?"

"Sano," the affable child replied.

Brul smiled at him. "Would you be a good boy and say hello to those children?"

Kokor nodded to the White warrior, who nudged his waifs forward. Sano introduced himself and asked their names.

The White children looked up to their father, who said, "Eelik and Toli," and shoved them closer. Toli half smiled and reached over to feel Sano's patched cowhide vest, running his fingers along the hide, stopping at Sano's plump belly.

"Ooh!" he cried.

"Vest," said Sano as he ran his finger along Toli's jutting ribs and hollow stomach. "You must be hungry." He reached into his pouch, handing the boy a strip of dried meat.

Toli took it, looked at his father, who in turn looked at Kokor, who nodded. The boy tore the strip in half, mouthed it, ran to his sister, and gave her the other piece.

"See, all children are born kind and curious," Brul said. "We could teach them how to work with animals and plant food. They would seldom go hungry and grow big and smart."

Eyeing Toli's beaming father, Kokor rubbed his chin before coughing hard, causing his body to shake. Clearing his throat, he asked, "You give all these gifts for what in return?"

"Only that we live together in peace, no longer fight."

Kokor stared into Brul's eyes. "Why would we do that?"

Brul patted his stomach. "So all people can raise their own food. Grow fat. Let wild animals live and grow alongside us."

"How can this be?"

Brul looked to the ground, then up to the setting sun. "My father gave me the power to see new ways and follow my heart."

Kokor narrowed his eyes. "Do we have to give up *our* ways?"

"No. As long as you do not harm other people."

"How do we…?" Kokor coughed and struggled to finish.

Brul spoke solemnly, "You only need to decide." He extended his hand toward Kokor. "What kind of people do you want to be?"

"Eeyii!" A scream pierced the air. Holor bolted to stand protectively above Kokor. "Father, what are you doing?" He raised his hand for the warriors to draw their bows.

Countless arrows and spears pointed at the terrified Wolf Tribe.

Kokor yelled, "Son, you don't need to do that. There may be another way."

With his arm high and taut, Holor said, "Father, our people are starving."

All eyes fixed on Holor's white arm as it quivered against the dark sky.

"Holor," Brul called, "there is another kind of power."

Holor looked at Kokor. "Father, can we trust another tribe?"

"Wait. Listen!" On his sealskin-strewn litter, the White chief strained to rise.

Holor's hand twitched.

A round, silver moon rose above the ridge of pines. Keelo raised her head and let out a soulful cry. The sharp fear in Brul's gut loosened as he closed his eyes, pondering what his father had left him and what he wanted to leave his son.

Glancing back at Kokor, he whispered, "When I see a new moon rise, I call for all on earth to live and love in peace."

Epilogue

WAS KEELO'S CALL ONE OF sorrow or hope? Would Brul's commanding spirit, under the specter of death, win over the Whites? Asked another way, did your journey with Irik's family open a window on your beliefs and the future of our species?

Our story speculated on how the ancient ancestors adapted, invented, and survived, and how they not only came to see ahead, but to see inside themselves and change. Along the way, we marveled at how a different animal species could have become a loyal ally to the human animal.

By looking way back into the beginnings of humanity, we can better ponder its future. In the end, we are left with a conundrum. Some assume the beast of violence is inherent in human biology. Others feel virtue abounds when empathy, reasoning, and social structures curb aggressive impulses. What do you believe and hope to leave your children?

No one knows for sure when our earliest ancestors first used symbols to communicate, developed a conscience, or even attempted to farm. Will we, as individuals, members of a tribe or a species, evolve from each for themselves, into one for all? In the long meantime, our imaginations can follow Irik the younger into the next millennium with another story of becoming who we are.

FREE E-BOOK

THANK YOU FOR READING MY book. If you enjoyed it, please tell others and consider reading my first novel, Stalking Los Angeles, about a lonely Native American boy and a lone mountain lion. You can find the free ebook download on Amazon or, https://www.barnesandnoble.com/w/stalking-los-angeles-tom-berquist/1123297015?ean=2940161060964/free, or Stalking Los Angeles eBook by Tom Berquist - 1230005494439 | Rakuten Kobo United States or Smashwords – Stalking Los Angeles – a book by Tom Berquist

While on Amazon or any of these platforms, please consider writing a short review of my books. Thanks again and happy reading.

Tom Berquist

About the Author

GROWING UP IN THE BOONDOCKS of Northern Minnesota, Tom loved exploring the woods and wildlife with his dog, Pal. He dreamed of becoming a game warden and vowed he'd never sit behind a desk working in an office. After Graduate School, he left home, moved to New York and started a new career in a cubicle as an advertising copywriter.

After a lifetime in the business world and living in Connecticut, the journey of a wild animal caught his interest. A young male mountain lion travelled seventeen-hundred miles from South Dakota in search of a mate. He was killed on a highway not far from Tom's home. Soon after Tom moved to Santa Monica, California another mountain lion had to be killed by police a few blocks from his house, on his birthday.

Tom's love and respect for wild animals was re-kindled. At least he could now tell stories about them. So, he wrote his first novel, Stalking Los Angeles, about a lonely Native American boy and a lone mountain lion. Since then, he has written two other novels, this one, about how wolves co-evolved along with early human beings to become our closest spiritual allies. He has just finished writing Somewhere Beyond the Sea, about how the love and respect for a fellow mammal, the dolphin, brought two people and different cultures together to save thousands of lives.

All Tom's stories are written to inspire young people to care about protecting fellow species who share our home planet, and he donates most all his profits to wildlife conservation. Please have a look at his author website https://tomberquist-author.com to find out more how we can share ideas and actions about caring for all our animals.

CPSIA information can be obtained
at www.ICGtesting.com
Printed in the USA
LVHW041323140123
736914LV00007B/483